CROSSING THE SHELIKOF

Alaska Adventure - By Land, Air, and Sea

BY
MARALI SARGENT-SMITH

PUBLICATION
CONSULTANTS
WE BELIEVE IN THE POWER OF AUTHORS

PO Box 221974 Anchorage, Alaska 99522-1974
books@publicationconsultants.com, www.publicationconsultants.com

ISBN Number: 978-1-63747-016-9
eBook ISBN Number: 978-1-63747-017-6

Library of Congress Number: 2021910657

Copyright 2021 M. Marali Sargent-Smith
—First Edition—

Cover art: Collage by Marali

Manufactured in the United States of America

DEDICATION:

This book is a work of fiction, well, partly, anyway. I'm dedicating it to all the women who won't lie down, give up, or go quietly away and the men who recognize that equal doesn't have to mean "the same as."

PROLOGUE

I'm burning as I freeze. The icy ocean mauls me, sucks me in, spits me out, and sucks me in again. Flaming debris drifts nearby. My fingers claw for purchase on something, anything. Grabbing at passing objects, I clutch at a partially burnt plank. The water is purple-black, yet the tops of the waves reflect the firelight. Is the ocean on fire? That can't be real. I'm unable to make sense of where I am, why I'm in water. My head throbs. My brain, stunned, is slow. I see the fingers of someone pushing through the swell, swimming toward me, and I reach out to pull them closer so they can grab the board I'm clinging to. As I take hold, I find the arm is not attached to a body, and I stare at the gold ring on the icy finger of the hand I am gripping, for what seems like a very long time before I let it go. This urgent need to move. Somewhere in my head, my father repeats, "Get out of the water, Loren, Get out of the water." The shooting starts.

CHAPTER 1

Months ago, working my garden in a silence so deep I could pick out the crash of waves collapsing on the shore below, a sharp echoing crack resonated through the trees. Muscles tight, I raced for my house, locked doors, and closed my shades. I sagged onto the floor, panting. Was that a rifle shot? My dirty fingers smeared my face as I wiped tears away.

I used to hike around the Kenai Peninsula with my friend Belle. After being hunted like an animal, the woods seem no longer friendly, no longer a refuge. One afternoon last April I left for a walk. As I pushed through swaying trees, branches grabbed at me. My eyes skittered in every direction. My walk turned into a run. Squirrel chitters, limbs creaking, the natural sounds of a forest filled me with apprehension. I fled at the rustle and snap of something moving through brush behind me.

Frightening dreams threaded through my nights last winter. Dread, cold as the waves I attempted to paint, surged over me. I turned on lights, read books, and played soothing music. It helped, but intermittent nightmares and anxiety describe my life for months.

I'm an artist, working with oils and acrylics. The buttery smoothness of rich oil pigment sliding across canvas thrills me. Turning juicy colors into something that looks three-dimensional satisfies my soul, always has. I live alone on five acres north of Homer, Alaska, in a house that my husband Brad, a commercial fisherman, and I built together four years before a drunk driver killed him. After seeing my two adopted sons off to college, I converted the family room into my studio and accumulated a jumble of paintings, canvasses, frames, and art equipment, filling the entire first floor of my home.

Once noisy and fingerprinted by the busy hands of my two boys and their friends, the walls have a fresh coat of paint but are silent. After last summer's misadventure, my sons took turns flying home to help as I healed from my injuries, then returned thousands of miles away to school and jobs, one in Colorado, one in Maine.

Friends came to see me after I arrived home from the hospital. In a small community, word gets around fast. Jess, a retired social worker I met while volunteering at the library, showed up at my place often. She was a thoughtful listener. The aroma of her salmon casserole brought me hurrying from my studio. She watched over me, sharing homemade gourmet goodies until the day she moved to Florida to be with her daughter. Soon after, I ended my volunteer work, but took her advice and met with the therapist she'd suggested. Arriving for my first appointment a few weeks after Jess left, I saw a large, comfortable-looking woman with crayon art crowding her walls. She had a streak of bright blue dyed in her hair and "Dolly" hand-painted on her nametag. Dolly listened to my frightened rambling, and after our session ended, asked to pray with me. She seemed compassionate, but my guilt over my best friend's injuries, as well as the therapist's offer to pray, bothered me all the way home. It reminded me, painfully, of Belle's sacrifice and her prayers on my behalf. I decided I wouldn't go back to counselling. Nightmares continued to interrupt my sleep, so, after considering, I set up another appointment. Dolly, gracious, listened. During subsequent sessions I told her my story. She suggested I write my experiences down; so, here goes:

Tonight, is a quiet, unremarkable, August evening. Tonight, marks the one-year anniversary that began the most frightening days of my life. Tonight, even though my physical injuries have healed, when the tiny whisper of sound drifts into my studio, I stiffen. Another soft flutter, and for a micro-instant, my heart stutters.

I slow my breathing, then trace the noise up the stairs into a bedroom where an enormous, emerald-winged moth bumps against a window. Relieved, I open the louvered glass to free the fluttering insect, but stumble back at the sudden appearance of a helicopter overhead. As it disappears into the mist, my hands tremble, remembering the helicopter ride to a beautiful lodge that catapulted my friend and me into the middle of a desperate struggle for survival. I trace my fingers over faint burn marks left along my arms. Those perilous days gave me the scars, along with an injured left hand. My friend, Belle, took a bullet meant for me.

This series of events began with a trip across the infamous Shelikof Strait of Alaska legend. A tale that started with a bang, so to speak, but I'm getting ahead of myself. Before I begin, I've got to run and pick up someone at the airport.

Just a warning: according to the FBI, the account I'm writing never happened. People who died, "were killed as a result of human error that led to a gas leak explosion," my days struggling to survive in the remote Alaska wilderness explained as "confusion" from my "head injury" due to "the blast." They described our capture by drug runners, or terrorists, or whoever the bad guys were, as "an unfortunate event involving a group of drunk hunters" who got "carried away one early fall weekend."

Who would believe nefarious international goings-on of that sort, way up here in the north, anyway? California or Washington D.C., sure, but come on, Alaska? Much easier to label everything as a series of "unfortunate" happenings.

My misadventure began in early August, one year ago.

I stood in my studio sipping coffee and staring at a half-completed painting of Tutka Bay Lagoon. This little cove radiates beauty, but rough brushwork showed my frustration. I tried to get a snow patch on a faraway mountain glittering like I'd seen it from the deck of Belle's catamaran the week before. We'd driven her boat over to fish, but I'd gotten so goggle-eyed over the scenery I almost fell out of the vessel as wake from another craft set ours bucking.

Back in my studio, I loaded a brush with paint for another try as my phone rang.

I glanced at my caller ID, hoping to ignore it, but saw Belle's number, picked up, and said with a marked lack of enthusiasm, "Hey, you."

Her voice bubbled. "Just got wonderful news. Remember that opportunity I told you about, the Seago Lodge thing?"

Belle, a high-energy, successful realtor and my best friend, was often in the middle of some big-money deal. I remembered she had an opportunity to show a pricy, tourist-type lodge located on the Alaska Peninsula that had recently come on the market. Before I could answer, she said, "I think we're getting close to a sale. The lodge manager, Howie Nilsson, said a Native Corporation and two other groups are interested. I need to fly over and meet with them. I want you to come with me."

I set my mug down too hard. Coffee splashed onto my palette. "I think I've told you I'm kinda busy, painting for my show, remember?"

"That's over two months away. Besides," Belle continued, pausing, I guess for emphasis, "I want your help. If I can get the place sold, I'll end up with an excellent commission. With the twins going into collage, I need the money."

"Mmhmm," mumbling, tapping my brush and peering at my unfinished canvas; I wondered what excuse I could trot out this time.

"You even listening?" she asked, impatient. "You know your boys have been telling you to take a break. We've only gone on one hike this summer and one short boat trip. Compared to last year, that's just about nothing."

She was right. We usually spent a lot of our free time together. For the last eight months, however, I had worked long hours, painting in my studio when it was too cold outside or painting out of doors when the weather warmed. My only other extracurricular activity was exercising on my elliptical and watching the many small birds that flitted from tree to tree in my yard as I paused between brushstrokes.

Still holding my cellphone in my left hand with a dripping brush in my right, I looked out my window and watched her climb from her decrepit Jeep Cherokee, two rescue mutts barking after her. She closed her phone and hurried in, briefcase swinging. Medium height, well-rounded body, wide hips, and waist-length black hair, her Aleut heritage showed in an almond complexion and the attractive tilt of her smiling black eyes.

She slipped out of her "extra-tuffs," knee-high rubber boots, obligatory footgear for most activities around our waterfront town, poured a cup of coffee, set her case down, and handed me a colored brochure. Her bright eye, bushy tail demeanor said she was in salesperson mode.

"Isn't it gorgeous?" She pointed to the photo of a large, three-story, timber frame building covering the front. "That's the main lodge." She opened the glossy booklet, and we looked at another picture of the imposing structure built on a rock cornice jutting out above the ocean.

The brochure described the high-end retreat as accessible only by boat, helicopter, or floatplane. Even so, it boasted electricity, running water, and a five-star restaurant, rare amenities for a remote Alaska location.

"Why do you want me there?" I swirled my brush into a glass of water, cleaned up my spilled coffee, took the booklet from her, and sighing, flipped through the pages.

"It's only for a week, you need the break, and I don't want to go by myself," She explained in a rush. "Besides, you can hike or take supplies and do art outdoors."

My attention caught by that same troublesome area on my painting, I picked up my brush, swiping irritably as I said, "Can do that here."

"The scenery is incredible. I know you haven't seen that part of Alaska, yet," she argued. "There's an amazing waterfall which would make a gorgeous painting. Besides, I'm starting a new diet, so you can help keep me away from all that wonderful food. Howie said the chef is fantastic."

I wondered how long her sales pitch and superlatives would continue as I stirred white paint into a blob of Prussian blue. Inwardly groaning, I decided I should at least listen to her spiel, so asked, "Tell me why you need to be over there for that long."

"Like I said, three groups are coming during the week. The lodge workers will provide a meal, and except for the last group staying overnight, they'll fly in and out the same day. I'll guide them around the place and show them buildings, boats, and acreage and try to answer all their questions."

"Isn't this a lot different from the way you usually sell real estate?"

"Yeah, it's not the typical way to sell property, but the location is difficult to get to, and the lodge will shut down soon for winter, so the owners want to get as much exposure as they can while everything looks as good as this brochure shows it to be."

Three weeks later, Belle and I loaded our baggage into her decrepit jeep, grabbed a coffee as we drove through town, and rumbled down a narrow, rut-filled road to the airport. Colorful bush planes lined the edge of the runway. To my surprise, we drove past Homer's commercial terminal, and she brought her rig to a shuddering halt next to a rusting, corrugated metal building with a half-round roof, called a Quonset hut, originating from the Cold War era, or earlier.

"Why are you parking here?" I questioned.

"It's a surprise. Put your bag on the luggage wagon."

A frisson of alarm rippled through me, but I brushed it off, piled my bag onto the cart, and helped her pull it into a building that smelled of pine-scented air freshener and resembled a set from an old military movie.

Belle said, "I've hired a helicopter to fly us."

I hid my shaking hands in my pockets. "That'll be spendy. Why not jump on a commercial jet to Kodiak and go from there?"

"It's the fastest way to get to the lodge from here. Besides, I'm not paying money for the flight. I'm selling a couple lots for Daley to cover our charter, so it'll all work out."

The waiting room contained two wooden chairs, a military surplus desk with a black, dial telephone that looked like one my great-grandmother had owned, and a gurgling water cooler. A closed door near the chairs had a lacy embroidered sign announcing, "The Head." I couldn't help wondering what excitement occasioned the command scrawled in extra-large print on ripped computer paper and taped below it, which read: Danger! Do Not Overfill.

While we stood waiting, two twenty-something guys sporting buzz-cut hair and matching, grease-stained, gray coveralls with "Daley's" embroidered on the back, argued over an aerial map thumbtacked across one wall. In the corner, a skinny woman with a puffed stack of box blond hair giggled into a phone.

A fit-looking man wearing sunglasses, gray t-shirt, and carrying a leather flight jacket hurried through the door. He set a duffle bag on our cart and stepped over to Belle and me, introducing himself. First impression: He was tall, had a Roman nose, great tan, and firm handshake. He said he was Daley's new helicopter pilot, Jay Carrel. After collecting our information for the charter paperwork, he grabbed the cart handle, and smiling, ushered us out to what he said the guys at Daley's had nicknamed Big H. 'H' did not look big to me.

Jay loaded the luggage. He grunted in surprise when he lifted Belle's bright red bag.

My eyes traveled over the helicopter.

"You're kidding, right?" I whispered, watching Jay stow our belongings. "Wasn't there anything else we could get there, in?" My vocal cords felt so tight my voice squeaked. "This dinky machine is what you chartered to fly us over all those miles of ocean?"

I think Jay caught on because he pointed toward two canvas covered objects on top of what he called skids, which I thought of as the helicopter's feet.

"Those pontoons will inflate, floating Big H and us if we have to land on water. Problem is, climbing over them to get into our seats isn't easy, and stepping on them could cause damage. Here, I'll be glad to help you."

Reluctant, clutching his arm for support, I clambered into the cabin and strapped on my seatbelt. Muscles taut, I waited while Jay helped Belle into her seat. I unbuckled my seatbelt, tried to tighten it, refastened it, and wondered how long it would take for the Coast Guard to rescue us if we ended up bobbing around in the ocean. What if a storm blew in while we were in the air?

Outside, Jay walked around the small craft, touching this part, turning that. I knew he was doing a preflight check.

"This thing looks kinda like a plastic bubble," I commented. I realized I was picking at a fingernail and made myself stop.

"And you get to sit closest to that tall, handsome pilot," my friend said, grinning.

"He does smell nice," I responded, attempting to calm down.

She patted my arm. "Aren't you glad you got your hair trimmed and put on makeup?"

CHAPTER 2

Belle, her sturdy frame sporting a navy-blue power suit, tooled leather boots with a high, square heel, and designer sunglasses, fished a vintage compact from her purse, checked her lipstick, patted her thick black braid, then aimed the small mirror in my direction.

Jittery nerves and generous coats of fiber-laden mascara made my blue gray eyes stand out more than usual, a kind of unflattering, bug-eyed, cartoon look. My angular face was pale, lips a tense line. I'd already chewed most of my lipstick off. My shoulder-length, streaky brown hair looked decent, I decided, relieved. So much time alone in my studio doing art projects didn't leave a lot for styling my hair or putting on makeup. Besides, I asked myself, what was the point? Yet, I still felt guilty going to the grocery store in old sweats.

As a young girl, living in a remote part of Alaska, what we called the "boonies," I remember seeing my determined mother, with no benefit of electricity or running water, hair permanently curled, wearing crisp dresses and click clicking on dainty heels as she did hours of housework for her family of six. I had raided my closet, trying to find clothes for this trip. Belle often made her wardrobe selections into a design extravaganza, so I didn't want to look like something pulled from a thrift store donation bag. I refused to wear heels, however, and hadn't felt tight curls from a perm bouncing around my head since my mother's hairstyling experiments when I was in second grade.

Does anyone get home permanents, anymore? I was working diligently to distract myself. Enough fingernails chewed, I decided, so pressed my chilly palms together. At least my hands weren't paint-stained today.

Were those storm clouds out over the ocean?

I still wasn't sure why Belle had asked me to act as her assistant, and hoped new jeans, a black leather blazer, and the silver earrings I had cut out and spent hours fabricating looked professional.

Jay climbed in and gave a concise safety briefing that included showing us how to activate what he called a "federal aviation mandated personal floatation device." He helped us strap these on.

This safety talk did not make me feel better. He gave us headsets and set up the intercom so we could converse without screaming, then started the turbine engine. I caught a faint whiff of exhaust. The helicopter blades rotated, we lifted off, and soon were buzzing over the water as the late summer sun shimmied with the waves.

After we crossed Kachemak Bay, Jay said, "Look for the towns of Seldovia and Nanwalak on our left, then we'll head out past the Barrens toward Cape Douglas."

Belle rolled her expressive eyes, giving me a goofy grin, then explained in answer to Jay's question; she'd been born on Kodiak Island and had relatives in Homer and Kodiak, and was familiar with the area.

Chuckling, teeth bright against his weathered skin, he said, "I guess I can stop my tour guide routine, huh?" I gripped the edge of my seat, grimacing at the whitecaps below. My stomach hurt.

Jay explained he worked flying both fixed-wing and helicopters for the last fifteen years in various locations and flew up from his hometown in Durango, Colorado, for the summer.

"Why are you two going out there?" He looked over his shoulder, "If you don't mind me asking."

"I'm hoping to sell the lodge we're flying to, and my artist friend, here, Loren, is taking time off to come with me," Belle said.

I passed Belle's brochure to Jay.

"I flew over that place, last week," he said. "Took a wealthy, vacationing couple from Ninilchik. The lodge looks impressive, at least from the air."

"What brought you to Alaska?" I asked Jay.

"A great opportunity to see amazing scenery and animals and help my cousin Daley after his knee surgery."

The small chopper hit an air pocket, zoomed upward, then dropped. I let out a muffled shriek and, reaching blindly for something to hold on to, grabbed Jay's shoulder.

He flashed a dazzling smile. Flushing, I let go, apologizing. Belle winked at me again.

I grew up in "bush" Alaska. I had flown in single-engine aircraft many times, but this peanut-sized flying machine made me feel I was bouncing around out in space on the string end of a balloon. If those rotors stopped turning for any reason, we would drop like a rock, whereas small, fixed-wing airplanes might at least continue to glide for a bit. I told myself to relax, but my stomach didn't get the message and kept jumping into my throat, making it hard to swallow.

After passing the Barrens, a rock formation jutting from the ocean, which was our halfway point, we headed directly to Cape Douglas across the south end of the Cook Inlet entrance.

Now we were flying over untouched mountains, valleys, and lakes.

"When in doubt, find out," someone once told me, so thinking information might help calm my trepidation, I began asking about Big H's capabilities.

As hills covered in riotous pink fireweed slipped beneath us, we learned this craft with its 278 horsepower, Allison turbine had a cruise speed of 125 knots, or 144 miles per hour.

"Depends on the load, but Hughie can travel around 301 nautical miles on a full tank of fuel," Jay said, as he hovered high over a lanky moose crowned in velvet.

I scowled through the windshield. All I cared about was that this little flying machine packed enough power and carried enough gas to get us landed safely at our destination. My anxiety lessened as I leaned forward, even forgetting to cling to my seat while I watched the huge animal below us, standing proud and elegant under his heavy rack. I saw the bull moose shake his head and bolt.

Vivid colors painting the earth and water stunned us silent. We stared through the helicopter windows. Jay, a rangy, well-muscled, thirty-something guy with short cropped brown hair, confident movements, and quick smile, seemed dazzled with the scenery passing below; but so were we, although Belle and I had lived in Alaska for most of our lives. Far away, we saw a herd of creamy mountain goats strung like tiny pearls high along a chain of jagged rock.

Belle pointed, laughing at a black bear sow sprawling in lush grass near a stream. A red cloud of spawning salmon sparkled the water. Two fat cubs wrestled nearby. Sunshine glazed the tips of jutting peaks, and glimmering lakes shone like polished turquoise. Because we spent time sightseeing, our flight took almost an hour and forty minutes. I timed it, and although I was now much calmer, I almost cheered when Jay set the craft down in a clearing cut in the middle of lofty spruce.

The rotors slowed, we removed our headsets, and Jay popped the door open. I got a glimpse of vivid green eyes as he slid off sunglasses, jumped out, and helped us pull our belongings from the little chopper.

Belle struggled with an enormous, shiny red piece of luggage she'd designed and had a local company fabricate. She said the bag was a fireproof floatation device packed with survival gear and safety gadgets and insisted the contents would keep her and at least two other people fed and warm in an emergency. Stubborn, she lugged it everywhere, even though it weighed half a ton. I called it her "Santa sack" and could never talk her into bringing something lighter.

"Would you like me to carry your stuff to the lodge?" Jay offered, pointing toward the bag as he watched Belle tug at it.

"Thanks, but someone should come along soon," she said, dropping her load with a sigh. After her wrestling match with her luggage, her face glowed almost as bright as the fireweed surrounding us.

I looked around, wondering when that "someone" would show up. Out of habit, opened my cell phone, only to see no bars.

Belle said, "Oh, yeah, forgot to tell you. There's no cell service, landline, or internet here."

Again, sounding like a tour guide, Jay agreed, "Radio is still a lot more reliable than cell phone in remote areas of Alaska."

"I should have known that; I'm way too addicted to this thing," I said, dropping it into my bag.

"And this from the girl who spent her early years living off the land with no electricity or running water," Belle said, smiling at me. "But the lodge has both radio and satellite phone available, if we need."

Jay waved, lifting off. The sun flashed across the whirling rotors as he flew toward the ocean. Belle turned from watching and remarked, "Daley said Jay is about the best pilot he's ever known. Said he's flown many types of helicopters and airplanes for the military in some tricky situations, hauling troops under fire, emergencies in Afghanistan and Iraq. This is a vacation for him."

While I had seen nothing from Jay's flying skills that alarmed me, I knew sometimes being an expert pilot wasn't enough. For me, flying in anything smaller than a 737 brought painful memories of a tourist-laden, Cessna 206 cartwheeling into the surf one foggy summer morning, killing everyone aboard. That pilot had been excellent, too. That pilot was my father.

A profusion of late summer flowers bloomed at the edge of the clearing, and the sweet aroma of moss and ripe berries should have been relaxing and familiar. Yet I shivered, feeling disoriented and alone.

Something rattled toward us, and before long, a four-wheeler arrived, pulling an aluminum trailer with a bench seat and room for luggage. A scowling guy with tangled black hair and a grubby hoodie, braked, climbed off, introduced himself with a heavy accent as "Leo," and loaded our baggage onto his rig.

"I got get back to lodge quick because they need me for help with boat," he said, voice brusque. He reeked of sweat and fuel oil.

I climbed into the small trailer, leaving Belle to squeeze onto the four-wheeler's seat behind Leo. She stuck her tongue out at me. I wondered if Leo's accent was Russian as we rumbled down the trail toward the lodge. Having flown in from the north, we hadn't seen buildings from the air, so it was surprising to jolt suddenly out of the trees onto a broad field of cut grass with picturesque cabins in front of us. We rode between these peeled log structures positioned like extras pointing toward the star of the show, the magnificent lodge. This large stone and timber frame edifice had all the drama of a posing prima donna as it stood, the restless ocean as backdrop.

Leo drove to our cabin, stopped with an exaggerated lurch, dumped off our luggage, and without speaking, kicked his machine into gear and sped away.

"Whew, that guy needs deodorant," Belle said, as we toted our bags inside.

"Russian accent, huh?" I asked, looking at varnished logs that formed walls up to an open ceiling crowned with roughhewn rafters.

Belle was friends with a large group of "Old Believers," a close-knit clan who left Russia before World War II to escape religious persecution and eventually settled near Homer. A lovely young lady from one of their several villages worked in her office. Belle was three-quarters Aleut. Many of her Aleut ancestors on Kodiak Island suffered harassment, assault, slavery, and death by Russian explorers, hundreds of years earlier. Her great grandparents had struggled through the Jim Crow era, yet a gracious commonsense ruled her life. She was independent, determined, outspoken, and opinionated, but she never played the victim card, nor was she vindictive or bitter.

I moved further into the room. Two, well-crafted spruce beds and a small sitting area with several paintings distracted me. Curious, I examined the art, oils, unfamiliar signatures but all originals. Everything scrubbed clean. The scent of new wood lingered.

"I'm impressed," I said, touching the marble tiled shower with inlaid agate accents.

Enthusiastic, Belle said, "If the rest of the place is this nice, then the $16.5 mil. price tag makes sense. But I'm starving. Let's go check out the dining room."

"Didn't you ask me to help you with a diet?"

"Well, yeah, but I need to start by checking the quality of food and service for myself, so I can be accurate when I represent to the buyers."

Heading toward the lodge, we passed guests piling suitcases outside their cabins.

"Howie said today is the last day the lodge is open," Belle explained, as we worked our way around stacks of baggage.

We strolled on raised boardwalks connecting the buildings and entered through over-size, iron-clad doors adorned with North Pacific Sea plants and marine animals. I slid my hand across details carved on a wooden octopus shown just emerging from its hiding place and felt the knobby structure of a lifelike barnacle, all professional quality and hand made.

"I want those doors at my house," my friend declared, bustling toward the reception area where she gave her name and business card to a flame-haired young woman busy behind a counter. Guests milled through the lobby. With no hesitation, the pert young receptionist asked Belle to come with her as she marched through an inner door into a large office. I followed. A short, rotund man engulfed a sagging office chair.

He barked into a handheld transmitting device of some type, "… and remember to lock that bear gun back in its case and leave the radio there, this time. We don't need more trouble." He cut his conversation, removed his glasses, rubbed his large, veiny nose, bumbled to his feet, hurried over, and thrust out his arm saying, "I'm the manager, Howie."

Belle shook his hand and introduced me. Howie's wispy hair stuck up like dandelion fluff all over his round head, and his pudgy fingers thrust against my palm felt as soft and damp as warm dough. I had to concentrate to keep from jerking my hand away. I decided I would probably never make homemade pretzels again.

He launched into talk about the prospective sale, but less than a minute into his monologue, Belle interrupted with, "How's about we get some lunch and go from there?"

No argument. Howie grabbed a thick folder, and we followed as he puffed his way up the polished plank stairs to the dining area.

CHAPTER 3

A server brought us a meal of clam chowder, sea kelp salad, and sourdough bread. I watched the rotund manager happily smack his way through six slices as his greasy fingers smeared butter over the lodge paperwork. The view of the twinkling ocean through cathedral-shaped windows made a welcome distraction.

A few days before our trip, Belle and I studied a detailed map and knew this part of the Alaska Peninsula's coastline consisted mostly of fiords: deep, narrow inlets with steep mountains rising from either side. All wild, uninhabited country; the closest town, Larsen Bay, populated with about 85 hardy, pioneering souls, sits on the island sixty miles southwest of the city of Kodiak, requiring a lengthy boat ride across Shelikof Strait, a treacherous waterway.

After lunch, Howie gave us a tour. The main, three-story building appeared to be in excellent repair. A well-appointed, top floor contained six luxury suites with floor-to-ceiling windows. The second floor had the dining room, kitchen, bar, and game room, and the ground floor included the lobby, a small gift shop, snack area, offices, and storage rooms.

We ambled back through the lobby to the bay side of the building, out through another pair of carved wooden doors that echoed the sea theme, and found ourselves on a broad, spruce slab deck, facing the fiord. Overdressed clientele crowded tables as they waited to get on the lodge's private ferry, *Sea Dragon*, for the open water run carrying them to Kodiak Island.

Howie motioned to the other moored craft. "Most of the workers are leaving with the guests today, so we'll only have a skeleton crew here the rest of the time. The last boat that'll head to Kodiak Island is our fifty-eight ft. charter rig, the *Sea Princess*. I'm driving it over with the rest of the staff after we get everything cleaned up and shut down for winter."

Leo and another lodge employee pulled a cart stacked with suitcases through the lobby doors. We followed to the edge of the deck and watched them trundle it down a freight ramp to the pier.

"The lodge has two large boats you see tied to this dock, and two more thirty-footers and several kayaks and canoes about a mile down that way on a smaller pier. The *Sea Princess* is for guests who want to charter extended camping trips around the area, and then, as I said, that's our ferry," Howie stated, pride in his voice as he pointed again. "It runs twice a week during our season."

He and Belle began going over the details of operating and maintaining the watercraft, all information she would need to regurgitate to prospective customers. Bored with the logistics, I ambled away and looked down onto the dock. A man carrying a wooden crate climbed from the *Sea Princess*, looked about furtively, darted under the ramp and disappeared. Belle and Howie were engrossed in their conversation; they didn't seem to notice. I walked down rough stairs onto the dock, where I pretended to examine wood carvings fastening to railing. Actually, I was snooping, trying to see where the man had gone.

Too dark. I saw nothing. Staying away from the crew loading the ferry, I wandered to the edge of the wooden pier and squinted through sunshine into the water, noting massive pilings driven deep into mud and rocks below. I was sure someone had gone under the ramp, but no one came back out. I turned back toward the lodge, surveying the scene. Two, large, pricy boats moored here, and more recreational craft at another location, expensive construction on the entire set up. Someone had spent big bucks on all this.

I wonder if this place is making money.

I turned back toward the stairs as Belle walked up.

Her eyes, usually lit with fun, flashed. She grabbed my arm, jabbering, "Lor, we gotta talk, now."

She sprinted up the stairs, me behind her. I followed her around the outside of the lodge, avoiding the gaggle of visitors trooping toward the boat. We hurried into our cabin, breathless.

Once inside, she plopped onto the edge of her bed and turned toward me with a sigh.

"Something's messed up, here," she burst out.

"Messed up? What do you mean?" I was still trying to catch my breath.

"Howie," she said, drawing his name out for added emphasis, "Just informed me there are not three groups of prospective buyers coming. There'll be one group flying in today by helicopter and staying the night. After you and I show them the place, we'll have to leave, at the latest by day after tomorrow."

"How did scheduling get so confused?"

"I don't know," she muttered, scowling and flipping through pages in her notebook. She extricated a much written over calendar. Pointing to penciled dates, she said, "Katrina, my assistant, organized this. She's usually on top of every detail. I was out of the office showing a house."

"But we planned for Jay to pick us up this coming Sunday."

"And that's six full days from now." She slapped her notebook onto the bed.

"Ok, thinking, thinking…" I said, rubbing at a mosquito bite on my ear. "Can't we get a ride out on the boat, day after tomorrow, with everyone else?"

"I hope so."

Someone tapped on our door. Belle opened it. The red-haired receptionist with "Seago Lodge" stenciled on her shirt handed her a folded paper, turned, and left. Before she closed the door, I glimpsed the *Sea Dragon* chugging toward Kodiak.

Belle unfolded the paper. "It's a note from Howie. He wants me to meet him in the lobby before the prospective buyers get here."

"Let's use their satellite phone, call Daley's, and get our return flight changed," I said. "We need to get a message to Jay."

I was surprised she hadn't already suggested this, quick as she usually was to jump into problem-solving mode.

Not wanting to keep her waiting, I slicked on lipstick, grabbed a sweater, and headed toward the door. Once outside, noticing she was not with me, I turned back and saw her slumped on the bed.

"What's going on?"

"This has become so convoluted," she blurted.

"What has? Just tell me what you're thinking." I pulled on my sweater, working to hide my impatience as I waited for her explanation. I was hoping this was not yet another of my charming, but unpredictable companion's impulsive schemes. After a friendship solidified in grade school, we'd had many adventures over the years, some with happy endings, others that had become more exciting than either of us wanted.

"I had this idea," Belle began, picking at a thread trailing from her sleeve.

There must have been something about the way I narrowed my eyes, because she jumped up and erupted, "You weren't getting out or going anywhere, and I've been worried about you. I tried to get you to go with me to that string orchestra concert in June. I even asked you to go with me to Juneau on the ferry, but you kept saying no."

She was right, but getting ready for a show, I buried myself in the process. I worked long hours, unable to relax, as I tried to make every tiny detail perfect.

"Matt called me and said you pretty often don't return their text messages, and he and Ryan worry about you, too."

My heart warmed at the mention of my sons. They worry? I knew they cared; most boys love their mom, but with college, jobs, and girlfriends keeping them occupied, there wasn't extra time.

"When I'm painting, I 'pretty often' forget where I set my cell phone, so by the time I get around to reading their messages, the moment is over, and they've moved on. It seems absurd at that point to text back." My voice sounded too loud.

Staring out at the ocean, I considered, "Not sure why I feel displaced and set aside. It's hard to know when to call because they both seem so engaged in the business of their lives. Feels like I'm intruding, especially now they both have girlfriends."

Moving toward the bathroom, I cleared my throat, not wanting her to see tears in my eyes. I didn't need those layers of mascara streaking my face.

"They're maturing into wonderful young men, and I'm happy about that. I've got friends who complain their kids don't want to find a job or take on adult responsibilities. The hard part is balance. They make decisions, and I wonder whether to offer advice or keep my mouth shut. And, yeah," still not looking at her, feeling foolish at my outburst, "I realize texting is what everyone does now, with lots of emojis, but there are times I just want to hear their voice." I grabbed a tissue and blew my nose.

"This empty nest business calls for a lot of adjustment." I sighed, swallowing more tears. "I sound pathetic, sorry. Not sure why all that came pouring out, right now." Walking back, I leaned against the door.

Great, here comes a headache.

Belle's voice was soft. "We're both kind of young to have kids in college. And the first year they take off is rough. They say it gets easier, but I can't testify to that, yet." She sighed. "Family stuff. Often perplexing and complex, isn't it? You know mine's been. Remember when my cousin was fighting breast cancer and gave me guardianship of her twins, and my sweet baby, Jakey, wasn't so sweet, anymore, because he was going through his terrible two's? About the same time, I found out my brother, Cody, was doing cocaine. Those years were chaotic. I was a young single mom trying to help my sick cousin; I mean, the twins having to adapt to a new living situation was hard enough, but with the added pain of a terminally ill mother, so, so difficult. And with Cody, I learned more about drugs, trying to help him get away from that garbage, than I ever wanted to know. Good ole Cocaine Cody; thought we wouldn't survive. But back to the subject at hand; your sons are kinda worried, and me too."

She paused again, then flung out, "So, here's what the deal is."

Oh, crap. I shut my eyes. *Whenever she says, 'Here's what the deal is,' it's going to be sketchy.*

"I told them I was planning a trip for the both of us," Belle said, her tone defensive. "We thought it would be good for you to get away for a couple weeks."

Peevish, I interrupted, "You know my show's happening in October; that's less than two months of work time."

"I also know you get so wrapped up in getting ready you forget to eat or sleep. Besides, you told me you have all your paintings finished, except the one with the sea otters in Tutka Bay."

She glanced at her phone's clock. "I gotta get over to the lodge right away, so I need to hurry and tell you the whole story."

I flounced to my bed and perched, stiffly. I'm sure Belle could sense my irritation, because she added, "You can tell me off, later."

Without waiting for me to comment, she rushed on, "Jake's doing this semester with my cousin's family in Texas, and I had vacation time saved, so

I thought I would plan a trip for us. I told you about the Seago Lodge sale and asked for your help, and I do need it," she said, noticing my deepening frown. "For moral support, if nothing else. The first part of my plan was arranging for Daley's, that is Jay, to fly us over here, and yes, I arranged for him to pick us up on Sunday."

She paused, then continued excitedly, "Here's where the surprise part comes in. I set it up for Jay to fly us to Kodiak on Sunday instead of back to Homer, where we catch the jet into Anchorage for a few days."

She picked up her notebook and I followed her out the door. She locked it, saying enthusiastically, "I thought it would be fun to rent a car and drive up to Denali for a day or two, see the sights and stop overnight in Talkneetna on our way back home."

"That sounds like fun." I toyed with her idea as we hurried toward the lodge. "I haven't done the tourist thing in years. But what about my garden?"

A golden crown sparrow whistled. Turning to locate it, I thought I saw someone slip from our cabin into the woods. Alarm, light as moth wings, brushed over me. I had watched Belle lock that door.

"My neighbor," she continued, oblivious, "Has five girls, and they know how to work. Their family grows a lot of their food. Anyway, I hired them to weed and water around your place and watch my dogs while we're gone."

"I saw that guy, again, Belle." Realizing I hadn't told her about the man under the dock ramp and realizing I didn't know for sure what I had seen either time, I shut up.

My friend steamed ahead, not paying attention. "Ryan and Matt know all about my plan and are in total agreement. They won't expect calls from either of us for a solid two weeks. Furthermore," she exulted, as we pushed open the entry doors, "They liked my idea so much they forked out money for our car rental. Said to tell you it was an early birthday present."

"Hey," I began again, but Howie hustled over, ending further conversation between us. He held a clipboard in one hand, a plastic drink container rattling with ice in his other and had donned a wrinkled brown suit. I smelled chlorine and peppermint and realized the odd combination was coming from him. He gulped his drink.

"Belle," he said, crunching ice, "You asked about freshwater storage and our generator, so I want to show you our filtration system and power sources before they get here."

I peered back through the lobby windows toward our cabin but saw nothing.

What if it IS nothing? Lodge employees move around the property for all kinds of legitimate reasons.

"Why don't I change our booking with Daley's?"

Belle explained we needed to make a call, and Howie pointed me toward the room that held, he said, a long-range radio and satellite phone.

CHAPTER 4

Inside a windowless cubicle, office supplies, empty cardboard boxes, and two printers crowded the space. I could see a narrow door beside the overflowing counter. Curious, I pushed it open. A picnic area with glass-topped driftwood tables sat on crushed rock. A raked gravel path led toward the forest. Closing it, I looked for the phone, locating it on a stand next to the radio in the middle of a tangle of wires that dripped onto the floor. I picked it up, staring at the unfamiliar buttons.

How do I make it work?

Didn't want to end up calling Tibet or making some other silly mistake. I scrabbled around on the messy counter looking for written instructions, not eager to show how electronically challenged I was. I also did not want to demonstrate my ignorance to that confident, copper-haired receptionist.

This is me not being too proud to ask for help.

At the counter, holding the intimidating little device out toward her, I said with exaggerated calm, "I don't know how to activate this. Will you help me, please?"

She sighed, pursed her lips, looked at her nails, all very long and very red, smoothed her hair with those same long red nails, plucked the phone from my fingers, sighed again and began punching buttons with a nonchalance I envied. She smiled condescendingly as she handed it back and made her formal pronouncement.

"There is password. You must have this to operate. We get older, we forget more, da?"

"Thank you," I said, forcing a polite smile. I walked away, muttering, "Older? Bet you can't drive a stick shift… and, not sure about those nails, but your paintbrush eyelashes are fake."

Unlocked, it behaved like any other cell phone. I dialed Daley's Flying Service. Several rings later, my call was answered by a disembodied, canned voice assuring me I could leave a message, after informing me that Daley's would be closed for the next ten days for the Silver Salmon Derby in Seward. I winced. Belle's fun adventure was fast turning into a problematic dilemma. We couldn't stay at the lodge any longer than the day after tomorrow, and we didn't have any way to get word to Jay about our schedule change. I left a brief message, anyway, just in case someone checked the machine.

Replacing the phone, I left the cramped room. The distinctive blap, blap of a hovering helicopter drew me to a window in the lobby. It set down a lot closer than the helipad we had used. A minute later, its twin landed. Two groups emerged, clutching their luggage, bent at the waist and scuttling clumsily from the still spinning rotors. My friend and Howie came into the lodge from the ocean side, and she motioned me over as they waited for the prospective buyers to enter.

"Howie said we can catch a ride to Kodiak on the last boat," she said.

"Great, because there wasn't anyone answering the phone at Daley's."

The helicopter's passengers were now standing upright and straggling across the rough field toward the lodge. Two men in winter hats and long overcoats, probably in their fifties, hurried from the first helicopter, followed by a team of six, rough-looking, younger guys in dark green uniforms. As they walked toward the lodge, five men emerged from the second helicopter, and two women climbed down after them and began struggling in spiky heels across the uneven ground. The last man out of the second copter was short, skinny, and frizzy-haired with an enormous, black mustache. He shoved a bulky red duffle through the helicopter door, wrestled, and dropped it. As his finale, he tripped and sprawled over his luggage, tearing the seat of his pants. I avoided looking at Belle, knowing we'd disgrace ourselves by laughing. The five men from the second helicopter bunched together, looking severe, organized, and fit; keeping the women surrounded as they walked. Big mustache stumbled after, towing his voluminous, red bag; a white flag of underwear signaling from the split in his trousers.

"Here comes your soul mate, Belle."

She blushed. "I will kill you."

Leo, another lodge worker, and the flame-haired receptionist raced past me and hurried outside, loaded themselves with suitcases, and lugged everything in, placing it in piles on the floor in front of the counter. Leo ran back and tried to take the red case, but the mustachioed little guy wouldn't turn loose. Our sweaty four-wheeler driver had cleaned up, I noticed, his long hair washed, combed, and tied into a thick tail. He wove in between the guests like a tango dancer. He and two other lodge employees had donned fitted blue and gold suits, heavy with braid. Their theatrical attire looked as if someone had cut the Alaska flag apart and used that cloth for their costumes. The outfits were so tight I thought they should have used a bit more material. I couldn't help smiling when I saw gold stars sewn across their shoulders.

The first eight men who came into the lodge were not speaking English.

"More Russian," I thought. The two older men in long coats stood close, talking together, while the others spaced themselves several feet away. The six were much younger; with steroid-pumped muscles straining their uniforms and fierce expressions, they resembled eager attack dogs. I didn't see any weapons, but their aggressive stance made it obvious they were guarding the older men. When the second group pushed through the doors, the Russian-speaking men stopped talking and watched.

Once the heavily made-up women stepped inside, I noticed their designer clothing and expensive hairstyles. One woman limped and, up close, her dyed hair, furrowed skin, and sagging neck telegraphed her age. Belle and I looked at each other, shocked, recognizing Charlene Chametz, Speaker of the House. Her blunt-featured face, artificially full lips, and painted eyebrows had been spread across the news for the last two years. Outspoken in hatred of whatever wasn't currently going her way in politics, she seemed to relish being at the center of any political fracas. The four men surrounding the two women looked like hard-eyed marines in dark blue, well-tailored suits.

Secret Service? I tried not to stare. And who was scrawny mustache man with the red duffle bag?

Howie cleared his throat. I glanced at him. Flummoxed, he gaped at the newcomers.

"Belle, Howie; look at Howie."

"U-huh, yeah," she answered, peeling her eyes away from the visitors. "Houston, looks like we have us a problem; Howie's systems seem to have shut down."

She stepped up close to his side, slid her right hand up under his baggy suit coat, and did something to his back that made the addled man wince and start forward. As she moved away, she patted his arm and said in an undertone, "Earth to Howie, you've got guests. Say something."

Whatever she did, worked, because he pushed out his chest and began, after clearing his throat and making a few false starts, welcoming every-one to the lodge and inviting them upstairs to the bar and dining room. The two, older, Russian-speaking men ignored him and approached the counter. Flipping her bright hair, the perky young woman waiting there fluttered her hands, batted her false eyelashes, and chirped a greeting at them in Russian. After his awkward speech, Howie turned, forcing Belle and me with a moist but resolute grip up the stairs where we stood in a huddle in the open area between the dining room and the bar.

He wheezed, "That's speaker of the House of our United States. That's Madame Chametz!" His breathing rasped like he'd just finished a marathon.

"Howie," I interjected, before Belle could say anything, "Didn't you know who was coming?"

"Howie," Belle said, taking her turn, "Seriously. What on earth? You've got the Speaker of the House with her group, and eight Russians, or at least Russian speaking guys who've landed here, and you're acting like you don't know what this is about."

Howie's ears pinked. "I don't, I don't," he asserted, slurring his words. "Was told there would be one helicopter, just one group of people who wanted to see the lodge. Guy on the phone said the Nontalwuk Bay Native Association. Don't know why they're here, or what's going on," he contin-ued, peering over his grimy spectacles, bloodshot eyes confused.

It was then Belle and I realized Howie was about halfway to soused. I guess his extra-large drink container had contained something besides ice water.

"Of all the times," I said, recalling a bit of snarky self-help I had read years ago on a social media site. "'This is not my circus; these are not my monkeys.'"

"Oh, yeah, desert me now," Belle said. I realized I had made my comment aloud. She grinned.

"When the going gets tough," she mouthed, and we both snickered, remembering Charlie, Belle's uncle, who had a habit of climbing partway up the local radio tower, using a bull horn and bellowing pithy quotations like, "When the going gets tough, the tough get going," every time he got snockered, which was twice a month or more during our long winters.

We helped Howie to a chair.

"You should stay here with him, since you've gotten to know him so well, already," I said, giving her my best, wide-eyed smile. "You encouraged him so nicely to make his welcome speech; weren't you massaging his back downstairs?"

Belle glared. "I pinched him, you nit. I was trying to make him say something."

"Still, you might need to pinch him some more. Anyway," I said, laughing at her disgruntled expression, "I'll go see if I can find someone who can step into this hot mess and take charge."

I dashed into the dining room, noticing a table heaped with an impressive buffet. My stomach recognized the scent of food and growled. I saw a door at one end of the room, pushed it open, and found a steamy kitchen with three workers scurrying about. The aromas were even better in here. Not knowing what else to do, I called, "Where can I find the manager?"

Curious eyes stared at me.

With a pronounced accent, someone answered, "Howie."

"Is there anyone else?" I tried again, "Assistant manager?"

"Just Howie," came the retort, and they all began working again, ignoring me.

I left the kitchen and grabbed a sliver of prime rib, medium rare, as I hurried back to Belle. Howie was gone.

"Hey," I said, my mouth full, "I barged into the kitchen and asked for the manager, and they said, 'Howie.' It appears there is no one in charge here except our Howie."

I could hear people climbing the stairs. "So, just where the heck is that Howie character, now?"

Charlene Chametz had reached the top. She marched over to us, followed by the other woman and three of her five bodyguards, secret service, Marines, private soldiers, or whatever they were.

An intense group.

No smiles. Ms. Chametz addressed herself to my friend. She did not speak to me.

It must be Belle's $600 power suit.

"What have you prepared for our meeting?" she questioned, and without waiting for an answer, walked away, glanced into the dining room, then strode over and inspected the bar.

"This will do," she called over her shoulder, and her retinue scurried to follow her into the lavish room.

The younger woman rushed back to us.

"Tell the Kazlov group we are ready to begin the negotiations. Also, have the waiters bring the food from the buffet to us, immediately."

For an instant, we stared at her. She grasped Belle's hand. I could see her polished, French-tip nails biting into my friend's wrist as she leaned toward us. An aggressively, cloying perfume wafted from her.

"You'll want to hurry," she insisted, tapping Belle's palm. "This is a crucial meeting, and we need everyone cooperating, doing their part." Belle jerked her arm away. Her dark eyes snapped.

"Look," she said, with a calm I knew she didn't feel. "I'm a realtor. My friend and I are only here to show this property. We are supposed to meet a group of prospective buyers and take them around to look at the place, nothing else."

Further conversation was stopped by noise on the stairs. The two older men, speaking Russian, swished by in their long wool coats. They located Ms. Chametz's group and stalked toward the room, ignoring us. The woman with the French tips and expensive clothes looked apprehensive.

She spoke again, her tone uncertain, "So, you haven't been cleared." As her voice trailed off, she smoothed her suit and hurried to rejoin her group.

"Well, now, she's a very important person with her Jimmy Choo shoes, Hermes handbag, and Gucci scarf," Belle muttered, annoyed.

"Jimmy Choo, who?" I asked, teasing her.

She made a face. "We've got to go find Howie and figure out where we go from here, 'cuz, honey, all this is getting way too weird for me."

As if in answer to my questioning look, she pointed toward the far wall. "Howie left the building, staggering through there."

A door I hadn't noticed stood half-hidden behind a large sealskin-covered room divider.

I was gripped by a peculiar sense of urgency. Belle must have felt it, too. By the time we reached the exit, we were almost running. Anxious, I scanned our surroundings as we slipped through. There was no one behind us; no one had seen us leave.

"Rats," she said. "No din-din. I am so hungry, and that food smelled amazing."

Covered stairs led down the outside of the building. We came out into twilight. The sun had disappeared, and a chilly fog pushed in. Only one of the big helicopters was still there.

I had been so engrossed with the going's on in the lodge I hadn't heard the other lift off. A stocky, bald man I assumed was the pilot, leaned on the open cockpit door facing away from us; I could smell his cigar.

We were on the west end of the building by the patio. Belle headed off toward the trees. I followed her onto the path I had seen from the radio room. The trail led past blueberry bushes tangled with devil's club. Patches of glowing, green moss spread out like a luscious carpet. Forest smells were rich with late summer ripeness.

"I love these beautiful woods," I breathed, "Let's stay out here, eat blueberries, listen for birds and forget everything else."

"Would love to, especially the part with the blueberries."

CHAPTER 5

As we rushed along the path, we saw a row of rough-sided huts ahead. The contrast between these shacks and the luxurious guest accommodations was startling. Thick fog poured in from the ocean and curled around us, isolating.

"This must be where the lodge employees stay," I guessed. "How'd you know the buildings were here?"

"Howie showed me the layout during lunch while you visited the ladies' room. What took you so long in there, anyway?"

"I couldn't stand to watch him gobble down another piece of bread. He had butter all over his face."

"Well, I wish I'd eaten more," my friend said, as we walked up three stairs and knocked on the door. There was no reply, but we heard sounds inside. Impatient, she pushed it open. We stepped into an unpainted, particle board room containing a set of cheap bunk beds, a three-drawer dresser, and a broken chair. Howie, his back to us, stuffed clothing into a worn backpack. Realizing we had entered, he pivoted, pulling it close against his pudgy frame. His right hand remained hidden. He seemed a lot less drunk than the last time I'd been near him. Even his big, blue-veined nose looked pale. I decided he was sick, or afraid, maybe both.

Three sharp sounds, like far away gunshots, echoed through the trees. We jumped. The cabin door, standing open, framed the disappearing sun. Heavy mist now covered the woods.

Howie pulled his hand from behind his pack. We were looking at the business end of a shaking revolver held by a half-plastered, spooked little fat man.

"I don't know who you are," he quavered, "And I don't know what the Sam- 'ell is goin' on around here, but I didn't sign up for this, and I'm gettin' out, now."

"Howie," Belle began, in the gentle, placating, soothe the savage tone she'd used so many times with her drunken uncle, years earlier. "We don't know what's going on, either. We just flew over here to sell the lodge, remember?"

He peered at her, bloodshot eyes skeptical. I smelled his fear, or maybe that was mine. She kept talking.

"You and I had a phone conversation just last week about selling this place. Come on, put the gun down, Howie. We need to figure this out."

He glared at us a moment longer, then lowered his weapon.

"There's a man dead over there," he wheezed.

I shut and locked the door. More pop, pop sounds again. I was sure the noises were gunshots.

I said, "Belle, this has nothing to do with us. We need to protect ourselves." I had no clue what the danger was, or where it was coming from, but something told me we needed to get away from here.

"Where did you see a dead man, Howie?" Belle asked, as she pulled the curtain across the one window in the shack.

"In the radio room. I had a little too much peppermint schnapps and thought I was gonna be sick, so I ran down those outside stairs to get some fresh air. One helicopter flew off. I decided to call the lodge owner and ask what was goin' on, so I got myself back through that side door into the radio room. I was kinda drunk," he repeated, "And I didn't want no one to see me. Then I found the dead guy on the floor."

"You sure he was dead?" I asked.

"He wasn't moving, and he had a nasty big hole in his chest," he stammered. "Radio and the satellite phones gone. I came back out the side door and ran here to get my gun."

Moving determinedly, Howie picked up his pack in one hand and gripped his revolver in the other, waddling toward the door.

"Where are you going?" I asked.

"Takin' the boat," he retorted, "Not waiting 'til day after tomorrow. I'll try to call for help for you two, and everybody else," he added as an afterthought. "I don't know what's going on here and don't aim to be in the middle of it."

He clawed at the door, unlocking it.

"Wait," Belle said, "We're coming with you."

"You better hurry," he called, as he scrambled down the steps and fled.

We ran. Belle puffing in front and me following, haze so thick Howie looked like an overweight ghost floating ahead of us. My friend tripped over a root, and I grabbed her, pulling her upright.

Why does she insist on wearing those useless heels?

We rushed on, but Howie got further and further ahead. Panic iced my hands. Then a shot. Close. We stopped and skittered backward. I realized we were clutching each other. I held my breath. Stood still. Didn't know which way to run, or where the sound had come from. Couldn't see Howie. Slowly, we tiptoed forward. Nothing. Forced ourselves a few more timid feet, still nothing. The fog smothered. Creeping onward, we came to someone crumpled across the path. Belle used light from her phone as we leaned over him.

It was Howie. Howie with a neat, round, bullet hole punched in the side of his head. Blood trickled. I fell to my knees, my fingers trembling on his neck as I tried to find a pulse. No signs of life. He still smelled like Clorox. The gun glinted from the grass beside him. Belle scooped it up. We came out of our shocked state, realizing how vulnerable we were. Belle shoved her phone into her pocket. Frantic, I grabbed her arm, yanked her back off the path, and right up beside a dead spruce. I'm sure I looked as pale and horrified as she. She clutched his revolver.

"We've got to call for help," I said, feeling dizzy.

"You know there'll be a radio in the boat," she said.

"We have to make a survival plan; it's getting cold out here, we don't know what's going on, and I'm not going back into the lodge to find out. Let's go to the boat, now." My voice shook.

"I have to get my survival bag. We'll need warm clothes."

"I don't want to take any extra time; it should be warm enough in the boat."

"We might not be able to stay on the boat," she said, plunging into the brush, heading for our cabin. She was right. I caught up to her, and we began working our way back. It was now dark; most of the fog had disappeared, replaced by a stiff wind. I felt the first drops of rain. Faint light shone from the lodge on our right, and we used it to help aim ourselves in what we thought was the right direction.

We straggled through devil's club and other undergrowth until we reached our cabin door. It stood ajar. Inside, afraid to turn on lights, we used illumination from her cell phone. We looked around, dismayed. The contents of our purses, suitcases, my art supplies, and Belle's briefcase spilled onto the beds and floor. My cell phone sat underwater in the toilet bowl. Belle's survival bag was mostly emptied; draped over the threshold with items strewn about, but she didn't think anything was missing. She slid her phone from her pocket and shoved that into her bag along with everything else she repacked. In a terrified rush, we changed into hiking boots and pulled on our coats. I headed toward the door and the wind and rain outside. My friend tugged at my coat sleeve and motioned me back to her bed, where she said, "I need to pray about this. God can help us."

"Now?" I questioned. I bent forward, exasperation and fear making my belly cramp. "Can't you?" I began, but she had already started talking in a low, earnest tone. I made out, "and protect Loren by your mercy…"

That was so like her.

The thing was, she believed and lived it. She believed there was a great big God out there who cared for us.

Prayer completed, Belle gripped her red bag in one hand and Howie's gun in her other and bolted toward the door.

I stopped her. "Why are you so stubborn? Your survival bag is going to slow us down. We have to move fast."

She stood there, looking at me and said, "You know what? We might need it."

I wanted to out-argue her, for once, but knew we didn't have time, so I clamped my mouth shut, grabbed one end of the red sack, and pulled her, with more force than necessary, out the door and into the shadows under the trees.

Rain pelted. The wind had picked up even more and now drove into us, relentless. Our first, late summer storm had arrived. Small twigs and leaves flew about, stinging exposed skin. We needed to stay off the boardwalks and away from the buildings to keep from being seen. Once more, we thrashed our way through thick bushes. A loud crack when a tree broke. Our progress was agonizing slow as we floundered. Lights flashed in the darkened lodge building. What was going on up there?

The handles at the ends of Belle's survival bag helped us support each other and kept us together as we stumbled through the dark. We stopped under wind-whipped branches near the edge of the deck. I squinted, breathing hard, trying with my whole being to penetrate the darkness.

"I don't see anyone, do you?"

"No lights outside, anywhere," she said.

We would cross about thirty feet of landing with nothing to hide behind, carrying a big, bulky bag between us. It felt like two miles. Yeah, I said a few naughty words, but under my breath.

"We need to go as fast as possible," she said.

"No kidding," I returned, and got a firmer grip on the handle.

"Three, two, one; let's roll," she said. As we ran, I thought of the heroic people all those years ago in the hijacked airline on 9 11, who'd said similar words as they headed forward into the last valiant stand of their lives. True warriors, everyone. I wished I could be one-tenth as brave.

A noise. I jumped as a fox veered in front of us, looking for shelter. Moments later, we reached the stairs: no shots, no shouts, nothing but wind. Waves punished rocks below. Rain drummed. We felt our way down water slick steps and reached the dock. A man yelled from somewhere above. His voice seemed to echo from right outside the lodge.

We froze.

Was he shouting at us?

"Hide!" We squeaked in unison, then ducked under the freight ramp. Sneaking back into shadows, we waited, panting. I recollected seeing a man earlier today carrying a box under this ramp and wondered if his actions had anything to do with what was happening now. After the burst of shouting, minutes passed with no sound but more furious weather.

Belle said, "We really need to get to that radio on the boat."

I knew she was right, but boy, I did not want what had happened to Howie to happen to us. We crawled out and sprinted down the dock. In our mad rush, Belle, who was again in front, wobbled, lost her balance, dropped her end of the bag, and fell with a soft cry. Rain blind, I crashed into her, and we sprawled in a messy heap. The dock smelled of creosote and diesel oil. It must have been adrenaline, because I jerked her to her feet and scampered like a scalded cat toward the bobbing *Sea Princess*, towing the bag with one arm and pulling her with the other.

I slowed at the boat, let go Belle, dropped the bag, and began sidling along the edge of the dock, trying to find a way up and onto the rocking craft. Earlier that afternoon, I noticed deckhands tying the *Sea Princess* to the pier in three places, at the bow, midway back along its side, and close to the stern. Now, it shifted like a restless behemoth with the force of the waves, rubber fenders keeping it from damage against the dock's pilings. Belle moved further down the side and found a narrow aluminum ladder hanging near the stern. We would need to grab onto a rung, hoist ourselves and the bag up. We had both clambered around on commercial fishing vessels for years. Still, it would not be easy because it was black dark, and the boat never stopped moving. We decided Belle should go first.

She climbed into the boat. I tried pushing her bag up after her, but wet and slippery, it kept sliding back down. Belle could not reach over far enough to grab it. Finally, I stuck my arms through the dangling straps and hefted it across my back like a clumsy pack. Up the ladder, muscles straining, I delivered myself and her bag, sprawling onto the deck. As I staggered upright, gunfire rattled again. Lodge doors burst open. Light spilling from the interior outlined a group straggling toward us. Rain and wind made it impossible to determine details, but we could see people carrying flashlights. They moved toward the stairs which led down onto the dock. Just before the door slammed shut, I glimpsed someone bringing up the tail of the group, reflected light glinting off what looked like an assault rifle.

My friend still crouched, but I could barely see her.

"They're coming here," I said, sliding flat onto the deck in alarm. "We've got to hide. There's no time to get back off this boat."

My mind churned. I thought of places a person could stow away on a craft this size. The *Sea Princess* wasn't that big. Any halfway thorough search would find us in no time. I shifted, reaching down under my hip. Something hurt. I was lying on my car keys. Next moment, remembering I hadn't brought keys, I realized what was under me. A small, stainless-steel ring lay on the deck surface.

"Hey," I whispered, "Looky here." I got to my knees and tugged on the ring. It was a handle, and I knew, pulled on hard enough, it would come up like a trapdoor with an opening down into the hold.

How tiny is the space down there? I chewed my bottom lip.

I hate going into small places.

Crap.

Although it was too dark for Belle to see what I had grabbed onto, she reached out and felt the metal shape and guessed what I was going to do.

The group from the lodge shambled down the stairs. As they reached the bottom, I forced the hatch upward. We slid into a wooden storage area built under the boat's deck. Belle first, with her bag, and me, last, tugging the lid shut over us.

CHAPTER 6

Soft something's covered the floor of our tiny compartment, piled every which way. The odor of damp clothes greeted us.

"We're sitting on life jackets," Belle announced, her mouth against my ear.

I decided not to think about our cramped environment, instead concentrating on the noises above us. My resolution lasted about twenty seconds.

I hate going into small, dark spaces.

Older cousins talked me into playing funeral when I was four. They assigned me the role of "dead person." At the time, I didn't know what being dead meant. They promised me a tootsie pop. Rolled like a sausage in an old blanket, they laid me in an antique trunk, latching the lid. Every time I yelled for them to get me out, they insisted they were still mourning and said I had to be quiet because dead people didn't make noise. The trunk smelled like mice. I fell asleep; I don't know how long, but I remembered waking up, not knowing where I was.

I opened my eyes. Dark. Closed my eyes. Dark. I cried. I kicked at the enclosure. There was no other sound. Earlier, the cousins talked about putting dead people in the ground. I wondered if I was under the dirt, all covered up. I had to get out. I made myself stop flailing and worked at breaking through the small holes in that old rusty box. These grew bigger and bigger as I scratched and picked my way to freedom. I peeked through the opening I'd broken. I was still in the basement of my aunt's house. I made the void bigger, pushed my fist through, got the trunk latch undone, and climbed out, only to discover the cousins had forgotten about me and run off outside.

People began stepping onto the deck right above us. We cowered. Loud voices in a foreign language.

"Russian," Belle whispered.

Much shouting and laughter. Someone started a raucous song. No one seemed scared or angry. The celebratory sounds continued as the boat squeaked and bounced against its bumpers, but later we thought the group must have moved into the cabin because the noise became muffled. We waited. It grew colder. We huddled together in the claustrophobic space and strapped life preservers around ourselves to help conserve body heat. I must have dozed.

Then a sudden, rapid, boom, boom, boom; followed by a gigantic mind-stopping explosion.

Silence. Spinning. The shock of cold. *Where am I?* Underwater. *Why am I in water?*

Into my mind a line from a poem: *"In the echoing chamber, cold womb of the North Sea, I feel the sounds of darkness and ice, the sounds of death and silence."*

I'm floating down, or up? Numb, I can't tell if my eyes are open, but I am trying to see. I know that I'm supposed to do something. Now sensing nothing, now a burning sensation, now icy cold, I feel pressure. Pressure on my chest with this growing, insistent need to do something, but what?

I break out above the waves, gasping as my body sucks in air. My head pounds, and my ears full of seawater are ringing, ringing, ringing. I see flickering light and fire. In and out, breathing, my body does the work for me.

Where am I? Dizzy, confused, I move cautiously, trying to remember. Flames reach skyward. I stare, not comprehending the flying sparks, the floating piles of burning. There is no sound but the ringing. Devouring cold tells me I need to get myself out of here. The lifejacket floats me, but it won't keep me warm in this frigid bay. Somehow, I know this.

Debris drifts around me. My fingers claw for purchase. I grab and cling to a shattered board. The water is purple-black, yet the tops of waves reflect firelight. Is the ocean burning, too? That can't be real. I'm unable to make sense of where I am, why I am in water. My head throbs, my stunned brain is slow. Someone pushes through waves, swimming toward me, and I reach out to pull them closer so they can grab and hang onto my plank. As I take hold, I find the arm is not connected to a body. I stare at a gold ring on the icy finger of the hand I am gripping, for what seems like a very long time, before I gently let it go. Again, this insistent need to move. Somewhere in my head, my father repeats, "Get out of the water, Loren, Get out of the water." The shooting starts.

Bullet's zip over the waves, over my head. The sound seems far away, but the men are close. Are they shooting at me? Someone screams. I look up over the edge of my splintered plank; water blurs my vision. The floating blaze all around me silhouettes a man crawling across an undamaged part of the deck. It's Leo. He's dragging the left side of his body. Why do I know him? Another man runs from the shadows and shoots him. Point blank. In the face. In shock, I let go of the board. A wave slaps into my open mouth, choking me. I swallow seawater. I vomit. Now under, now bobbing up, I grab the unwieldy chunk of wood again, struggling for breath—my head pounds and pounds. I thrash, trying to escape. The fragment of board I'm hanging onto is so heavy I can barely push it through the churning waves, and I know I won't be able to use it to get away. I cannot get out of the bay close to where I am now, for fear of being seen and killed. I must remain hidden.

I scissor my legs underwater, maneuvering the plank away from the ripped open, wave-swamped *Sea Princess*. Sluggish, I crawl through the swell around the broken boat, trying to avoid burning wreckage. *Belle.* Her name comes into my mind, then her face, her smile.

Why can't I think? My best friend, Belle. I can't remember.

Where part of the dock is still standing, I let go the wood and propel myself between two pilings. I'm hidden down here, but icy waves bully me, pushing and pulling, sucking my life away.

Fatigue is setting in.

I must get out of the water soon, or I won't be able to.

Something bumps against my back. Without looking, I attempt to push it away but find my hand tangled, so I turn around to free myself and see a big bag bobbing against me.

It's floating high. I grab it, sobbing. I remember. My friend's luggage. Now, it's my home. Blinking away salt, I make out someone dangling from a piling brace. Belle. I drape my body over her survival sack and dog paddle to her. Her weak smile is my sunrise.

"Thank God, it's you," she bleats.

We used her big red bag like a raft, working our way from under the dock into the windblown night, from the lodge and fire and shooting and smoke. I swam much further than I thought I could, buoyed by finding my friend, my head becoming clearer even as my strength ran out. Judging we were far enough away to escape detection, we crept from the water onto rocks in the darkness and sheeting rain.

My toes connected with something sharp. I'd lost a boot. We tottered up the beach, knowing we must get warm or perish. Death from exposure in Alaska, even in summer, is a frightening and real possibility. We shambled forward, dragging her bag behind us. Fortunately, the tide was high, covering most of the beach and making our walk into the forest above the waterline short. We swam around a tree-covered promontory in the fiord and could no longer see the lodge or fire.

"It's around here, somewhere," Belle said. Her face was next to mine. What was she saying? I did not understand and wondered if hypothermia had set in. I shivered violently as fear chewed me. She plodded back toward the tide line, still towing her luggage. I groped after, wincing, as my bootless foot came down onto rough beach rocks.

"What're you doing? We've got to get warm." My voice sounded muffled; my ears felt stuffed.

"Howie showed me," she mumbled, wobbling forward, "I know it's close."

"Belle," my voice cracked as I touched her arm, worried now, "What're you talking about?"

She stopped and turned toward me. "The generator," she said, voice shaking, "They put the building around here somewhere to keep the noise away from the lodge. If we can locate that," she stuttered, "We'll be ok."

And we did. Belle had a great sense of direction. She could somehow align herself with trees, a stream, a mountain, and find her way anywhere. I could get lost in a Safeway parking lot. While I was using the satellite phone, Howie had shown her a map with a bay depth marker that indicated the channel and tide level to passing boats heading along the fiord. He said the generator, the lodge's primary power source, was in a small building in the forest about fifty feet above that marker. From there, workers buried electrical wires to the lodge to keep the area as pristine as possible. Howie showed her the control panels and, as she watched, shut the power plant off for the winter. He said the lodge would use stored solar energy for the remaining two days until he got everything closed up.

Rough wood covered the building. At least that's what it felt like, when we found it by colliding with an ocean-facing wall. We searched for a door. Locked.

"Lost my boot," I mumbled, sinking to my knees. "Let's rest here for a while, then try to solve our problem." I wasn't making sense at that point, even to myself, and think I was crying, but it could have been the rain.

Belle pinched me. I teetered upright.

"Let's look for a window," she said.

I stumbled and fell against the door. It opened a crack. My mistake: it wasn't locked. We staggered inside and shut it behind us. The room was dark, but we felt it. Heat. While no longer running, the big engine still emanated warmth, and its radiance welcomed us like our mother.

"Thank you, God," Belle said.

We felt our way toward our new friend and pressed our hands to the warm metal. Delicious. I turned and stood with my back against the steel. Diesel oil perfumed the room, but I didn't care. The balmy temperature was bringing me back to life. With life came pain. I realized I was still wearing a life jacket. I stripped it off and removed my shredded and sopping coat as well, hanging it on a metal knob protruding from the generator. I discovered scratches, cuts, and burns all over my arms and hands. My left shoulder throbbed; it felt wrong, like something was twisted. My neck ached. When I tried to sit, I discovered a large splinter lodged in my back; I pulled it out, cringing from the pain, but glad at the same time it hadn't gone in deep enough to puncture something. I worried my hearing loss might be permanent and wondered how Belle had fared.

She groaned, "I think I might have a cracked rib or two. Everything hurts, but we've got to get dry clothes on."

No wonder her bag is so heavy.

I removed the rest of my ripped and tattered attire. We'd survived and found our way to warmth. Part of me felt giddy with relief; the other part wanted to wail. Belle handed me dry clothes. Her size, they were roomy, but I crept inside them; at least they were dry. She gave me footgear. Although I knew they would be too big, I was thankful. I took my socks off, wringing them out.

Thankfully, the floor wasn't cold. I edged back to the door, hoping to lock it from the inside. There was a handle above the knob, the same type of deadbolt as on the back entry at my house. I felt the bolt slide into place, and relieved, eased back to the generator. Belle was still poking around in her bag.

"Food," she said, pushing something foil wrapped into my hand. I struggled to hear; my ears were still not back to normal.

The storm snarled outside, but we didn't care. There were enemies out there, bad people probably still doing bad things, but we were too tired to think about it, talk it over or make plans. We sagged to the floor. I leaned against the machine and, clutching my energy bar, fell asleep.

Click. I awoke. My ears worked. I knew that sound. Door handle, turning. No time to warn my friend, no time to hide. Dim, foggy light and gusting rain splashed into the room. I struggled to my feet. Belle hurried in through the open door. She saw my expression, blurting, "Just me, sorry I scared you. Needed to visit the little girl's room."

I eased back against the power plant. It cooled during the night, but the room was still warmer and drier than the storm outside. Up near the roof, two skinny windows glowed with pale dawn light. Although we couldn't make out much of anything outdoors but fog, they let in enough light for us to see each other.

"Whoa!" I stared at Belle's blood-caked nostrils. She had a scraped, raw spot on the left side of her head that looked as if someone had tried to scalp her. A split top lip, still oozing. She showed me a gash on her calf that would need several stitches. Burns spotted her hands, but her biggest complaint was the injury to her right side. Had to be a cracked rib or two, she said. Her breathing seemed ok, so we didn't think she had punctured a lung. We took turns assessing each other's wounds. We decided the jagged cut on her calf needed antiseptic, one item that must have fallen out of her bag in the cabin. I moved stiffly around the building, looking for a first-aid kit. My swollen eyes stung. I ran my fingers over bald patches on the back of my head. My neck popped. My shoulder twinged. I walked behind the generator and rummaged around, pulling drawers open on a steel tool chest, remembering Howie talking on his little handheld receiver as we walked into his office the day before. He was instructing someone to lock up a bear gun and leave the radio.

As if reading my mind, Belle limped over, grinning triumphantly, waving a rectangular, black plastic box. It looked like one of the first mobile phones manufactured. With a long, braided cord dangling from its handle, the clubby device was huge compared to current cell phones. She'd found the radio. We pressed switches and buttons, me saying, "S.O.S.," and Belle calling, "Mayday, Mayday," and near the end, both of us desperate, "Help, somebody, please help."

Hoping to receive a response, we were unsure how far it would transmit if we got it operational. It could mean more trouble if we alerted the wrong people.

My socks were dry, so I slid them on and stepped into Belle's borrowed boots. Grabbed my coat, saying, "I think this is where the bear gun is," as I walked over to a narrow cabinet and pulled on the door handle. "Why don't you figure out how to get this open? My turn to run out to the little girl's room."

Almost back to our hiding place, a low growl and a hulking, shadowy shape, lumbering through a patch of salmonberry bushes told me why a big gun was kept in the generator building.

CHAPTER 7

I rushed through the door, turned the deadbolt, and found Belle cutting industriously at the cabinet lock assembly with a hacksaw.

Stuttering, "There's a brownie out there. A big male."

She stopped sawing. We listened but heard nothing.

"It could've been passing by," I said, hoping I was right. We waited a few tense moments, still nothing. I had just decided the beast must be gone when a soft "woof," followed by a rhythmic thump, bump, rubbing commenced. Mr. Bruin was scratching his back against the corner of the generator building. He wasn't leaving.

We took turns sawing through the lock, working the blade as rapidly as we could. It was miserable, tedious labor. I could tell Belle's right side was giving her a lot of pain, because she didn't argue when I took over the job. My fingers began cramping, so I rested for a moment. Slipping my hand into my coat pocket, I discovered a pen-sized flashlight I'd forgotten last winter. I flicked the switch. It must have been waterproof, because it still worked. The cheerful beam felt like a victory of sorts, lifting my spirits. I shined over the dark room, noticing one wall with cartons stacked against it. Curious, I edged over and began examining them. The box at the top had split corners. I saw plastic-wrapped packages nested inside. One had leaked a pearly thread of powder. I moved closer. The glow picked out a cardboard container on the bottom of the pile with one end torn away. I saw the butt ends of four rifles.

My light aimed at the contraband; I said, "Guns, and that's got to be drugs. Wonder if this stuff had anything to do with the explosion last night? We really, really need to get out of here."

I picked up the saw and began cutting furiously. My shoulder burned from the repetitive motion as a blister blossomed on my thumb. The aggressive smell of diesel was making me nauseous. Belle took my penlight and examined the stack. She came back, showed me a few grains of powder on her palm, touched her tongue to them as I watched, and then spat in disgust, saying, "It's cocaine. Drugs and guns, but no ammunition, at least in this load."

Finally, after cutting halfway through the door handle, it broke, and the locking mechanism sprang free, allowing us to open the cabinet. The bear gun was propped inside with two cases of bullets beside it. I lifted it. The rifle felt heavy, solid. The label on the ammo read Remington 45-70. I held a bullet so she could see, asking, "Have you ever shot anything this big?"

"Nope. Biggest rifle I ever shot was my uncle's 30-06 on a moose hunt when I was seventeen."

Crap. Neither have I. Bet it kicks.

"Think the bear left?"

"Don't know," Belle replied, "But like you said, we've got to leave. At some point, unless they're dead, someone is going to come after that stash. I don't think we want to be here when they show up."

From the floor, the radio made a blip, blip, noise and a tiny red light began blinking atop the stubby antenna. I picked it up. Someone was speaking, but I could not tell what was being said. I found the volume knob and turned it up.

"Do… need help? Where… you? Over." There was a pause, then the voice repeated the message. Belle and I bumped heads, trying to get close enough. Was the person on the other end friend or enemy? I pressed the talk button, saying, "I pledge allegiance to the flag of," and released it, waiting.

From what sounded like a million miles away came the response, "… United… of America and… the."

"Republic for which it stands," I continued grimly.

Abruptly, Belle grabbed the radio and spoke into it, "Where are you?"

"This… Jay Carrel…," the faraway voice came back, "… camping Balashof … need…elp?"

"It's the helicopter pilot guy, Jay," I said.

My friend's voice trembled. "I need to make him understand. We don't know who else can hear us talking on this thing, so we've got to say only what's really important for our rescue; at the same time try not to draw attention to ourselves from the wrong people."

She began, "We're your passengers from yesterday. S.O.S. Trouble where you dropped us off. We need to be picked up. S.O.S. ASAP. Original location unsafe. Alert, appropriate people. S.O.S. Urgent."

Jay replied, "Radio… help… cabin. Fog… go south… fi… miles. I… fly… or… boat…"

A jet of tinny music cut off his transmission. Nothing more from him, even though frantic, I turned the dial, searching for the sound of his voice. Feeling discouraged, I turned the volume down and said, "Weird, how a radio can sometimes pick up stations from hundreds of miles away and not be able to transmit from somewhere close. Anyway, we need to get away from here and start south to that cabin."

I walked toward the door and tripped over the life jacket I'd dropped. That soggy object transported me back to last night, with icy waves washing over me, bullets spraying through the stormy darkness, and Howie lying dead on the path with blood dripping over his face. Again, I saw Leo with his bright blue and gold suit crawling across the deck; I closed my eyes and rubbed my forehead, stopping those thoughts, lightheaded. My hands shook as I examined the big rifle. It was a lever-action and loaded. No way could Belle pack the gun with her side injured. My shoulder throbbed. I dreaded having to carry the thing; it was going to be a pain, literally. I put more bullets in my pockets and tied her survival bag on her shoulders. Her red bag was much lighter now because we were wearing the heavy clothes she'd packed inside before leaving home, but it still contained survival food and other essentials. Her face paled, and she grimaced, adjusting the weight. The radio had a strap, and not knowing what else to do, I slipped it around my neck, letting it hang against my chest under my coat.

Belle said, "Sounded like mariachi music coming out of that thing. We can't receive Jay's message, but we're getting Mexico?"

"Or maybe Anchorage. We used to pick up Korea occasionally out on the fish boat," I said, as I hefted the rifle. The large-caliber gun had its own thick leather strap; but fearful of being attacked by a brown bear, I would carry it, pointed in front of me, ready to fire. While both Belle and I had gone on our share of hunting trips, involved in everything from shooting and gutting the animal to loading four-wheelers with field dressed meat, neither of us had ever been on a brown bear hunt. I wasn't sure how she felt, but I'd never had any desire to pursue or trail those animals. Although I had seen my share of bears, alive and in color, sometimes roaming where we hunted deer near Kodiak Island, I respected the savage ferocity and cunning of these enormous creatures and grew twitchy at the thought of being in their vicinity.

We crept to the door and listened. My scratched face and hands rankled and stung, and my shoulder pained with every step.

"At some point," I said, "We'll have a conversation about this fun trip you talked me into. You were right about the scenery. It's amazing, but as for the rest of it, not so sure."

"I am so, so, sorry, you know that; but be fair, you also know I'm as confused about what happened last night as you are."

I knew yesterday's events were not her fault, but I was hungry, hurting, and scared. There was at least one energetic carnivore out there, on the other side of the wall, less than two feet away from where we stood, and I wanted someone to blame.

Her voice broke. "Poor Howie."

We waited. Minutes passed—no more bear noise. Just as we were about to slip from the building, I remembered to pick our discarded clothing and life jackets off the floor. We didn't want to advertise our presence to whoever came for the cocaine and guns. I stuffed them under a pile of greasy rags in a corner, and because nothing that sounded like Mr. Bruin happened for several minutes, we crept from the building, me in front, rifle ready I hoped; and began picking our way due south.

We were hiking parallel to the beach but doing our best to keep hidden by creeping from tree to tree. The wind had calmed, but the haze was back and so cottony it was doubtful that anyone could have spotted us twenty feet away, let alone from the water. We also knew the misty drizzle would hamper any rescue efforts. We were jittery, peering into the brush, listening and sniffing for bear. Those animals stink. With the cream thick fog, I knew a bear could probably not see much; however, their sense of smell is acute, so one could easily find and overtake us. The rifle thrust out in front of me felt heavier and heavier. My arms ached, and sharp darts of misery screamed across my shoulder. I thought I must look as ridiculous as Elmer Fudd in those old cartoons. The pain intensified. Agonizing minutes passed. When I couldn't take any more, I hefted the big gun onto my right shoulder, hoping to get it aimed in time if a bear charged.

After plodding along for well over two hours, growing more tired and hungry as we walked south, I stepped on a rope tied around a spruce snag. It lay strung on the moss and down over the rocks to the water. I showed Belle. We knew it was a running line placed to allow someone to easily move their boat so it wouldn't go dry on the beach at low tide. A few yards above the rope we found a narrow, twisting trail leading toward the mountainside. Although it could not have been past midmorning, the gray mugginess made the day dark. We picked our way quietly along the slippery path.

In the bay below, the strident whine of an outboard alarmed us. We hunkered in place, frozen. Belle was pale. The motor sputtered, died. Friend or enemy? We knew whoever landed that craft could be either.

I dropped the rifle, waded through sodden moss to my companion, and whispered, "Let's hide in the trees somewhere near the cabin and see who's coming."

"What I was thinking," she shot back, as she bounded up the slope.

The energy of fear. I picked up the rifle, forgetting aching muscles as we ran. We came to a patched-together, beat-up, log building sunken into moss. We left the path and wrestled our way through brush. Crouching behind a spruce, we used its wide split trunk and long sweeping branches for cover. Belle slipped off her survival bag and hid it beside a rotted log. Nerves taut, we waited. A few minutes later, someone jogged up the trail. I held up one finger, a second later changed it to two. Belle held up four, as three guys appeared, single file. They carried rifles and appeared to be heading for the cabin. The third man lumbering along had no weapon but was bent almost double, hat pulled low over his face, loaded like a pack mule. The fourth wore a cowboy hat and bobbed and crouched behind the first three, obviously using them for cover. They closed in on the cabin but never noticed us.

Several events collided. An enormous, woofing, tooth-popping brown bear charged the four men, a spindly geezer with a wild shock of snowy hair appeared on the roof of the cabin, waving a rifle, cussing and blasting away, and heaven dumped barrels of rain down on everything. Time and the exact sequence of these occurrences seemed confused in the chaos. The aggrieved bear swatted a man who fell and lay still. As the geezer on the rooftop kept firing, another man screeched, clutched his chest, and crumpled face first in the mud. The old guy on the roof disappeared around that time. The bear bit into the pack carried by the guy loaded with supplies and began shaking it and him. Belle made a small, strangled sound and lurched forward. I grabbed and pulled her back. The terrified man shucked his load, wobbled sideways and fell, rolled, picked himself up, and tore off down the path toward the beach, while the guy with the cowboy hat kept shooting the bear until it no longer moved.

Then Cowboy Hat man, ignoring his fallen companions, entered the cabin. We sat motionless.

Belle's face was ghastly. "That's Cody," she mouthed, rain plastering her hair. "The guy that ran down the path is Cody."

Belle's brother, 'Cocaine' Cody. What on earth is that useless dipstick doing here? Why isn't he still in jail?

Guess we now knew these guys weren't our rescuers. I realized I was panting. We hunkered in the rain, aching and exhausted, trying very hard to stay still, waiting and watching and getting wetter and wetter. No signs of life from the two on the ground. Cowboy Hat sauntered back out of the shabby residence, walked over, and nudged them with his rifle barrel. They lay graveyard still.

My thoughts careened like the marbles in my grandpa's pinball machine. *What should we do?*

We thought Jay wanted us to come here and wait for him, but now? Two bad men wiped out, which helped, but we needed to stay far away from the guy with the cowboy hat. He was armed and dangerous. I knew Belle did not trust her brother, Cody, either. Experiences with him had taught her he would betray her or anyone else for his one love, drugs. I briefly thought about blasting Cowboy Hat man, an easy target with this rifle, but rejected that idea. I knew I couldn't wind up and shoot someone. I tried to slow my breathing. The towering spruce gave us some protection from the rain, but we could not stay out here, indefinitely. I wondered what happened to the grizzled old-timer on the roof, and then I sat there worrying about Jay showing up and then I sat there worrying about Jay not showing up.

The wind returned with gusto, and we shifted, trying to reposition ourselves. The once sheltering tree whipped us, its branches flailing. My friend huddled, head down, despondent. Her brother appearing with those men had been a blow. Last she knew, Cody worked at a gas station in Billings, Montana, doing well, no drugs.

Cowboy Hat disappeared once again into the cabin, and the men on the ground stayed right where they'd fallen. I was sure they were no longer among the living. The bear lay in a matted heap, shot to pieces, jaws open, and very dead.

CHAPTER 8

Before I could plan, I glimpsed motion nearby. The old man who disappeared from the roof during the shootout limped through trees behind his home. Mud smeared; his weedy shoulders sagged. Rainwater dripped down the creases on his face. He was leaning on a broken branch, using it as a crutch, trying to be stealthy, but that wasn't working for him, either. Belle looked up and waved to get his attention; he didn't notice. I handed the rifle to her, whispering, "Here, in case someone looking for trouble comes out the door." I crept over to the old guy, who now leaned against a thick tree trunk.

"Hey," I began, with no idea what to say. He squinted through the rain. His deep-set eyes were the same pale blue as a husky pup I'd gotten on my tenth birthday. His Adam's apple crowded his sun-charred neck; wet hair straggled.

"You two came up my trail first, today," he murmured.

I nodded.

"What're you doing?" He jerked his thumb back over his shoulder. "You with them?"

"No," I said. "We're in trouble. We were at the lodge yesterday; there was an enormous explosion, a gun fight. We escaped. We found cocaine in the lodge's generator building where we stayed the night." I couldn't tell if he was listening, but I kept babbling, anyway. I knew I sounded desperate.

"Please come further over into the trees and talk with us so we can figure out what we should do. I'm afraid that man with the cowboy hat might come out and start shooting, again."

"You go that way, girl," he motioned, pointing away from the ocean, "Up against the side of the mountain. Climb over a hedge of rocks, and you'll see a thick group of hemlock. In through those trees is my steam bath. Go inside and wait for me."

"I could help you walk up there," I offered, pointing to his leg, but he waved his hand at me in dismissal.

"I've got a situation to take care of; you go ahead, I'll be along, directly."

I didn't want to leave. He seemed feeble and in pain. After a moment, not knowing anything else to do, I motioned Belle to follow, wanting to get out of his earshot. After we discussed our options, basically none at this juncture, we started in the direction he had pointed. We didn't have a choice.

Rain pounded, soaking us and making it difficult to see. We thrashed through the brush. Why wasn't there a trail? Instead, we battled through thick undergrowth. The hill we climbed rose at a sharp angle. We scrambled up and over a craggy grouping of boulders and arrived at a thick clot of interwoven hemlock, just as he'd described. After struggling between overlapping branches, we discovered a miniature, bark-sided hut so well camouflaged, we might never have found it without the old guy's instruction. We crept inside, grateful to get out of the miserable deluge. I leaned the rifle against a stubby wall, reached up, and touched the low ceiling. We looked around, waiting for the elderly man. No talk, we were in trouble, there was nothing to say.

Half an oil drum fashioned into a wood stove sat in the room's center with a rusty metal chimney rising above it, sticking through the roof. Wood benches nailed around three walls completed the furniture, and a battered, aluminum suitcase hung on the inside of the thick plank door, tied shut with rope. Stacked towels sat on a bench; a basin and covered wooden water barrel filled one corner. Copper pipe hung above it. The little room smelled like pine tar soap, spruce ashes, and burnt plastic. Belle's parents had a steam bath, called a banya by the Alutiiq in Kodiak. Like this, these little buildings were commonplace throughout Alaska villages. Small groups would crowd the hot interiors, men and women separately, soaping up, then pouring water over their naked bodies and "steaming" in the intense heat. Lifting the lid on the water barrel, I remembered taking "steams" as a child with Belle and her aunts and cousins. It was a social time, unselfconscious; I loved these gatherings and always felt included.

A dipper, made from a tin can nailed to a stick, hung by the barrel, and I dropped it into the water and drank. Just as I thought, rainwater. Collected somewhere outside and brought in through the pipe. Belle opened the metal box. She tugged at the rope, found it knotted and uncooperative. As she pulled the lid open, someone fired a gun, then four more shots in rapid succession. The contents of the box spilled onto the floor. We waited, jumpy and afraid, but after that noise, there was nothing. We continued to wait. Where was the old man? To avoid thinking about what we were stressing about, we examined the items that had fallen from the box. He'd wrapped each in oilcloth, the way I remembered from my village childhood of keeping possessions, tools, and other metal objects from rusting. We unwound each package. I found two spark plugs, four cans of clam chowder, and a .38 caliber revolver with a box of bullets. Belle found a first aid kit. She smeared some antiseptic on the gash on her calf and taped a bandage over it.

I said, "I want to go back. That must be the cabin Jay meant us to find. We need to be there."

Truthfully, I did not want to go back after the battle we had witnessed, but we had to get to a radio, and we needed to check out why the owner of that cabin hadn't shown up like he said he would.

We argued. Belle thought she should go because her brother might have returned. We decided we both would. I left the heavy rifle in the steam bath and loaded the small revolver. We stuffed the contents of the first aid kit into Belle's survival bag. I pushed my arms though the straps.

"Give me my survival bag. You have the gun to handle, and you might need both hands."

After several more minutes of arguing, I gave in, gently hoisting it back onto her shoulders, hating her sudden intake of breath as the weight settled. Although she had picked up Howie's gun in that forever of yesterday evening, it had gotten lost in the explosion.

We sneaked back. It was a little easier going downhill. The wind increased, and I thought the swaying trees' creaking and groaning made more noise than our clumsy struggles, but I felt apprehensive just the same. There was no sound, light, or movement from the cabin.

Behind the same spruce, we huddled, watching and waiting, but saw nothing. We crept behind trees and brush as we moved around the side of the building—still nothing. The door stood wide open. My legs wobbled. I clutched the gun; my fingers hurt; I was squeezing it way too hard. The two men we had seen lying silent in the mud were no longer there. We sidled around the enormous dead bulk of bear and peered inside.

Where was everyone?

A groan greeted us. I pointed the weapon. We edged forward into the dim interior like actors playing cops in movies when they "clear" a house. My heart hammered. I sucked in huge gulps of air, but it didn't seem like enough. Belle spotted the man first. He lay on the floor behind a make-shift table. She dropped her bag, rushing over to him while I peeked into the bedroom and looked around. There was no one else in the two-room building. Blood spattered the man's coat and shirt. As Belle peeled torn clothing off him, we smelled something oily, foetid, like punctured deer gut. An ugly gash low on his belly continued as a deep tear into his left side. Part of his intestines hung from his wound. Although he lay curled in a pool of blood, there wasn't much coming from his gunshot anymore. His injury was terrible. Not knowing what else to do, I looked for a clean rag and ended up grabbing a sheet off the bed, which we wrapped around him.

"I need to get up," the old guy insisted, trying to right himself. "I was bleeding like a stuck pig out there in the trees but got myself back in here after I ran him off." Shifting, motions weak, he said, "The bullet's gone through my side and missed everything important, so I'm ok. I winged him, so he ran off," he repeated. We tried to help ease him back onto the floor. As soon as we let him go, he struggled to a sitting position.

"Put me in that chair and hand me my rifle. I want to be ready when those s…scumbags come back."

Together, Belle and I hoisted him to his feet. The effort of lifting him must have hurt her ribs because she made a soft groaning sound and clutched her side. I knew her injury was most likely causing her constant pain; my shoulder throbbed. We half drug him to the closest chair.

Panting, I said, "Can you tell us your name?"

He ignored my question, saying, "Check how much water is in the barrel, there; if it's full, bring me some, then bar the door."

I looked for a glass and found an empty jelly container. It looked clean, so I filled it with water and held it while he drank. The barrel was full.

He sipped, then pushed his drink away, closing his eyes.

"Can you tell us who hurt you, and why?" I asked, once I'd set the jar on the counter.

Instead of answering, he said, "You two should have stayed hidden in the steam bath. I would have gotten there." I glanced over at Belle. She grimaced. He certainly didn't doubt his abilities. Pointing at her, he said, "Light the kerosene lanterns, girl; the matches are in that drawer." He looked at me, "When she's got the lamps going, you lock the shutters. Bears are why I only have two windows. I built inside shutters to keep them out; well, hold them off at least until I could get my gun, anyway. That dead boar out there is likely to draw in others. No cabin will keep a brownie out if they want to get in."

I shivered. He struggled with the lever action on his rifle, finally managing to jack a shell into the chamber.

When he stopped bossing us, I said in a rush, "I'm Loren, and this is my friend, Belle; she's in real estate, and we got flown north of here to the lodge yesterday so she could show it to clients. The prospective customers never showed up, but two helicopters landed and fighting started, and we tried to get to a boat and call for help, but they blew the boat up, and people got shot, and we ended up spending the night in the lodge's generator building where we found cocaine and guns. Our friend, the helicopter pilot, told us to come to your cabin, and he would try to get here and pick us up, but when we arrived, there was more fighting." I stopped to catch my breath.

The old guy said to me, "You already said most of that outside, earlier." He looked at Belle but pointed a trembling finger at me.

"She always talk this much?"

Belle ignored his question, asking, "Why did those men show up here, today? What was the shooting, about?"

"I left here to get doctoring done in Anchorage, and when I got back, I saw these guys took over my place and stored drugs in here. I tried to burn the stuff, but it took too long, so I hid everything up by my steam bath and camped out in a cave I used many years back. That's where I lived when I first moved over here." He coughed and continued, "I want to show the troopers the drugs, soon as I get the chance. Those no-account rats stole my skiff and trolling stuff. Destroyed a lot of my supplies around here. Ding wads thought I wanted to sell the drugs myself; the pile they left here is worth a lot of money. They chased around through the woods after me for over a week. Soft, citified idiots. They never found my steam bath. Lived out here too long to let them catch me. In fact, I lived in a cave for years and survived just fine. I wrote a book about that; I'll show you girls, sometime."

He rambled on. "Hadn't seen 'em for several days, so I'd just come back this morning to my house, and you two came along, climbing up my trail. Trying to figure if I knew you, when I recognized the sound of my outboard motor. I put it on the skiff before they stole that from me and so realized they were back."

"Ok," Belle said, once he'd stopped talking, "Where's your radio?"

"There," he said, pointing.

We hurried into his bedroom. It smelled like damp wool. An iron cot with musty army blankets and a ramshackle wood box appeared to be the only furniture. A green case covered with buckles and straps that looked like it'd come from an Army/Navy surplus store sat on top. We rushed over, opened it, and saw an old school, transmitter/receiver device, smashed. Belle's face fell. I was so disappointed I wanted to cry. Instead, hearing a retching sound, I hurried back into the kitchen with her right behind me.

The injured man sagged in his chair, forehead sweaty, eyes shut. Vomit dripped down his chest. I touched his leathery neck, almost no pulse.

"He's still breathing, but I think he's passed out," I began.

She pulled the rifle from his relaxing grip. We felt helpless.

"I'm going to try this, again," I said, pulling the handheld radio from under my coat.

Someone pounded on the door. My stomach muscles knotted.

Eyes wide, Belle aimed the old guy's rifle, and I crouched, gripping the .38 in both hands. She growled, making her voice sound low and harsh, "Who's there?"

"Listen, you stupid old man, better open up, or we gonna burn you bad."

Belle, face angry, leaned the rifle against the wall and tried to lift the thick wood bar that locked the world out.

Fear made my voice crack. "Are you nuts? What're you doing?"

"That's Cody," she hissed. "Help me get the door open."

"No, wait. You're forgetting the other guy. What if Cowboy Hat's out there, too? Besides, you know you don't trust your brother."

"If it's Cody by himself, I can handle him."

"If it's not?"

"Cody," she called, no longer trying to disguise her voice. "Who's out there with you?"

There was a long, heavy pause.

The same male voice said, "Sis? Is that you, Sis?"

"That's my brother."

After another, extended silence, Cody said, "There's no one with me, Sis."

Belle opened the door. Her brother stood there, although I wouldn't have recognized him. I remembered Cody as a senior in high school, handsome, well-built, athletic, a young man that teenage girls surrounded, giggling. Now he was glowering, gaunt, and gray faced. Under his ratty stocking cap, his eyes looked like cigarette burns in a dirty blanket. Cody gawked at his sister, confused, then turning, squinted at the path behind him.

"Sis, the h… heck? What you doin,' here?"

CHAPTER 9

"Hmm," Belle said, "What are YOU doing here, brother of mine?" Wind whipped his torn raincoat as he peered first at Belle, then, fearfully into the trees at the edge of the yard.

With anxiety crawling spider like, across my back, I slipped the revolver into my coat pocket. I could barely stand still. Cody was not my favorite person. I managed to stay hidden behind the door.

"Look," he said, gathering himself, "You can't be here."

Belle asked, "Cody, where is that super brave guy with the cowboy hat?" She quickly handed me the old man's rifle. Cody didn't notice as I slipped into the bedroom and shoved the gun under the mattress.

He appeared puzzled by her question, asking, "How do you know about Jim Daumier?"

"We watched all four of you walk up the trail to the cabin," she replied, voice extra sharp.

"Jim is CEO of the company I work for," Cody began.

Near the door, I stood where he could see me and interrupted by asking, "Where is this Jim Daumier, now, and when will he get back here?"

Cody squinted at me. "You? Why're you here?" Sounding fretful, he turned to his sister and said, "I can't believe you're still hanging around with her." He turned and scanned the woods again, as though he expected to see someone, adding without meeting her eyes, "Daumier took off to do some business at the lodge. Weather's too rough to get any construction work done. They said they're staying there, tonight, and they'll pick me up in the morning."

"Cody," Belle scolded, sounding like the older sister I remembered from school days, "What kind of constructing are you doing? We saw two men killed outside, today, then later the coward with the cowboy hat shot him." She indicated the injured man.

"He sent me ahead to talk that geezer into giving back the merchandise he stole from us," Cody whined.

"Stop lying. Daumier and you, and I don't know who all, took over this man's house when he was gone and stored drugs in here. When the old guy got back, he saw you had it stashed in his cabin. He then spent days hiding out while you and the rest of your brave friends chased him through the woods. He's injured because Daumier shot him today. You just now showed up here saying you'll burn him out, so stop making up stupid stories and tell us what's going on."

Cody wilted. "I'm in trouble."

"I thought you were in Billings, Montana."

The injured man groaned. I reached his side and grabbed him just as he toppled from the chair.

"We need to get him into bed," I said. "Cody, your sister's hurt, in case you hadn't noticed, so why don't you come over here and help me carry him?"

"Look, Sis," Cody said, squinting through the open door at the old-timer. "I don't know why you're here, and it's too bad you're hurt, but all I can say is, you need to leave. I've got to find where that guy hid our stuff, and I've got to have it ready when they show up in the morning, or I'm going to end up as dead as that stinkin' bear out there."

"Cody, who made your breakfast every morning for over six years and helped you with your schoolwork?"

"Come on, Sis. Don't do that. You don't understand."

"Who got you into re-hab not once, not twice, but three times?"

"They're going to kill me."

"And last, but not least, who saved your bony butt with Naloxone when you overdosed?"

Cody swore, walked over, picked up the unconscious man, and dropped him on the cot in his bedroom. I pulled a blanket over him. I couldn't tell if he was asleep now, or comatose. Back in the kitchen, he frowned at his sister.

"You," he said to her, then growing aggressive, pumped two fingers in my direction, "And your ugly witch of a white friend from school days need to leave, now. The old man will stay here."

He still hates me; I thought, my pulse jittering.

"I'll watch the old gentleman awhile just to make sure he's ok," I volunteered, wanting to get away from Cody and wanting to try the radio I'd carried around my neck all day. Cody stood near the table with his back to me, so I walked into the bedroom, checked that the feisty sourdough was still breathing, pulled the radio from under my sweater, and flipped the "on" switch as Belle asked, "Why are you here with these guys?"

Cody began his story, but didn't get far, before she interrupted him.

"What trouble are you in?"

I listened, amazed she hadn't added "this time," because, for as long as I could remember, Cody jumped whole heartedly into any trouble he could find. Sadly, but not surprisingly, his behavioral issues started when he was in seventh grade, which was the same winter his mother, out ptarmigan hunting, had fallen through the ice and drowned. There had been many visits to counselors, and then during high school, temporary stays in jail and foster care and a week in the state's psychiatric institute after he'd dismembered a neighbor's pet. With their father working out of town, Belle, who was a kid herself, raised Cody. Their uncle Charlie tried to help when he wasn't drunk; he even tried to help when he was drunk, which rarely ended well. Life wasn't easy in an outlying village, even with aunts and cousins bringing meals and supporting when they could.

Their voices became heated, louder. It would help to mask the chitters emanating from the little radio, I decided. I pushed buttons and whispered into its mouthpiece as I remembered the start of our friendship on a field trip way back in fourth grade. Tasked with finding a razor clam, we were instructed to dig it out and bring it back to school to dissect. Many of the children had never harvested from the sea and did not understand what to do. Our unhappily single teacher was not paying attention to her class; instead, she strolled along the shore, aggressively flirting with the nervously quivering fish and game biologist who discovered that what he was there for, was not what he was there for. While most of the students milled about, Belle and I grabbed shovels and began walking the beach, looking for the minute round indentations that signal a marine mollusk is under the sand in that area. Once we'd located the telltale dimple, we dug. A few other kids followed our lead. The class bully, jealous, threw rocks at us and punched

Belle. I ran to her aid. Together, we dragged him behind a brush clump and stuffed wet seaweed down his pants. We then got back to digging and found over half the student's clams. That day we became best friends, and to cement our alliance agreed on a "top secret" codeword, "seaweed," we'd use if either of us ever needed help. Silly, yes, but we were nine years old.

Kids often had to grow up fast in "bush" Alaska. Both our families lived a subsistence-type lifestyle, miles from a town of any size. Our parents and grandparents taught us to contribute to the family gathering and harvesting enterprise very early.

Things got rough after Belle's mother died. It was easy to see she had been the rudder in that family. My friend and I often spent hours together at her house, completing our homework and doing chores. Cody never seemed able to cope after his mother's accident. The bereft little boy wandered like a waif, trailing around after his sister and me or hanging out on the docks until chased away. As he grew older, he stayed in his room for hours, reading graphic comics, creepy Stephen King novels and making dark, grisly little drawings.

Although he grew from a runny-nosed kid into a lean and handsome young man who excelled in basketball, and made good grades, there was something troubled, an eerie emptiness dulling his eyes.

Deep in my memories, Cody's angry outburst brought me back to the present.

"I got to work for Jim because I owe him over $365K."

I looked through the doorway and saw the shock on Belle's face as she registered his words. In the silence that followed, the radio made an odd, drawn-out, farting noise. I grabbed at it, fumbling with the volume, turned it down, and hid it back under my clothes. Cold and tired, I despaired. How were we supposed to get word to Jay? The wind and rain showed no signs of abating. The storm had picked up in intensity. I knew enough about ocean conditions and weather to realize the gale-force winds made it perilous for anyone to fly or travel by boat. Without a radio, how would we send word we needed help? No friends or family expected a call from us for at least two weeks. No one would realize we needed rescuing. As I glanced at the critically injured man on the bed, trepidation settled over me. Without help, he would not make it. With no help, were Belle and I going to make it? I feared we were on our own.

Again, I checked his injury; there was no fresh bleeding. As I rearranged his covers, he muttered but did not wake. Cody still droned in the other room. I pulled the radio out again, turned the volume back up, and listened for a few minutes more. Nothing but static. I wanted to hide it from Cody, so decided to go outside and try calling Jay from there. I stuffed it back under my shirt, covered everything with my coat, and stepped into the kitchen, pulling my hood up.

"Think I'll visit the outhouse." I opened the door, only to have Cody grab my wrist and jerk me back toward him. I screamed. His breath reeked, rotten teeth and stale beer.

"Cody, let her go!" Belle yelled.

"I thought I'd never have to see your pale, trouble-making face, again," he rasped, looking down at me, eyes slitted like a feral creature.

The real Cody comes out; I thought in the millisecond before I responded, "Get your grimy hands off." My instant anger surprised me. It startled him, too; I wasn't acting like the shy kid he remembered. He let go. Woozy, off balance—bolts of stabbing pain shot through my shoulder. Belle jumped in between us and slapped her brother. I felt lightheaded for an instant, but pulled the revolver from my pocket, turned, and aimed at him.

Cody backed up, hands in the air.

Belle cried, "Wait!"

Holding the .38 in my shaking fingers, pointing it at Cody with sweat running into my eyes, I felt scared and a bit idiotic, but more angry than anything else. I had never aimed a gun, any kind of gun, at anyone.

"Cody," I said, "I will shoot you; if you touch me again, I will shoot you. You are a worthless, cowardly, trouble-making, piece of…" I started over—no cussing around Belle. I had promised her. My arm wavered. My voice shrilled, but I was too tired and too indignant to care.

"You've caused your long-suffering sister more pain and trouble than you'll ever know, and I will never be sorry I reported you to the police for hurting her. You've bullied her for years, and she's put up with it, trying to help you make something of yourself. I would love to put you out of her misery; you…you… weasel."

I motioned with the .38, growling, "Sit down, there. Now!" as Cody hesitated. "Belle, lock the door," hoping she would do it.

"Ok," I said, wanting to put the gun down, knowing I was making this up because he forced it, but refusing to let myself back away. Fourteen years old, taking a shortcut home by crossing the cannery dock, I'd found myself caught in the middle of a strike by dock workers, an angry mob melee. I escaped with only a sprained elbow and some fast talk about my cousin and his friends being a few steps behind me. The rabble's unruly behavior terrified me. My mother's inebriated rants scared me. I grew into a frightened and cowed adult, priding myself on my ability to remain neutral and slip away from any dispute. If I were honest, most of my pretended tolerance was more from cowardice than anything else. Anything to avoid conflict.

"Ok," I said again. "Cody, you need to answer some questions, and you need to do it, now. No more lies, no more bull."

His palm struck the table. Scowling, "I told my sister everything, few minutes ago. I don't talk to you, bossy white cow."

He launched, lunging toward me. I shot. He squealed and crashed back onto the chair.

Eyes enormous, Belle hurried over, looking for injury. I hadn't shot him, but firing the pistol made a horrendous noise and jolted him into believing I could and would kill him, which is what I wanted.

Cody curled like a question mark, eyes shut, arms cradling his head when the gun fired. Belle looked at me in what I could only call astonished dismay; I winked at her and tried to smile. The smile didn't come off so well because my teeth were chattering.

"Look," I said, "The explosion at the lodge that you probably had a hand in, almost killed your sister and me. All you've done is run your mouth and make yourself out a victim; most of it lies. Look at your sister's scraped face. Have you seen the gash on her leg? You self-centered cretin. You haven't even cared enough to ask what happened."

Cody mumbled, scratching an ear.

"Enough from you, shut up," I said, my voice knife blades. "Now talk. Give us the truth about the drugs and the explosion."

Belle was looking at me funny. I realized I might be confusing her and Cody a bit, but she knew I was an amateur at handling confrontation, and I figured I would get better with practice.

CHAPTER 10

Cody told us he became friends with Jim Daumier in jail. Daumier's father sold meth from some homestead near Denali. Jim learned to cook the stuff and began selling throughout Alaska. When Daumier's dad died in a meth lab fire, Jim took over. His number one "mule," an aging hooker, bombed out of her mind walking through the airport in Anchorage, burst a paper bag loaded with meth on an escalator, and got herself arrested. She ratted Daumier out. Daumier's first arrest, he got twenty months. He expanded contacts while inside and brought Cody into his confidence, supplying him intermittently with opioids flown in on drones. The state released Daumier ahead of Cody, who was in for eighteen months for assault with a deadly weapon. Jail time over, Daumier picked Cody up in a brand-new Ford truck outside the prison entrance and drove him to a roadside steak house.

"He bought me the biggest steak I ever ate," Cody bragged. Daumier introduced him to his associates, then showed him how to mainline minute quantities of various drugs to get high, but not become so addicted he would be 'wrecked by the need.'

This last, self-delusional bit made me laugh, more like a derisive cackle, I'll admit, and Belle said, "That's absurd."

As his addiction grew, Daumier withheld drugs and taunted him about using.

"I stole coke from Jim. I felt really crummy about that. One day he took me for a ride with two of his guys." Cody pushed his sleeve up, showing a long, puckered scar. Daumier's flunkies burned him with a propane torch as punishment for stealing.

"He said if I wanted to live, I better repay the $170K I owed him. I ran off to Billings and got clean after that, but they tracked me down and brought me back. Then today, Jim told me to get over here and finish the job with the old dude," Cody complained. "I said no, but he said I now owe him over $365K, and he'll kill me, and I know he will."

Cody looked at his sister. He stopped talking and stared at the floor. Was that fear or shame I saw, or more playacting?

"Then what, Cody?" Belle asked. Her features looked pinched, but I couldn't tell if that was pain from her injuries, or her brother's meandering saga.

My muscles ached from holding the gun at arm's length, so keeping it aimed at Belle's brother, I dragged a chair over and sat, resting my arm on the counter.

"Jim restarted his distribution ring by buying drugs from Central America, but the step-up in security made it hard for him to get enough stuff to build his business. Plus, on probation, he always felt like cops were watching him. The business was a real headache." Cody spit on his thumb, then rubbed at a mark on the wooden tabletop.

Repelled, I burst out, "Are you trying to get us to sympathize with that lowlife?"

Cody glared at me, and the weapon still aimed at his belly, sighing, enjoying the drama.

"Still mean as when you called the cops on me in Kodiak, aren't you?"

"No," I answered, waving the .38 and doing my best to sound threatening, "I'm much meaner, now. What's the Russian connection?" I bit my lip and hoped he couldn't see my knees jiggling.

Cody said Jim Daumier and he took a flight to Fairbanks three years earlier to "discipline" one of Daumier's sellers, Rolf, a military reject who started an attention-getting turf war over towns between North Pole and Anchorage.

Served watery booze during their crowded jet ride, they rented a beater of a car that popped a tire down a slimy mud road close to Rolf's house. Daumier was in a foul mood. He ordered Cody to break Rolf's legs with the sledgehammer they bought earlier at Home Depot.

"He told that stupid Rolf," Cody said, "To, like, cool it. You know Jim Daumier is no dummy."

"Even if that's how his last name is pronounced, huh?" I interrupted. "Where do the Russians come into all this? Finish your story."

"He started making me do all the dirtiest jobs," Cody moaned.

"We left the guy crying in his shack like a little kid, even though I kinda felt sorry for him and only broke one of his legs. Jim had already gone to the car, but he still made me change the tire. Mosquitoes ate me alive. Jim sat in that rusty Honda, playing on his phone and yelling about how slow I was. He kept saying we should go back to Home Depot and return the sledgehammer and get our thirty-two dollars and twenty-seven cents back because I didn't mess it up or nothin,' but I talked him into stopping at this bar we passed earlier, instead."

Cody said they met two guys from Yaroslavl, Russia, dressed in camo, who came into the place soon after Daumier downed his third black Russian. The camo guys sat near them, boasting about poaching polar bears in northern Siberia, and ordered black Russians, also. They noticed Daumier and began arguing with him about the coffee liquor the bar used to make the strong, vodka-based drink. The four men moved to a secluded corner. The Russians were flying to Kodiak to go brown bear hunting. Daumier introduced Cody, bragging up his hunting abilities, saying he was a genuine Aleut, big-game guide, raised on Kodiak Island. The Russians slammed down drink after drink. One of them jumped on a table and tried to dance like a Cossack. He smashed a chair, broke several glasses, and the bouncer threw them out. Daumier and the Russians were so inebriated by two in the morning, Cody had to drive. They ended up at a cheap motel. Cody paid, helped them into their rooms, and stayed outside in the car like Daumier ordered, watching the Russian's door so they wouldn't take off in the morning without them.

"Is there a point to this, Cody?" I asked.

How long would he keep yapping? He relished being the center of attention. *Nothing new about that. Where, oh, where is Jay?* The storm seemed relentless. Savage wind drove through cracks in the rickety building. The room grew chilly; my clothes were damp. I wiggled my sore feet as my arm holding the gun cramped.

"What does this have to do with the explosion?"

Cody squinted at me, reproachful, "You said you wanted to know. We flew to Kodiak, and Jim made me get hunting supplies rounded up."

Cody had no supplies of his own and hadn't lived in Kodiak for the past ten years, so he ended up "borrowing" from an elderly relative who had gone to fish camp.

"Decent of you to steal Uncle Robert's stuff," Belle said in disgust.

Cody said, "Those guys, they brought lots of money." The Russians chartered a plane. They had a map and knew what they wanted to see. No airfield, so a floatplane landed on the bay. Daumier, impressed with the Russian's money, determined to stay friends with them. The men did nothing but slug vodka and wander a few feet from their tent to the relief of Cody, who had never killed a brown bear or guided a hunt. The tall Russian bragged his boss back in Moscow had bought the property they were camping on and would build a lodge for hunting, partying, and tourism but said it would mostly be used as a stopping-off place to bring drugs from Asia through Russia; drugs they would spread around Alaska and down the Inside Passage and beyond.

Belle and I were familiar with the Inside Passage, as are many others. This waterway links Alaska to Washington state. Both Canada and the United States use this route to ferry supplies and people between communities.

Cody picked at a scab surrounding a crude star newly tattooed on his neck and said, "On the fourth morning, I woke up early to pee and overheard those Russians. I couldn't understand everything, but they said they could tell the pilot we left to hunt and never returned. The tall one with the pierced ear kept arguing for killing us, leaving us curled up under a bush somewhere, he said, but the other one who was boss, said it'd be less hassle if they let Jim and the Nif," Cody's face grew angry at the slur, "Have the drug running job as a trial to see if their business plan could work. If the plan failed, they could, for sure, kill us then and go back to Russia. I told Daumier. He said hide the guns. Next day the floatplane picked us up. We flew over two brown bears on our way back to Kodiak. They made jokes about their stupid Aleut guide not finding them a trophy," he finished, looking miserable.

"You continue to choose the most wonderful friends. Daumier must be right at the top. Such an honorable person. He helps you get re-addicted, uses and humiliates you, makes you his minion. Mama would be proud," Belle said.

She got up, eyes snapping with suppressed fury, limped over and looked in through the bedroom doorway at the unconscious man. I saw her stare at him for a long moment, hurry over and feel his neck and wrist for a pulse, then check his wound. She tried to find a pulse, again. Putting her ear on his chest, I knew she was listening for a heartbeat. Her eyes were bleak as she glanced at me and shook her head. I tried to swallow. My stomach knotted. Cody realized something had happened and stood.

"Sit down," I stammered around the lump in my throat. I waved the pistol again. I needed to keep him off balance. "You haven't finished your story. The explosion last night, remember?"

Eyes loathing me, he sat. Belle pulled blankets over the body, moved from the bedroom, and opened shutters on a window. Rain beat on the glass, wind moaned through crevices; daylight drained away. She refastened the shutters and resumed her seat across from Cody. She rubbed at tears on her face.

"Cody," she began quietly, "That elderly man in the bedroom is dead."

"He caused us a lot of trouble," Cody stuttered. "He wouldn't leave our stuff alone."

Belle looked at her brother. Her expression hardened.

Cody shuffled his feet. He pulled his hat off, running his fingers through lank hair. Before Belle or I realized what was happening, he stuffed a flat, round, object that looked like an antacid tablet, into his mouth and swallowed, saying, "It wasn't me. I didn't shoot him."

"You might not have pulled the trigger, you blinking idiot, but you were still part of what killed him," I shouted, enraged. "Did you just take some kind of drug? Belle, you saw him stick something in his mouth, right?" I thrust the pistol at him. "Give me the rest of your pills."

"That's all Jim gave me. He said I could have more when I find where that geezer hid our stuff."

Is he lying again? Suddenly, I didn't care. Weariness clouded my thoughts. My eyes burned. Neither Belle nor I had eaten since that one energy bar. Blinking back tears, I felt sadness swell my soul until my chest hurt. They bullied and finally killed that old-timer—what a tragic death. I didn't even know his name. And Howie, too. What had either of these unlucky men done to end up murdered?

If only this were something I could delete from my phone or take back to the library.

Wrung out from hunger and fatigue, I wanted to be home, sleeping, making something good to eat, or happily painting and listening to a recorded novel. An Agatha Christie, Frazier, or even an old Louis Lamour. A book that spun an entertaining tale without me having to leave my house, go hungry, or without sleep. So tidy. I liked fiction, because most problems got solved by the end. The significant characters eventually overcame their challenges and often lived to have another escapade. I wriggled my icy toes, trying to generate warmth. Our experience was no audio book; I could not press pause, get a cookie and come back later. I thought of my friend Joan, who churned out easy-read romance and argued reality was dull.

Well, wish you could see me, now, Joanie ole pal, 'cuz this is turning into my very own, real-life thriller with murder, mayhem, conflict, and danger, and here we are, only the second day into it.

I needed a plan to get myself and my friend out of our predicament. Cody's boss and the drug-running Russians were ruthless; they had weapons; they had more people. We had nowhere to hide; the storm was making it impossible for a rescue. We didn't know where Jay was or how to contact him. I was positive the only reason we had survived so far is that the bad guys either didn't know we existed, or they knew and thought they had killed us. How did Charlene Chametz fit into this, and what to do about Cody? I didn't like or trust him, but I didn't plan to kill him.

Controlling my voice, I said, "All right, Cody. I don't care if you swallow fifty pills. Fact is, this ugly white cow kinda hates you and wishes you would."

Changing the subject, I said, "Who does the lodge belong to?"

Cody thought for a moment, slowly scratched his belly, shifted on the wooden chair, and said, "See, the land we camped on for the hunting trip was where the lodge got built. They brought in lots of workers, and it still took almost two years to get finished. Some rich Russian guy owned it. I don't know his name. But we ran the Russian drug operation, and there was this wild girl…" He smiled, voice trailing off dreamily, restarting, "Then, in June, the Ru-Russians got in a fight over the lodge."

"Why?" Belle asked.

He pouted, mumbling, "I don't know, I don't know." He leaned over, cleared his throat, held one nostril closed with a finger, and blew a gloppy wad onto the floor.

I tried not to flinch.

"They said a big stakes poker game happened somewhere in Russia, the lodge owner lost, and Daumier said he lost the lodge to some high up, Russian military or political guy. The owner, Vitaly, claimed they cheated him. They started fighting over who owned the buildings and even the drug business, too." Vitaly has a nephew, Sergei, who used to hang around the lodge, especially when they brought in those Spanish hookers.

He paused, "You guys heard about the boat that caught fire and sunk near Sitka early this summer, right?"

His words were slowing, slurring, "That was the boat we used for getting stuff down to Washington state and we made a deal to sell the drugs off that boat to Sergei, but Daumier kinda double crossed him."

"Last night was fighting over the lodge. I think they were trying to blow up the boat we were going to take since the other one sunk. We need to find the big stash we stuck in here and get our drugs sold." He yawned, trailing off, "Dude, we're businessmen and we got bills to pay. That old goat caused a lot of trouble. He hid our inventory and I got to find it, fast.

"Yesterday, Cody, we were at the lodge when two helicopters landed. We watched Madame Chametz climb out of one and come into the building where she had a meeting with some Russians that landed in the other one. You know anything about that?" Belle asked.

CHAPTER 11

Cody twitched. He seemed unable to focus. There was genuine bewilderment in his voice. "Madame Chametz? Who's that? Is she one of them hookers?"

"In a manner of speaking," Belle said thoughtfully. I interrupted, asking, "Where were you and Daumier, yesterday?"

"We heard Sergei was looking for Jim, so we hid the cocaine and rifles under a tarp in the trees up the beach," Cody gabbled, voice vague. His eyes looked glazed. He scrubbed at his face with one knotted fist and stared at the floor, blinking slowly, seeming to lose his train of thought.

"Jim said there was going to be trouble, so we unloaded it from our skiff just in case. Jim got on the radio with someone, and later in the evening, he told us bad weather was coming in, so we had to go back and pack all the stuff through the woods and sneak it into the generator building so it wouldn't get wet. The guys were pretty dang mad about carrying it so many places. Just when we got it inside, there was this explosion. The building rattled, even that far away. We ran out and got into our skiff and headed across the fiord. It was dark by then and raining hard. We could kinda tell the explosion damaged the *Sea Princess*, but we didn't know what all had blown up, and we didn't know how many guys were over there."

"Doesn't it seem odd, Cody, that Daumier would send you back over here to get drugs from the old man that he couldn't get earlier, and not even give you a weapon?" Belle asked. She reached for a pen and appeared to be doodling on a scrap of paper she picked off the table.

Cody looked at her for several long seconds, eyes half closed. "He told me the old man was dead. He said he didn't have time to get our stash because I run like a chicken from the bear, and he had to hide Juan and Cal's bodies by himself."

"Use your head. What do you think Daumier wanted to happen over here?"

Cody seemed to consider, then, his words barely intelligible, "He-he told me not to quit until I did the job. He said I better have the drugs found by tomorrow when they come by." Muttering, "He was trying to get me shot by the old man."

"Belle," I said, "We need to go."

She ignored me and, leaning forward, spoke earnestly, "You're still alive, Cody. You're still young. You can still walk away from all this and do something better with your life."

Cody hunched, resting his chin on his hand. Rheumy eyes and lines carved into his face by years of hard living left me unconvinced of his youth, but I said nothing. His sister's impassioned plea was genuine.

"Cody," I said, "Why are you so sure Daumier isn't coming back over here, tonight?"

He sniffed and yawned again, smirking.

"He's visiting that red haired lady at the lodge and don't want to be disturbed. And you know something? He's scared to operate the boat in the dark. Has a hard time keeping that kicker running, and he can't swim so good." He chortled drunkenly. "It's pretty rough out there, you know." He closed his eyes, and said, "After what he did to their boat near Sitka, I don't care what he says; he's no hot-shot boat captain, thas' for sure."

We watched him slide down like a dirty chunk of sea ice melting on a warm April beach. His head landed with a thump on the scarred wooden table. He snored. Belle got up, leaned over her brother and gently lifted one of his eyelids.

"He's zonked," she said. "Stoned."

"Have any idea how long he'll be like this?"

"No. Don't know how much he took or what it was, but he could be passed out for hours."

"I hope he is."

Belle motioned me to the corner of the room farthest from her brother.

In hushed tones, she said, "I know you think I'm a nitwit letting him in the cabin. But I worried he'd start the place on fire with us in here."

She looked at him for a long moment. "I've been thinking about something the old man said." She handed me the scrap of paper she'd been doodling on earlier. Her note read:

We should look around cabin for book or diary old man wrote before we leave.

"Why?"

She wrote: Remember he said cave he stayed in?

"So?"

She wrote: Find map, cave may be place for us to hide.

I took the scrap from her and wrote: Morning light's coming, need to find book fast.

We began searching for anything that looked like a journal. The cabin was small, with few places to hide a book. We found bullets for his rifle, thick perfumed letters from someone named Clara, an unopened cardboard box which claimed to contain forty-eight toothbrushes, several containers of outdated scientific magazines, but no journal, no book.

Cody's mouth hung open. He drooled, snorted, and snored but, other than that, never moved. I tiptoed around him, trying to imagine where the elderly man hid a diary in this small space; wandered into the bedroom, and looked at the meager furnishings again. Did not want to feel around under the mattress with a body lying there, so tiptoed back into the kitchen. We were running out of places to search. My eyes rested on the water barrel.

Laying the revolver on the counter, I removed my coat, picked up a dented saucepan from the dish drainer, and grabbed the gun again just in case. I filled the pan from the barrel, dumping it quietly down the sink. Belle knelt near the woodstove, searching through a cardboard box of old magazines. As I neared the bottom of the barrel, I could see something glimmering—a translucent plastic container.

I haven't seen Tupperware in years.

I sat on a chair by Belle, checked to make sure Cody hadn't awakened, pried off the lid, and lifted out a thick, leather-encased book. It was hand-made, hand-written. Hours had gone into working the leather and sewing the pages. After leafing through a few, I handed it to her, whispering, "Here's a map he drew. What is this? His magnum opus? Think this is what he was talking about?"

She took the volume from me, running her fingers over the drawing I'd found. "This is what I was hoping for," she gestured.

We examined a sketch that included part of the fiord, the cabin we now sat in, and his steam bath. Looking closer, we saw a series of consecutive landmarks with arrows that pointed to what he called "his cave," located according to his notes, about one hundred feet up the side of a mountain.

Belle wrote on the scrap again: I want to go find this cave.

Of course, you do.

Dubious, I scribbled: How far away you think it is?

She shrugged and wrote: One to eight miles.

Another long trek through the brush. I sighed, "Let's go somewhere we can talk."

We collected the few items we had brought. I walked back into the bedroom and slid the old guy's rifle out from under his mattress, trying not to look at his waxy, bluish face. I picked up ammunition we had found while searching his place and stuffed it in the pockets of my coat, watching for movement from Cody. Belle removed the hand-drawn map, put it into her pocket, folded the leather cover back around the book, and placed it into her survival bag. I grabbed two of the new toothbrushes, a jar of peanut butter, a box of pilot bread, two cans of tuna, a can opener and rusty flatware and crammed it all into a canvas backpack I found hanging on a nail. We looked at Cody one last time, walked through the door, and shut it behind us. The wind and rain had slowed. Traces of morning sun teased the gloom overhead. A bossy blue jay chided as we walked away, rasping his demands, no doubt used to scraps.

We moved west through the forest, heading uphill, away from the water and the cabin. It didn't take as long this time to reach the steam bath.

Once inside, we collapsed on a bench. We didn't mention Cody. Belle pulled the map from her pocket, and using my small flashlight, poured over it. I took his book from her bag, flipping to the page where she'd torn it out. I read and reread, hoping for direction, but what I saw looked like something out of an amateurishly written, fantasy novel.

Dismayed, I stood, stumbling over the cans of chowder we'd dropped hours earlier. I grabbed my flashlight away from my friend, shone it on a paragraph, and read aloud, "The wizard walked into the magical cavern. Strange, multicolored orbs floated above his head, and he sensed the Lady of the North's calming presence."

I discovered I was chewing my bottom lip when I tasted blood. Turning to the inside cover, I mumbled, "By Arthur Cook." Slamming the book onto the narrow bench, I said, "This is all made up! I'll bet there's no cave."

In the dim light, I could see tension etching Belle's face. I knew it reflected my worry.

We had hoped for somewhere we could hide until rescue happened.

"This Arthur Cook guy wrote some goofy fiction, so he wouldn't die of boredom, I guess." Inexplicably, I felt anger toward the elderly man.

"Crap! Wonder what else he made up?"

Belle closed her eyes, slumping against the plank wall. "What about the smell of burned plastic?"

Stepping to the rusty barrel stove, I jerked open the door, shone my light inside, and pulled out two partially burned loaf shapes that looked like the packages we'd seen in the generator building.

I bolted out the door, scrambling around the perimeter of the miniature building looking for the rest of the drugs. Arthur Cook said he tried to burn them and couldn't, so hid them by his steam bath to show to the troopers. At the back of the hut, pushed under the branches of a sizable hemlock tree, my flashlight found a tarp draped, wooden box with kindling scattered nearby. I ripped the tarp away. Plastic packages filled it.

I rushed back inside, carrying one and dropped it on the bench next to Belle. She had pried open a can of the chowder we'd found earlier. She opened another for me, and ravenous; I gulped it, hoping it wasn't too many years past expiration. We each chugged two cans of the pale, bland soup dotted with chewy chunks of something brownish, the clam, I supposed. When she handed me an energy bar from her survival bag, I accepted and ate it in four bites, almost imagining a flavor. We drank rainwater from the barrel in the corner and huddled on a bench, afraid to light a fire. She picked up the book, and using my flashlight, began turning pages, stopping to read a section here and another, there. I stretched, moving my shoulder from side to side.

"Hey," I said, trying to get her to look at me. Arthur's writing engrossed her.

"Belle," I said again, louder. She stopped reading. I couldn't help giggling. "Cody might have done me a favor." She gave me her complete attention.

"I'm not joking," I said, seeing her frown. "When he grabbed me today, uh, yesterday, and yanked my arm, I thought I was going to pass out, it hurt so bad. I think that explosion dislocated my shoulder, and his pulling on it might have popped it back into place. It feels better."

"That's good," she said, smiling for the first time since I'd found her clinging to a piling under the dock. She read for a few minutes more, then closed the book, saying, "Arthur Cook hid the drugs. You found them as he described. So, the old guy wasn't making that up. I realize his book sounds like unskilled nonsense, and I'm sure a lot of it is, but something made him want to write it. The parts I've been reading describe a cave. Remember, he told us he stayed in one for years. I still think there's an actual cave, and he lived in it."

"And you want to find it."

"I don't know what else to do, and I'm worried my brother will tell Daumier about us to curry favor, maybe blame us to buy time for himself. They can't afford to stop looking for their drugs. I'm also worried if they look long enough, they'll find this steam bath and us if we stay here."

We hadn't talked about leaving Cody in the cabin. I didn't have a problem with it; I couldn't save him. For years, I witnessed Belle helping him out of one predicament after another, often to her detriment. I was surprised when she walked out of the cabin and away from him, but relieved. Daumier and his crew would keep looking for the drugs. He and several others might end up dead over the loss. I was no expert on the going retail price for cocaine or heroin, but I'd seen media coverage and pictures of triumphant cops standing next to piles of confiscated bundles. The box outside the steam bath was full, and there were about as many packages as anything I'd seen on the news; I guessed we were looking at several million dollars in substance, worth enough to get a flunky like Daumier butchered for losing it.

"What I want to do is get across the fiord and find the dock that Howie told us about, the one with the smaller boats, take one of them, and head for Kodiak."

"Yes, I know," I continued, seeing her doubtful look, "We would have to hike back by the lodge and get to the other side of the fiord without being discovered. Even if we stole a boat, got it running, and escaped to the open ocean without being chased down and shot, we would never make it across the Shelikof in this wind."

I sighed, moving around the space, "It's just that the boats he told us about are real, and I don't know for sure the cave is."

"We could flip a coin," she said, "If we had one."

The radio hanging around my neck gave a sudden squeal. I jumped, stumbling backward, the bulky device thumping onto my chest. I yanked the strap, pulling it over my head, and began working the tuning dial back and forth.

A faint whisper of a voice almost covered by static said, "… is Jay." Another burst of static, and then it appeared to go dead. Flipping the volume as loud as it would go, I shook the radio, realizing at the same time why it was fading. It was my fault. I had forgotten to turn it off down in the cabin the last time I tried to call for help. More white noise, quieter this time. The batteries were almost gone. Shook it again. Dumb of me. I knew that wouldn't help. We heard a faint hiss, a mere breath of sound. Belle squeezed against me, almost climbing into my lap.

CHAPTER 12

The transmission was quiet, but crystal clear. "Jay calling realtor and artist, storm hindering contact." A pause. Was Jay finished talking, or were the batteries gone? I took a chance, pressed the talk button, and yelled one word, "Cave."

Releasing the button, I listened with my entire body. Belle jammed against me. We pressed our ears against it, her right, my left. From a million miles away, these last words before it went completely dead, "… go to cave."

I set the radio on the bench beside me. "What do you know, Jay is still trying," I said.

I saw Belle's lips moving and realized she was praying, "… and thank you for watching out for us and helping Loren's shoulder feel better."

"I guess this means you're willing to go search," she said, as we gathered our meager belongings. I rammed the hat Belle had given me over my tangled hair and slid on the pack I took from Arthur's place. Belle lost her hat on our trek away from the generator building. I offered the one I wore, but she said no, and I watched her take an oversized bath towel from the pile and wrap it around and around her neck and head like a scarf.

We packed the items we'd taken from the old guy's cabin along with all the bullets and both rifles. We filled our water bottles. Belle had her survival bag with Arthur's book and map.

The distant rattle of automatic gunfire shattered the morning quiet. I spun toward my friend; she was already out the door. We hurried from the tiny building and peered through dense trees toward the cabin. Flames engulfed it. The roof had fallen. Belle made a strangled sound, flung her pack on the ground, and started toward the fire. I raced after and caught her arm. She tried to pull away, but I refused to let go, dug in my heels, and held on.

"Listen," I said, "There's nothing you can do, and you're going to get us both killed if you go down there."

She looked at me, eyes hollow with misery.

I pleaded, "We need to get ourselves out of here; we deserve a chance to live, don't we?"

She nodded and, without another word, hefted her bag, headed away from the steam bath and up the hill. I shut my eyes for a second, breathing heavily. That was close. I kept peeking over my shoulder as we moved farther and farther away, expecting armed bad guys to come running up behind us. Belle never looked back, staying silent as we picked our way through the undergrowth.

I dropped both rifles as I chased after her. Reconsidering, I chose the 45-70 but was not enthusiastic about toting it as I fought through the brush. My only consolation, it packed the punch needed to stop a Kodiak brown bear.

We both knew Belle would oversee interpreting Arthur's directions to find the cave. My job? To watch for bears and look for specific signposts Arthur had drawn on his map. He described the cave as up the side of a mountain and two to five miles away. Which direction? North would take us back parallel to the lodge but away from it by several miles. We headed that way because the mountains south were much lower and closer to the water, making it less likely that any cave would remain hidden. I hoped we were making the right choice as we pushed through undergrowth and fallen trees. The fog dissipated, but the wind insulted us, spitting rain in our face, making it difficult to see. There was no trail, so we hiked about fifty feet higher than the steam bath, looking for a sign that Arthur traveled this way. Above us, the mountain reached straight up. We shoved our way through bushes, spruce, and coarse grass, trying to get far away, fast, from the still burning cabin. Fallen trees, rocks, and organic rubble piled by yearly avalanches littered the terrain. We concentrated on looking for the first landmark Arthur Cook had drawn, which slowed us even more. I found it by chance when we took our second break. Was that a great gray owl? I looked up as it flew over us. A hemlock growing on the side of a rocky outcropping caught my eye. Shifting in the wind, branches at its broken top were swept back like wings. Belle crouched, filling her water bottle from a trickling stream that splashed silver down the mountain.

"Look," I said, pointing. "You think?"

"Winged victory," she replied, referring to the name Arthur had given his first landmark. "It looks like the famous statue in the Louvre; how weird is that?"

"I guess we're on the right track," I said, feeling relieved as we set off once more.

My relief was temporary as we clawed our way through dense wood. There were tumbling waterfalls, beautiful even in the rain but not fun to wade across, plus the challenge of climbing through and around the ever-present fallen logs and tangled branches. We fought to stay upright on slopes where loose stones and shale slid alarmingly under our feet. Sometimes, we crawled on hands and knees, inching our painful way forward. I glanced at my friend, wondering if my face was as scratched and dirty as hers. We found more landmarks, a dead tree with tangled roots that looked like Medusa standing on her head, a narrow waterfall that had carved an indentation in rock, a boulder resembling President Lincoln's profile, and an old rubber boot swinging from a branch. This last suspended over a well-worn path.

That we had found ourselves on a trail after struggling for what seemed miles should have made us happy, but our apprehension increased as we came to churned up mud and spotted two enormous tracks and several smaller ones. Fresh brown bear prints. I set my foot inside one and cringed. The bear's track made my footprints look diminutive. This was an animal thoroughfare. I knew a sow and her young had recently come this way. A few feet further, we saw bear scat, and yes, I touched it, and yes, it was slightly warm. My mind locked. My eyes searched our surroundings, where was she? I tried to draw air into my lungs. There had to be a tree I could climb, although I knew brown bears sometimes climb trees. I also wanted to scream, curl up on the ground and suck my thumb. Belle had earlier left the trail for a toilet break. She came up behind me, as near hysteria, I lifted the rifle into firing position and in the tumult of terror, jacked shells onto the ground. I was sure I could smell the brutes, even though the wind now howling around us made that improbable. After a long second, I calmed myself enough to clean mud from the bullets and reload. We continued struggling along the trail, me in front, trying to keep myself and the rifle ready. Gritting my teeth, crying, I moved forward. A fresh blister was being born on my foot. I was tired of flailing through the brush. I was tired of not knowing what the bears or bad guys were up to, and I was tired, tired, tired of this miserable storm. My head hurt. My scrapes and burns stung and my entire body ached. My list of wants included clean, dry clothes, a hot cup of coffee, and a bowl of real clam chowder instead of the goop we had inhaled earlier. Where was Belle? Turning, I saw her about fifty feet behind me, not walking, leaning against a rock. I hobbled back. Her breathing was loud and ragged, she looked sick. She bent over and barfed, sagging onto the wet moss. Her forehead felt hot. I leaned the rifle against a broken snag and knelt, rubbing her hands. We sat like that for several minutes.

I'm not sure what I said, things like, "It'll be ok and just rest here for a bit, and I think the storm is getting better."

The storm was not getting better. Rain now beat on us, vicious tormenting pellets that made our cheeks feel raw. I wondered if Belle and I should crawl under a spruce tree, try to rest, conserve body heat. Uneasy stopping in the middle of a game trail, I also worried about the ever-present threat of hyperthermia, and wondered what I'd do if she became too sick to go further. Meanwhile, my coat was leaking, both my boots had tears from sharp rocks, and my hat hung like a soggy sack over my ears.

Belle staggered to her feet. She pointed past me, murmuring something unintelligible.

I looked. The sow raised up on her hind legs, standing about eighty feet away. Huge front paws worked in a coordinated balancing act as she moved her massive head back and forth, grunting and sniffing the air. Steam puffed from her mouth. I glimpsed two cubs behind a tree as mama lowered to all fours, let out an angry bellowing roar, and charged straight at us. You cannot imagine how fast one of these gargantuan animals can cover ground until it is heading your way. Fur, fat, and muscle rippled as she thundered along the trail. Desperation. I tried to stand, reached for the rifle and tripped, which flung me forward onto my hands. A loud crack echoed above. I watched a great spruce crash down the mountain, where it smashed onto the path right in front of the bear. The ground shook, and football-sized rocks rattled down both sides of the trunk, bouncing and rolling away with a gravy of mud pouring after. The monstrous beast, all ferocity gone, scooted off the trail into the bushes and disappeared, her cubs tumbling after her.

After a minute or two, my heart started. I sat, legs splayed, gulping, knowing we had been seconds from disaster.

"Thank you, God," Belle said, and threw up, again.

I pulled two space blankets from her bag and wrapped us together. We shivered, a wretched, sodden pile of cold and misery.

After a few minutes, she spoke, "It almost ripped me in half, leaving my brother there. Over the years, I've spent so much time not knowing where he was, hurt, dead, or alive. The only time I ever felt I could relax was when he was in jail with someone else watching him. I can't stop feeling responsible, but I can't seem to do anything to fix what's broken in him."

"I know."

She wept. I put my arms around her, and we sat there, blubbering together.

"I've tried and tried to help Cody. He always seems bent on destroying himself."

"I know you've done your best," I responded. "But he has to get serious and take responsibility if anything permanent is going to happen. So far, he hasn't taken steps to make lasting change." I tried not to sound preachy or impatient, but I wondered why she had put up with his shenanigans for so long.

Who am I trying to kid?

And who was I to feel impatient? Why had I kept on living with my unfaithful husband? Each time, there was a reason that made sense. The boys needed a stable family, one more fishing season to get through, his mother's illness, a complicated list. I knew Belle loved Cody, but was my reason for staying married to Brad for all those unhappy years, love? Or was it fear? Was it the inability to contemplate losing my husband because of what I'd gone through losing my father? Shame washed over me.

Can't tell anyone, not even my best friend; when Brad died, I felt nothing but relief.

As if from a great distance, Belle said, "Time to move it. We've got to get ourselves over this tree and find that cave."

"You feel up to going on?"

"Yes, and no," she replied. "But it shouldn't be much further, now. If we believe Arthur's map, there's only one landmark left to find, and that's a pointy spire of rock right above where the cave is on the side of the mountain."

I worried about getting around the enormous spruce, but when I walked over to examine it, I saw a place where the tree had no limbs. Thick branches on either side of the bare spot held the trunk up high enough, so we crawled under and resumed our trek.

Belle handed me another energy bar. Mine had almost definite hints of raspberry and chocolate among the usual sawdust texture. We washed it down with water we'd collected and trudged on.

Keep looking up, looking up, looking up. After about two more hours slipping and sliding along the muddy path, gazing upwards with rain in our eyes and necks sore, Belle saw the spire. We were excited until we noticed the next spire, and not knowing what else to do, we continued walking until I spotted the third. These strange rock formations, high on the mountain, stuck out like the upraised fingers of a long-buried colossus, but fog shrouded them so we could only catch glimpses. We spent long minutes staring upward, trying to figure out which was the one above the cave. We decided it couldn't be the first, because it thrust into the air not over thirty feet above our heads with a sloping hill of nothing but loose gravel below it. Not at all as Arthur Cook had described.

Belle seemed to feel better. She walked with more energy and wasn't as pale. In other good news, the rain was now a light patter, and the wind had settled.

I handed her the rifle and said, "Since we don't know which pointy rock thing it is, I'm going to hike over under the second spire and see if I can find anything that looks like a cave. If I see nothing there, I'll go on to the next one."

Over her protests, I said, "It won't take me that long; rest here and try to stay warm until I get back."

The animal trail meandered down into a valley away from the mountain's base, so I left it and continued into thick brush and short, scrubby trees. No devil's club growing up this high, I realized, relieved. Overripe blueberries scented the wet air. Stuffing my mouth with the squishy fruit, I fought my way forward, wishing the energy bars my friend brought tasted this good.

And if it weren't for Belle's almost obsessive safety planning, we would be out here with nothing, I chided myself.

The .38 in my coat pocket seemed like a friend, even though I knew it wouldn't stop a charging brownie. I spent, what seemed to me, an eternity clambering around the mountainside about one hundred feet below the second spire, finding nothing. Slipping and scraping back down, I dumped out my boots, trudging off toward the third, disheartened. Passed that one without even seeing it and had to double back.

I whimpered and complained and was just about to give up searching when the mist cleared. There, the needle-like rock tower rose above me. My legs rubbery, I again began a long climb upward, telling myself it couldn't be far. This latest hike was much steeper than the others. Clumsy from fatigue, I snagged onto bushes and scrabbled over rocks, pulling myself higher. Nothing looked like a cave opening, just scraggy stones and more stunted brush. Up and across another jumble of boulders I toiled, pulling myself onto a narrow ledge where I slowed, winded, and sweating. Needing a breather, I stopped and looked down the mountainside. And that's when I heard them. Wolves.

CHAPTER 13

Far below, fog feathered in and out of trees like wandering spirits. I sat, quiet as the surrounding stones, trying to place the animals. I knew wolf sounds and figured these were tracking, chasing something. It sounded like several young in the pack. I strained, trying to make sense of their yips and other noises. Could be a training mission. Two summers north of Fairbanks during high school with my biologist aunt, Fern, taught me a little about these animals but the wind now whipping through tree branches made it challenging to figure their direction. Were they somewhere down in the valley? No, nearer, much nearer, and moving fast. My stomach churned. Were they on the trail between Belle and me? Had they found her?

Oh, please, no!

The wolves ran closer. I pulled the revolver from my pocket and checked to make sure I'd loaded it. My hands were so icy, slick with sweat I almost dropped it. Even though Belle had the rifle I'd left and was an accurate shot, she also had a serious injury. The wind picked up and began slinging rain. The rising gale muffled noise, but now they were here. Movement. My muscles tensed as I aimed the gun, trying to steady my breathing. My friend limped out of the trees, and I lowered it, relieved, until I saw a heavy-bodied timber wolf appear, stop, and face her. Belle backed against the rock-strewn embankment at the base of the slope. Another wolf appeared out of the mist, ghosted forward, stopped, and stood silent as if waiting. The animals were silver and grey and black and beautiful. Belle hadn't seen me. Suddenly, she shouted at the pack in

Aleut. A warning? The leaders, one male, one female, advanced swiftly, silent, intent. More wolves crowded into the clearing; half-grown pups, moving in sync like choreographed dancers. The pair leaped for Belle. I screamed. In one quick movement, she jerked the big rifle up and shot. One wolf down, I emptied my .38 into the other as it slammed into Belle and grabbed her by the throat. Confusion. Animals, growling, backed away, startled by the sudden noise and movement as I hurtled down the incline, bringing a shower of stones with me. The beast lay on my friend. More bullets shoved into my gun. I leaned over her, trying to keep the wolf pack in view as I looked for injuries. She opened her eyes.

"Are you hurt? Are you ok?" Stammering, my heart doing a funny little dance.

"Can you get that hairy lady off me?" she asked, pushing at the lifeless animal.

I tugged at the wolf, all dead weight, struggling to drag it away from her. Belle sat up, retrieved her rifle, and got to her feet, panting.

"Can't believe I'm not dead! You saved my life; you saved my life! Thank you."

We stood, side by side, guns ready. Wolves milled around, feinting in, running back, not leaving, but cautious now. My friend seemed calm, but I shook so much, I wondered how I'd been able to kill the animal that attacked her.

"I thought she had you by the throat," I quavered. "It looked like she got your throat."

"She thought she had me by the throat, too," Belle said with a sideways grin, "But she had me by the towel."

I looked. The female had died with her teeth clamped around Arthur Cook's bulky bath towel. I remembered Belle wrapping it around her head and neck that morning in the banya because she'd lost her hat.

And what if she hadn't lost her hat?

"We need to get the rest of the pack out of here," I said, stating the obvious. "I'm scared to turn my back on them."

"One time I stayed at our camp on the river helping my grandparents make dry fish. I started singing, and Grampa Lukie told me my voice could panic a pod of killer whales," she said, and added, "Why don't we make a racket and see if that scares them into leaving?"

We bellowed. I thought we sounded like our library's recording of Walrus Island during mating season. When Belle broke into her peculiar rendition of "We Will Rock You," I almost plugged my ears. The wolves backed away, uncertain. I knew how they felt. Her enthusiastic screeching had made our pep club infamous back in high school.

Grampa Lukie was right.

With the two adult's dead, the remaining animals seemed to lose their will to attack. It was apparent they did not understand what had happened or what to do. Not taking my eyes off the pack, and keeping my revolver ready, I said, "Never thought I'd be shooting one of these wild beauties. You ever hear of wolves attacking people like this, before?"

"When I was a kid, village elders told stories about lean winters where wolves chased and killed people. I didn't want to shoot, either, but I also didn't want to die." She rubbed her hand across her throat, grimacing, and said, "It isn't personal, you know, to them you're no different from a caribou, fox, or moose, just food."

"I stayed with my aunt Fern, after my tenth and eleventh grades, two summers' up north of Fairbanks, and we followed a wolf pack. We wrote notebooks full, describing their habits and activities. I'd never left our tent if I thought they might turn on us. You're saying they sometimes track and eat people?"

"Summertime is when the living's easy for most animals in Alaska; food is plentiful, no reason to attack two bony women when fat caribou and moose calves are right in front of them. We get used to ascribing human characteristics to animals, but wolves hunt, kill and eat. It's not a moral or legal choice for them."

"I guess I thought they would be more afraid of us because, well… we're humans and supposed to be at the top of the food chain," I said.

Belle's tear-filled eyes and shaky laugh showed me she was feeling the aftereffects of her experience. She said, "Yeah, we like to think we're the hunters, not the hunted. These animals might never have encountered people before today. They usually take down the weak and injured, although sometimes they'll go on a killing spree. I once watched a pack near Denali kill four young caribou, then run off, not eating anything."

She shifted, leaning against a large boulder. "They may have sensed my injuries and decided to take an easy meal."

We gave up shouting and stood braced against the rocks in the pouring rain, waiting for the group to leave. The two animals lay where they had fallen; shiny fur coats mud-splattered, diminished in death. I tried not to look. A moment later, as if by signal, the pack silently slipped away. Daylight was fading. I could see Belle shivering. We decided we'd better continue looking for the cave; there seemed nothing else to do, and we needed shelter and rest. I took the heavy rifle from her. She did not protest. My teeth chattered, making it difficult to speak. We began climbing. She groaned as she edged up the slope. Tedious and rough. Rain beat on us. I helped her onto the same ledge I'd reached before. She sprawled on the jutting rock platform, breathing hard. I knew she was close to complete exhaustion. I placed the rifle and everything else I had lugged beside her and scrabbled on, desperate to find shelter. Those wolves might come back. I believed they could see much better in the dark than us, so I didn't think spending the night shivering under space blankets at the base of the mountain was an option.

Arthur Cook said his cave was about one hundred feet below a rock spire.

I had tried to measure and count as we climbed, but lost track in my faltering assent.

As I hooked my arm over a protruding rock, using it to steady myself, I saw what appeared to be a narrow opening above me, almost hidden behind house-sized rocks. That was about one-half second before the stone I'd grabbed came loose. I lost my balance and shrieking, flopped onto my side, skidding back down the incline, jolting and scraping as I fell. I stopped upside down about a foot above where Belle waited. Our eyes met for a second or two, and we began giggling, I guess, because we were so tired. When I could get my breath again, I said, "Think I found the cave."

Without further ado, we headed skyward again, towing our belongings a few feet, resting, panting, faltering, then fumbling our way in the loose shale and grit as we dragged our stuff laterally up the mountain.

Am I hallucinating? Where is the opening?

I stared into the rain. With full darkness almost upon us, everything looked blurry and gray. Crawling forward, I pinched my thumb between two rocks as I tried to get another handhold. I wanted to bare my teeth and shriek angry words into the night, but I didn't even have the energy to snivel.

Belle nudged me, pointing, "Is that what you're talking about?"

Close to ten feet above us, the rock-strewn mountainside turned into a solid mass of overhanging granite. We couldn't go any further. At its edge, right above where I'd grabbed the loose rock, I thought I saw that narrow sliver of black, again.

We crept forward, still on our bellies, still eating grit until we hauled out like two tired seals, up over the edge of what turned out to be another rock ledge, wider this time. After a moment, we staggered to our feet.

The opening was a narrow slit between enormous boulders. It was barely more than a crack angling down to our ledge.

It appeared to be a diagonal wedge of darker-colored rock from just a few feet away, which is why I hadn't spotted it from below. I turned on my miniature flashlight. I was not eager to go further.

"What if there are bats in there?"

Belle grabbed my light and shined it into the rift.

"Don't see any bats. I'm going in."

She squeezed through the opening and disappeared.

Crap.

I moistened my lips, trying to swallow. I am not fond of these furry, flying creatures. And yes, I know how they eat insects and help the environment and all that. They give me the willies, always have. We discovered little brown bats in the attic of one of the abandoned houses we'd played in as children and startled them into squeaking flight. As they dipped and fluttered in terror around us, I'd run wailing down the stairs, fallen and scraped my shins. I was six years old. I had bad bat dreams for weeks.

Light bounced through the narrow entrance.

Belle called, "This is a teeny cave. Come on in, no bats, I promise; there's not even any room for them."

I squeezed into the den-like space. Belle played light over the walls and ceiling.

Staring in disappointment around the cramped chamber, I said, "Do you believe Arthur Cook lived here for years?"

We brought the rifle and packs in and drooped onto the gravel-strewn floor, cold, wet, hungry, and discouraged. My flashlight dimmed, so Belle pawed through her survival bag and extricated a miniature battery-powered, LED lantern. I opened the crackers and peanut butter I'd taken from Arthur's cabin. It was a solemn meal. After, we turned off the lamp, wrapped the silver space blankets around ourselves, and huddled close, trying to get warm.

I didn't want to be a downer and say anything discouraging, but I couldn't help wondering how long we would have to hunker here. As I drifted off, I also knew, once again, I didn't have a clue how to get us out of our misadventure. We dozed in jumbled bits of time, shifting and adjusting. The granite wall we leaned against got no softer. At last, morning light shone through the constricted entry. We gave up trying to sleep. I stumbled to my feet and looked around. With daylight and Belle's lantern, we examined the room once more. It appeared to be an ordinary cave, if there is such a thing: pebble floor, rock walls, and a low ceiling.

"This is nothing like Mr. Arthur Cook, fantasy fiction writer extraordinaire, described," I griped.

"Had an idea," Belle said, with what seemed resolute cheerfulness. She had just returned from a privy break, except there was no privy.

"After you take your turn outside and we get a little something to eat; let's do some survival planning."

Although no idea what nuggets of life-enhancing wisdom I could offer to aid our preparations, I agreed. I slipped out, only to be grabbed by a wind so belligerent I feared it would throw me off the mountain. I completed my constitutional by clinging to rocks as my backside braved the elements, then crawled into the diminutive compartment, feeling whipped and humble.

Belle was bent at the waist, trailing her lantern close to all the surfaces, intently examining every bump and crevice. I still felt crabby, and it showed when I said, "I think we need to accept Arthur's book was fantasy, and instead, come up with another plan."

"Then how would you explain his landmarks? Why don't you help me look for a few minutes?"

"Look for what?"

"I don't know, anything unusual, out of place."

"I think it's out of place that I'm here." Feeling stubborn, I plopped down on the rough floor and dug around in my pack.

"I'm going to have more pilot bread with peanut butter and after getting my jaws unstuck, try to figure out where we need to go from here."

I watched her use the small lantern, running her hands over every inch of the miniature cavern.

"There's nothing here." I loudly crunched through another dry cracker. "We're running low on water and I'm sick of survival bars. I've already eaten more peanut butter than I've had in the last five years, and I think it's the reason I'm constipated. We're miles and miles from anyone who can help us. Dang it, Belle. No one even knows we're in trouble."

My optimism from yesterday had faded; my clothes were filthy and still damp, my cuts, burns and scrapes raw, and fear; like those long-ago bats, flitted through my tired thoughts. I drank the last of my water, closed my eyes to shut out my surroundings, and slumped against the unyielding wall. Belle was mumbling, probably doing her prayer exercises again. Frustrated and anxious, I drifted off to sleep. A mechanical whirring, and her excited voice called, "Wake up!"

CHAPTER 14

I felt a draft, opened my eyes, and stared as a door that looked like a rock wall a few minutes earlier slid back, revealing yawning darkness. I leaped to my feet.

"What in the world? How did you?" I began, and Belle interrupted, her face bright with amazement, "I stuck my fingers deep into this crack." She pointed. "You'd never know it was there unless you found it like I did. I discovered something that felt like soft plastic and pushed on it. That triggered the mechanism."

She shined her light into the opening, revealing a large room. We edged inside, but skittish, I stepped out again.

I thought of that old Tom Sawyer cave story from grade school and remembered news about an entire soccer team getting lost and stuck for days, deep in some dangerous underground pit.

I spluttered, "What if the door closes while we're inside and we get trapped? I need to know where that door opener, button is, before I go in."

"Yeah, you're right."

Belle showed me the slender crevice where she'd found the mechanism. I stuck my fingers into it and explored, locating a round, rubbery object. I pressed it, and the door shut. The entire setup was designed with such skill, that once closed; we saw nothing but a rock wall.

"We need to find something to put in the opening," I began as Belle interjected, "So we'll be able to get out when we want."

The wind growled as we emerged from the cave. Feeling the sting of hail, we worked in sweaty concentration until we maneuvered a basketball sized stone back through the entrance. Belle re-opened the door, and again we marveled at its artistry.

"Absolutely the coolest thing," she gushed. "I could play with this all day. I'd never have guessed it was anything but a rock wall." She limped through the opening once more, turned back, and yelled, "Now quit stalling and get in here. This is incredible!"

I stepped across the threshold, speechless.

What was this place? Belle's light picked out a flat wall covered in gray metal cabinet doors and right beside me, next to the entrance, a panel filled with switches. As we walked across a smooth cement floor, I noticed a miniature galley kitchen and bunk beds behind a curtain in another section. The room was large and airy, but not cold or damp. We traversed the place, gawking like tourists. Belle noticed another opening, and we glanced inside a room stuffed with plastic-wrapped pallets and containers.

"Batteries," she said, walking closer to inspect the bundles. "Kinda like the solar cells Howie showed me at the lodge, but these are way, way bigger."

Someone had crowded the large stone compartment with these monsters.

"Maybe," I suggested, "We should check out the panel by the door. I mean, we might figure out how to turn on a few lights."

"Yeah, this little light of mine is getting dim. We should at least try to find some batteries for it, if nothing else."

We returned to the door and studied the panel. There were neat rows of levers, each numbered with a hand-printed description. When I flipped the switch labeled, Main Room, the entire area glowed with clear soft light. I could see nothing above those fixtures, so couldn't tell how high the ceiling or cave roof was. More levers operated lights over the kitchen and bunks, and a tidy curtained space hid a chemical toilet and shower. While I explored, Belle disappeared, but soon came back, saying, "I found clothes. They seem to be of masculine orientation, but who cares? They're clean and dry."

"There's a shower and chemical toilet and a button for hot water," I offered, and she said, grinning and waving a bottle, "I found a pantry, cases of bottled water and freeze-dried food, enough for a very long time."

I was excited about finding food and shelter, yet uneasy. The cave did not fit with the remote Alaska wilderness I knew, and I couldn't believe Arthur Cook had built this by himself.

"I don't think one person constructed this. I'm standing here wondering who put it together, and why?"

When Belle didn't answer, I said, "This place reminds me of a submarine I toured with my boys one summer. All this gray painted metal looks military. There's no way Arthur Cook fabricated everything, even for an apocalypse type, hideout. Concrete floors? How could he have lugged bags of cement up that steep slope? Also, he couldn't bring those solar batteries or much of anything else through the same skinny gap we squeezed through."

Belle offered, between gulps of bottled water, "This is a government operation, military written all over it."

She'd spent six years in the Marines when she got old enough after 9 11; I figured she was right.

"I want to clean up and eat something," she said, "Then I'm going to look around some more."

"First, I want to check if this," I said, touching a lever labeled, Front Door, "Will open and close that entry panel from inside. Let's move the rock with you outside. Be ready to re-open the door from out there, if this lever won't do the job."

We shoved the rock away from the threshold, and I flipped the switch. The panel closed. I flicked the lever again, and just like that, it opened. Belle came back inside, and we grinned at each other like two toddlers with a new toy. Because we did not know how fresh the batteries were or how long they would last, we only used the few lights necessary. We pushed buttons to heat water and wash, hurrying, just in case. Showers in a cave. What a weird and wonderful thing. The water did not get hot, but even lukewarm; it felt heavenly. I put on the clothes she found. Everything was men's size, medium, so I rolled up pant legs, and pulled on two pairs of wool socks to fill boots she'd unearthed from somewhere. I felt clean, dry, and grateful to be alive. We attacked the food next, heating water in a saucepan over a fuel pack burner, pouring it into pouches of freeze-dried meals, and gobbling it like Thanksgiving dinner. After our meal, we looked for batteries for my flashlight and her lamp. We walked between high stacks of supplies and solar-related, electronic equipment to the other end of the crowded room. A wide, industrial-looking, green door embedded into concrete against the far wall surprised us. It stood locked tight.

"The mystery deepens," I said, knowing Belle felt as intrigued as I. We spent several minutes looking for a button, lever, or anything that might open it. After rummaging for a time, we discovered nothing, so we gave up and headed back to the compact kitchen, where we found stacks of AA's in a drawer.

"Wonder what's behind these?" I asked, walking out of the galley and over to the opposite wall. I grabbed handles, hearing metal squeak as I tugged. Inside, rows of levers and switches. Behind one, larger than the rest, thirty minuscule dials glowed. I rubbed away dust—vintage world clocks, which appeared to be keeping time. Overwhelmed, I forgot the storm, explosion, bad guys, and everything else. Arthur's cave did partly resemble his written descriptions. These rooms looked like something out of a sci-fi novel. Apprehensive now, I scanned the rows of switches, buttons, and levers again, noticing some numbered, others not. Why were they here? Why were so many of them lit up? Belle ran a finger over the buttons, reading labels aloud.

"This is a military setup," she breathed. I glanced at her.

"Oh, no," she whispered, wiping a hand over her eyes. No longer relaxed, she looked frightened. "I know what this place is."

I watched her open steel cabinets, running her hands over tags and markers. She blanched, saying in a rush, "I think I know what's behind the green door. This is a missile site."

"You're kidding, right?" I tried to laugh, but I couldn't get my breath. My chest felt tight. I sucked air through my mouth. "Why would the military put a missile, here?"

Belle said, "Military's primary job? Defend the good old U.S. of A. It could be they decided this is a prime place for strategic defense. This installation has been here for a very long time, way before we were born. So, maybe with more recent threats from North Korea, they upgraded or reactivated it. One thing I learned while I was in the Marines; under the umbrella of what is called, 'defensive operations,' all kinds of top-secret activities take place."

"Yeah, but weren't missile sites dismantled and taken out of operation, years ago? I seem to remember reading about an empty missile silo for sale somewhere in Arizona."

Wan smile. I almost felt her pat my head.

She said, "Two things I want to know, whether this is an active missile, if the meeting at the lodge with Madame Chametz and those Russians have anything to do with this place, and what we should do about it."

"That's three things. Besides, what can we do about it? All I want to know is when someone will show up and help us get home," I countered, irritable now.

Belle said, "Listen. If this cave is what I think it is, we need to let the right people know what's going on over here. This could be big, like the start of World War III."

Shocked, I stuttered, "You can't be serious."

Perhaps the stress of the last few days had gotten to her. We both needed rest. "Let's get some sleep and talk about it, later," I said.

"Yeah, I'm pretty tired," she admitted, "But I also feel like the responsible thing would be to check this place out."

"Once a Marine, always a Marine," I grumbled. I left her scanning dials and switches and wandered into the battery area, again. Thinking we could have overlooked something behind a stack of supplies, I scanned the walls searching for a panel, but saw nothing. A haphazard heap of mechanical odds and ends piled a pallet that set against the large door. I dropped to the floor, aiming my light under the stack. Couldn't see anything, so I lay flat on the cement, sliding my arm into the constricted space, feeling the surface. Nothing unusual. I wriggled closer and tried again.

This time my fingertips brushed what felt like a metal rim above the concrete. I couldn't reach any further, so I got to my feet, sneezing from the dust I'd raised, and began unloading old computer parts. As I finished, Belle walked up. We shoved the pallet aside and searched for what I had touched under it—a metal plate about four inches square with a raised edge screwed into the floor. A mechanical device placed there so someone could open the monstrous door without using their hands.

"I know how to work this," I said. I recalled seeing similar devices used to open doors in a cannery machine shop when I was a kid.

"We need a Philips screwdriver."

"Just so happens," Belle said, pulling a folded gadget from her oversized pants pocket. It was a "Handy Home Helper" with scissors, knife, pliers, and screwdriver, among other accouterments touted on infomercials as being the answer to every household challenge. I loosened the screws, and instead of trying to lift the panel, twisted it. Nothing happened on the first try, but after two more hard twists, I removed the lid, revealing a tiny compartment. Inside, we found a switch.

"Bet this lever means open, sesame."

"Somehow, I think you're right," she said, and flipped it.

"Hey, it was my turn," I complained, watching fascinated as the door swung wide.

A pungent sulfur smell enveloped us.

"Wow, stinks like Liard Hot Springs on a warm day," Belle said, ignoring my complaint. I noticed she was bent forward, hugging her injured side with her arm.

We stayed on the threshold as she ran light over the unlit, gloomy interior. I saw nothing except an empty cube about twelve feet by twelve, with an aluminum ladder fastened onto the opposite wall that reached up and up, probably into outer space.

Crap. Belle is in no condition to climb that.

She started through the opening. I stepped in front of her.

"No, you don't. It's my turn. I'll go up the ladder and describe what I see; you stay right here and make sure this enormous door doesn't close, shutting me in here, or would that be out here?"

"You don't like heights."

"It's a challenge I'm getting used to. We hiked most of the way up the side of a mountain in the dark, remember?"

I thought she'd keep arguing, but she nodded, leaning wearily against a plastic-wrapped pallet. I'd made it my practice not to climb ladders, cell phone towers or power poles if I could, and had been successful at avoiding anything higher than the stairs in my house. If she weren't injured and stumbling with fatigue, I wouldn't have gone near it.

"First, I'll look for a light switch," I said. I found nothing. With the miniature penlight clipped to the collar of Arthur's work shirt I'd buttoned on after my shower, I took my first step. The concrete space loomed above as invitingly as an elevator shaft in a haunted high rise. My underpowered light could not dispel the deep black, swallowing me. I counted twenty-five rungs and tried not to think how high I must be above the floor. Two more rungs and my light caught the reflection of steel framework above my head. My belly cramped as I pulled myself onto the platform. Frantic, I hugged the railing for support.

Note to self: Do not shine light down ladder.

CHAPTER 15

Noticing an access at the far edge of this steel floor, I stepped gingerly along, choke holding the railing until I reached it; a grey metal door that was closed, but not locked. It groaned as I pushed it open. I scanned inside this space, making sure there was something I could safely walk on. Steel grating formed a narrow deck surrounded by more railing. A few feet into this niche loomed a wall filled with dials, all glowing. At the right side of this display, my light caught a large, protruding red button, labeled "Missile Launch."

No. Way.

I stared. My stomach flip-flopped. I closed my eyes, opened them. It was still there.

An actual missile launch knob. That big red button we saw in old B movies was not just a prop.

How did I get myself into this situation?

Unable to take it in, bending double, gasping, eyes watering, I felt close to collapse. My guts churned. Not sure if that was from all the impacted peanut butter, or my close to melt-down, panic. Regardless, I had no desire to explore anything else. I had to face what Belle already knew. I took several slow breaths and flexed my icy fingers. Someone said reciting poetry was soothing. At that moment, the only thing that popped into my mind was a wacky tune a fisherman bellowed from his boat across the water one summer evening.

He crooned, "Keep your shades down, Maryann, keep your shades down, Maryann... last night, last night, in the full moonlight... I saw you; I saw you. You were combing your golden mane; they're sayin' you ain't sane. If you want me, for your future man, keep your shades down, Maryann."

It almost worked.

I needed to get down that ladder without passing out. I lowered rung after rung, mumbling words to the fisherman's ditty, my muscles tense and my mind ping-ponging with questions and supposition. Belle was right. We had stumbled into a missile silo. One thing I knew for sure, the narrow entrance we'd pushed our way through today could not be the cave's only opening.

We flipped the switch and watched the green door close as I described what I had seen. My friend didn't seem surprised.

"Can't think about this, anymore, Belle. I've got to go lie down."

My friend said nothing, offering no resistance as we shambled from the area. I leaned the rifle against the wall and set the pistol beside me. I closed my eyes, thinking I had never felt so grateful for a bed, even if it was an old, creaking, military bunk with no sheets and worn wool blankets. I let my sore muscles sink into the mattress, wrapping the blankets tight around me. My mind kept working, trying to process everything. It seemed like we'd been away from home for months, and I knew I was losing track of time. I began counting the days from last Monday when we'd flown to the lodge. We spent that night in the generator building after we survived the explosion, found the cabin the next morning, and stayed up through Tuesday night trying to help Arthur. Cody's monologue took most of the rest of the night. Early Wednesday, they burned Arthur's body and his home. We hiked miles, locating the entrance to the missile silo, or cave, later that day, yesterday. My thoughts turned to Matt and Ryan, glad they were unaware of what was happening in my life, hoping school and jobs were going well, wondering if I'd ever get to see them again.

It must be late Thursday night, so that's about four days so far.

Waking hours later, it was pitch black. It took a moment to realize where I was.

Before going to bed, we shut off every light, so the room was darker than imagination. I flipped on my flashlight and saw Belle sitting on the edge of her cot.

"We need to make plans," she said, getting to her feet.

In the galley, we prepared two more freeze-dried meals. We agreed it must be Friday, and a world clock said it was 7:30 am, Alaska time, so we made breakfast. I left the rifle leaning next to my bunk but placed the pistol on the table between us. I had a freeze-dried egg scramble; and she had a waffle. After she'd taken her last bite, Belle launched into conversation.

"You know I was in the military," she said.

"Six years," I replied.

"I didn't talk about it, much," she said, "Not because I saw all kinds of horrible things like some of my friends did, but, well, it was top secret."

I remembered those years. One year married, four months into opening an art gallery, busy caring for Matt and Ryan, my new husband's sons, and helping with his commercial fishing business. As a kid, I remembered relatives joining the Military after 9 11 or as soon as they were old enough. Belle and I hadn't kept in touch. I assumed she was enjoying her stint in the Marines; I hoped she was well, but she seemed worlds away, and we rarely spoke. She never gave me details; I didn't ask.

She said, "After boot camp, they took several of us to a facility away from base and tested us. I never saw the results of my tests or any grades, but they sent me to another location for specialized training. We wrote code, developed software, and learned to program drones, among other tasks. Everything was don't ask, don't tell anybody anything, and secret, secret, secret. We would spend all day in rooms with no windows, staring at a computer screen and click, clicking away."

She stood and moved around the space, opening drawers as she said, "I'm looking for something that resembles coffee." After a minute, she gave up and resumed her seat, saying, "I promised not to say anything, even after I got out of the Marines, but I'm very concerned, not only about what we've found here, but the weird Chametz /Russian angle, so I'm going to tell you a few things."

Do I really want this information?

"The reason I recognized this as a missile site is that one of my last jobs before I got out, was setting up computers to modernize missile bases all over the U.S. and a few other places, so people could operate, access, and control them via satellite. 'Missile silo' is an archaic name, not much used, anymore. To the public, they mostly don't exist. They didn't take me to a site," she said, "I didn't need to know where missiles were located. Other people built them and brought in whatever was necessary. Very few of us knew what others, even right next to us, worked on."

I ate the last bite of my scramble and said, "I remember seeing you just once at a community Christmas event after you joined the military."

"Yeah, I didn't get back often. We were busy. So many permanent changes implemented in our country after 9 11."

"Well, 9 11 is not that many decades ago. And with the little 'on' lights shining from behind buttons we saw yesterday, this missile might be armed and capable, or whatever they call it. What do you think we're in the middle of?"

Belle rubbed her eyes, and I noticed long scratches on her throat that hadn't been there two days ago. I realized they were from the wolf that attacked her.

She said, "I think we've found ourselves in the middle of a secret deal-making process between our esteemed Speaker of the House and some Russians."

"What is Chametz trying to do?"

"That's the big question." She opened a plastic bottle filled with water that boasted it was from a mountain spring in Colorado. She chugged, then continued, "These events are too strange. This isn't coincidence. Meetings take place all the time between different countries, even semi-private meetings, but for the Speaker of the House to fly up here, right next to an armed/ready missile, and have a clandestine, get-together with Vlodir Rafenski at a lodge supposedly owned by some Russian oligarch? That's over the top. Couple that with recent allegations of Chametz's ties to a secret anarchist group trained by Russia's FSB, and her open animosity against the president because he imposed sanctions on Russia. Something is going on, and I don't think it's good."

Breathless, I said, "What's the FSB?"

"The FSB is what Russia's KGB used to be, except worse."

"Who is Vlodir Rafenski?"

"He's …one of the older, gray-haired, Russian men that landed in the first helicopter. It took a while to recall why I recognized him," Belle said, "But last night it dawned on me. I remembered doing some specialty programming work involving image recognition and seeing him in several photos. He has a prominent forehead with an odd, protruding bump that his enemies call his 'devil horn.'"

"Horn? Weird, I didn't notice anything like that on either of the two guys we saw getting off the helicopter."

"Vlodir pulls his hat low over his eyes and keeps his coat collar turned up. Let's see, what else do I know about him? He wears these expensive, woolen, military-looking suits. You'd think all those heavy clothes would be way too hot during summer, but that's what he has on in every photo I've seen. Rumors say he has four children, a wife, two mistresses and is part of the Russian mafia. He's said to have sustained a serious head injury in a motorcycle accident running drugs when he was young, causing the malformation. No doubt he's cruel and tough, which is why word got around the growth on his head is a horn; another rumor says he's friends with the devil. I don't know all that firsthand, of course. A few years ago, I read an article online reporting Vlodir Rafenski had maneuvered himself upward to third in command over the entire Russian military and was working on moving into the top spot."

"Back to this missile," she continued, "With worldwide advances in computer technology, unscrupulous people, for enough money, have tried to hack into our military computers from time to time. Unfortunately, this sometimes includes citizens from our own country. We set these computers up to control missiles and many other mechanisms built for our defense. After seeing Chametz and Vlodir together, I'm worried something ominous is happening here."

A faint metallic pinging caught our attention.

Belle stopped talking. We both stilled, hearing the muffled clanking again. She jumped to her feet. "Hate to say this, but we've got something going on back there."

She turned, grabbed the .38, and limped toward the battery room, saying, "Hurry, get that gun and come with me," and as the disturbance continued, "Someone's trying to get in."

"I'm disliking this trip more and more," I said, approaching the imposing green door with the cumbersome rifle stuck out in front of me.

"I wish I had my Pop's sawed-off, twelve-gauge shotgun, illegal or not," I muttered. Much lighter, it could still scare the pants off anyone a person might have to face.

I don't want to be here.

Nevertheless, I stood braced, muscles quivering, mouth dry. I felt hysterical giggles bubbling inside me. Could my situation get any more absurd?

Ping, ping, ping, ping, ping. Was there a person rapping against the other side of the door? I'd seen no opening, yesterday, when I was in that concrete room. How did someone get in there? I wondered if it was Morse code.

Belle shouted in Russian. She spoke to her Russian Old Believer friends from time to time, so I knew she was asking, "What do you want?"

There was silence. Nothing. Centuries ended. The circle of life spun three times. My arms and shoulder sent slivers of pain screaming along my nerves, reminding me I couldn't hold the gun in this position for much longer. I shifted and watched the barrel of the rifle dip toward the floor.

Finally, a muffled voice answered in Russian. Belle translated for me, "I friend and you."

More time passed.

"That's no Russian. Why would anyone speak their native language so incompetently?"

"Jay?" I called out, more from wanting to drop the heavy weapon than anything else, right then. My arms burned with fatigue, and my shoulder ached.

From miles away, "This is Jay."

I moved to open the door. "One sec," Belle whispered, "The fact is, we don't know if Jay is our friend. How does he know about this missile? How did he find this cave? What is his agenda in Alaska?"

I stopped, appalled.

"Well then, what should we do?" I tried to keep my voice calm, but my high-pitched tone gave me away.

"We'll stand on either side of the door with our guns ready; when he comes through, we'll have him covered."

"Sure you didn't mean to say, we'll get the drop on him?" I questioned sarcastically. "Look, I don't know how to do this kind of thing."

"Just be fierce like you were with Cody," she retorted and, using her foot, flipped the switch. We moved into position. I stood behind the door with the rifle, and she aimed the .38 at the opening.

CHAPTER 16

Jay walked in and breezed past us like he owned the place. He carried a camo hunting pack, and his jeans and jacket were mud-spattered. His green eyes looked emerald bright in his dirty face. He acted as if weapons pointing at him, were an everyday occurrence. He kicked the lever. The door closed as we stood, watching. He faced Belle.

Pulling a paper from a breast pocket, Jay said, "According to the one radio call I got through, you're Melody Belle Engiak, and you were in the Marines. Where's Arthur Cook?"

"That info is correct," she said, still pointing the revolver at him, "But you need to call me Belle."

"Who are you, and how did you know about this cave?" I asked. My throat felt tight, and my arms shook from the weight of the rifle.

Turning in my direction, he looked at my jiggling gun barrel and smiled.

"Jay, if that is your name," my friend said, "Please identify yourself, tell me how and what you know about this site, and we can go from there."

I narrowed my eyes, sighing.

He researched Belle but didn't bother with my stats; I must look as non-threatening as I feel.

"Jay Brandon Carrel, but you need to call me Jay," he said, grinning.

"I started my career in the Marines. I'm now working for Department of Homeland Security. I've also teamed with a few other branches from time to time, freelancing. For the past few months, I've investigated a viable and present threat to this missile site. Why isn't Arthur Cook with you?"

"Because Arthur Cook is dead," Belle said.

He removed a worn leather case from a pocket and showed it first to Belle, then held it up for me. I saw his badge. It did not impress me, nor did it convince Belle, because she moved closer to him, her gun aimed at his chest, and said, "We're going to need more than that." Without waiting for him to speak, she said, "How's about I ask you a few pertinent questions only a guy in your position would know, and we'll see if you're who you claim to be. If you aren't, well…" She tapped her weapon.

"Sounds fair enough," he said.

As she began querying Jay, I sidled over and rested my rifle barrel on a stack of supplies. I had one job and didn't want to blow it. Making deliberate noise, I aimed it somewhere close to his belly button, but he turned and smiled at me, again.

Does he think I won't shoot if he keeps grinning? My charming husband smiled and still lied to my face, so don't think you'll win me over, big guy. I did not smile back.

After a few minutes of hushed discussion, Belle said, "I think he's legit. There's no way he would have answers to these questions, otherwise."

Jay looked at our ill-fitting clothes, my shaking rifle barrel, and our scraped and scratched faces, then said, "Just so you are aware, I could have gotten in here without your help." He looked straight at me. "Don't you know breaking into a missile site is a felony?"

I knew his question was fair, but his genial attitude and vigorously confident tone riled me, anyway.

Biting back an irate comment, I leaned the heavy rifle against the plastic-wrapped pile. Belle stuffed the .38 in the waistband of her oversize pants. She wasn't wearing a belt, and I hoped the gun didn't get away from her and slide.

"I don't think Loren and I being at this missile site is the biggest problem you've got to worry about," she called over her shoulder.

"You know how we ended up here, so why don't you tell us why you're in the area?" I asked.

As we walked back to the kitchen, Jay explained he was on assignment. Yes, he was spending a couple weeks flying helicopter for his cousin who had knee surgery; that was his cover. Yes, this cave was an active missile site, and yes, two years previous, the navy re-armed it, mostly, as Belle had guessed, because of the North Korean threat.

In the kitchen, Jay pulled out a metal chair and sat, looking from her to me. "You both look pretty scraped up," he said. "Do either of you need medical attention?"

"I think Belle has some broken ribs," I offered. She opened and closed cabinet drawers one after another and didn't respond.

"I'd like to know what happened at the lodge."

I didn't want to say anything that included Belle's brother, Cody, and I knew she wouldn't, so I searched for a way to describe events but leave him out. Before I could think how to tell our story, Belle walked over, sat down, and began relating how two helicopters landed at the lodge Monday evening, one carrying Americans, including Speaker of the House, Chametz, and the other, Russians, among them Vlodir Rafenski, for a meeting. She told about Howie getting shot and the explosion, continuing her tale with the rest of our adventure, as she called it. She included Arthur Cook's death, Daumier, drug runners, the cabin fire, and ended with us trying to get away, leaving nothing out except the part involving her brother.

I could sense her growing unease, so to forestall Jay questioning her in more detail, I jumped in with, "We found and read parts of a book that old guy at the cabin wrote. That's how we located this cave. Who was Arthur Cook, anyway?"

Jay said Arthur Cook was an eccentric scientist, brilliant and a self-described loner, working for a select, top-secret branch of the military. He told us Arthur took over the watchman's job of manning this missile site from an operative who retired in 2007.

"With no family, Arthur said this isolated area suited him. After building a cabin for his cover, he posed as a crusty sourdough who scorned what he called 'soft city living.'"

Jay went on to tell us intelligence agencies had suspected illegal interaction and deal-making between Madame Chametz and certain Russian government officials for some time.

"That's about all I can tell you, because it's classified," he said.

Belle resumed her noisy search for coffee.

"Try the pantry," I suggested, to stop her banging drawers.

"Why didn't I think of that?" She disappeared into the food storage area.

Jay set his pack on the table. From it, he pulled out a laptop computer and something that looked like a miniature flying saucer festooned with wires. Trying not to appear too interested, I dug around inside cabinets and found an old-fashioned coffee maker, a percolator, as my grammie used to call hers.

Belle reappeared with a package and bottles of water. She opened the pouch, filled the coffeepot from the bottles, then added grounds to the basket and set it on the burner. We drank our coffee as we watched Jay work.

"What is that?" I asked, pointing at the strange little object.

"It's a discombobulation machine," Jay said, twisting wires together.

"Uh-huh, right. That's classified, too?" I questioned, not hiding my exasperation.

"Usually," he answered—another smile.

Those white teeth. Even with dirt all over his face, Jay is almost ridiculously handsome. So, why do I feel slightly rankled every time he smiles at me?

Jay said, "Seeing as you are right in the middle of this and a good, upstanding, patriotic citizen, I think I can tell you." He tapped the compact device. "Some bright person invented a computer that works something like a satellite phone, only better. Among many other complex and sophisticated abilities, it can send and receive encrypted information. The encryption changes often, so even if what it sends and receives somehow lands in China or some other dodgy place, they won't be able to transcribe the data."

He turned toward Belle and said, "I know little about the drug selling end of all of this, yet. But I can tell you, it's not uncommon for Russian politicians to have their fingers in many illegal enterprises."

"Well, now, we sure wouldn't know anything about politicians and illegal activities in our country, would we?" I asked, sarcasm lacing my voice.

He stopped twisting wires and gave me a contemplative, measuring look, then continued, "We're not sure if drug running or the lodge's tourism business has anything to do with Chametz's deal-making with the Russians. She may have given the location of missile sites to someone in the Russian military in exchange for money or their help in some way. We also think she might have traded them some of our plutonium."

We're in way, way over our heads. Belle and I need to get away from here.

"Was the storm getting any better when you were flying out there?"

Jay took a swallow of his coffee and didn't seem to hear me.

"When do you think the Coast Guard or whoever you've contacted will get here, and we'll be able to leave?" I asked, knowing I sounded tense, and not caring. I watched him connect what looked like a tiny satellite dish to the strange-looking device.

"I haven't contacted the Coast Guard."

Not sure I was understanding, I tried again, swallowing my alarm. "Who is coming to help us?"

"I'm the rescue party," he said, so casually I wanted to slap him.

Was that a momentary twitch, or did he just wink at me?

I almost choked on my mouthful of coffee. "You're it?" I squawked.

He stopped, held my gaze for a moment, then resumed his work.

"Look, I'm not joking around. What are you saying?" I was spluttering.

"What it means," Belle said, "Is that no one else knows about this, no one knows we're missing, there is no Coast Guard alert, and there is no search happening for us."

"This is a priority mission," Jay added. "Top secret for some very valid reasons: one to avert an escalation of hostilities, another to get the missile issue resolved, and another to avoid the embarrassment of having the world know our Speaker of the House is a traitor and a sell-out."

How can he be so matter of fact? It sounds like he's reading from a manual on intelligence protocol.

I closed my eyes. "I guess that means, Belle, we have to rescue ourselves," I finished.

"Ain't no cavalry, coming," she said.

"I'll be happy to fly you two back to Homer or Kodiak just as soon as I've gotten my problem taken care of," Jay said.

"My problem is," I said, spitting the words, "I really, really don't want to be around here while you're taking care of your problem."

I walked over, punched the button, watched the rock door panel open, and stepped out into the confining space where we huddled the first night. I peered through the man-made, narrow opening and down the mountain, angry; but still marveling at the ingenious camouflage.

Blue sky. The storm had passed. From my vantage point, with no rain or fog obscuring my view, I could make out the faraway shape of the lodge, or at least part of a building I guessed must be the lodge.

Apparently, they haven't destroyed everything. Belle and I can sneak over and grab one of the smaller boats. Call for help and then start for Kodiak.

My friend walked up behind me. She peeked through the crack. "Storm seems to be over," she said.

"We need to go. See the lodge through the trees over there," I asked, gesturing. "I'm estimating it's only about five miles away. We can hike around to the other side of the fiord and take one of the smaller boats. Head toward Kodiak after dark and use the onboard radio to call for help. I'm betting the Coast Guard will come and meet us."

"I would love to sneak out of here," Belle said, "But, I can't."

I turned and looked at her, noting her red rimmed eyes and sallow skin; concerned. "Why? Is it your injury?"

"I think Jay might need our help."

"What?"

What is she thinking?

Fear, electric and hot, arced through me.

How can our world be so lovely and so messed up at the same time? I mind my own business, I don't make trouble, I recycle when I can, I don't support war, why is this happening to me?

I burbled, "I'm no Marine or secret agent or whatever Jay is. I know nothing about missiles or covert government operations, and I have no reason to get involved. I just want to get us home, get to you a doctor, get back to making art, and forget this ever happened."

"And how many times has, 'forgetting this ever happened,' worked for you?" she asked.

I turned back and stared out at sun rays streaming onto the rugged but majestic landscape spread below.

I knew what she meant. She'd watched me crying more than once over the state of my marriage, even while I refused to do anything more than feebly confronting my faithless hubby. Instead, being all too eager to 'forget this ever happened' until the next time rolled around and then the next. And so, I told myself I loved my handsome, erratic, fun-loving spouse. I knew I loved the two wonderful sons that had become mine after we married. He would stay faithful if I were a better wife, right? I read all the statistics about children raised in broken homes. His boys had already gone through that. More drama would bring more damage. My father's death had hurt my brothers, especially my younger brother, Ted. I knew, firsthand, the uncertainty and fear that follow us into adulthood after losing a parent and had experienced the blame spilled onto me by an angry, embittered mother for problems she couldn't solve. So, I sucked it up and became an expert at sticking my head in the sand. And yes, in the end, one careless act decided for me. I'd finally brought home divorce papers, and because he would never stop and listen to me, talked to him through the bathroom door, explaining politely, way too politely looking back on it, what I was going to do. He was getting dressed, taking much longer than usual, and I watched as he pushed me aside and walked into the bedroom, clean-shaven, spiffed up, and ever so good looking in a new, tailored gray suit I had never seen before. He grabbed my shoulders in both hands, laughing like I'd made a hilarious joke, ground his lips aggressively into mine, and told me to stop the hissy fit as he brushed past and rushed off. On another philandering jaunt, I found out much later, to a party somewhere near Moose Pass. He made it just past Cooper Landing with his new love of the month riding along. A young man, high on "crack," eager to get home to Kenai, passed a semi on a double yellow and hit Brad's car head-on, killing my husband and his latest fling, a young mother of three cuddled up beside him.

CHAPTER 17

"This is serious business," Belle said, touching my shoulder, bringing me back to the present. I turned toward her again, as she continued, "The warhead on that long-range missile packs an enormous amount of firepower. It could reach halfway around the world. We've got to disarm it. Jay thinks someone using a computer has hijacked the controls and reset them. The missile could fire at the hacker's command and head almost anywhere on earth they set it to go."

"Why don't they bring in an entire team and fix it?"

"Because Jay doesn't know what parts of the program they've messed with. He doesn't know who the bad actors are in this show, and he can't take a chance on letting the wrong people know the missile is compromised. The scary truth is, we've got traitors high up in every branch of our military and government, and it only takes a few, determined, evil individuals to do some real and lasting damage. The very people supposedly helping fix the problem might be the ones who would set it off."

"Ok, but why you?" I asked, querulous, still not wanting to understand.

"Wasn't my plan to get involved, I knew nothing about this missile site or Chametz and the Russians, and you know I only flew over here to sell the lodge. As I told you, however, I helped set up the computers for missiles and wrote programming; so, I'll offer what I can. My belief about this country is 'we the people,' remember?"

"Weren't you speaking, kind of philosophically, or would that be metaphorically?" I murmured, wanting to ease the tension and trying to sidle past her.

"Here's my speech," she said. "I believe every citizen of this magnificent land has a responsibility and a right to step up and do what can be done to keep our collective freedom. It is not just the job of those in the military or government."

"Yeah, yeah," I countered. "You were in the Marines. At least you have solder skills and high-tech, computer know-how." My voice rueful, "Like I could ever 'step up' and help my country."

"You might surprise yourself. Battles aren't only fought or won with guns and bombs. Think of all the non-military people who helped in hundreds of different ways during World War II."

Jay called from behind us, asking, "Loren, could you keep watch and let us know if you see anything?"

"What am I looking for?"

"Helicopters, airplanes, or anyone heading this way."

He and Belle returned to the kitchen.

She is going to stay and try to help Jay save the world. Should I grab a boat by myself, take off for Kodiak and call for help?

Hours later, Jay called to me from the kitchen, where he and Belle were hard at work. Crumpled papers littered the floor. His little spaceship machine made a constant whirring noise as it spit out a curling ribbon of paper.

Using Jay's laptop, Belle tapped keys and mumbled to herself. Anxiety marked her taut features.

Jay asked, "Would you hurry and go check on Big H for me? I'm in the middle of this transmission and can't leave. Also, think I might have dropped a small bag of tools on my way into the cave."

He didn't smile. He didn't even glance at me. His face looked rigid, neck muscles tight. He wiped his sweaty upper lip.

"Where's Big H?" I asked, hoping he didn't want me to go up that ladder.

"That's right," he said, speaking rapidly. "You two don't know your way around this site, yet. Make sure you're carrying a light. Open the green door, go inside the room with the ladder, look to your left. There's another large door that looks like a wall but isn't. Look at the opposite wall for a narrow vertical groove in the concrete about six inches above the floor. Slide your finger down the groove and press. The panel will slide open and close again on its own, fast. Go through it and follow the tunnel out." He turned back to the busy little machine. I saw Belle look over at him. Their eyes locked.

'Check on Big H?' Something's up. Why are they trying to get me away from here? What are they hiding, some kind of romantic event? I've never seen Belle like this.

I stood watching them for a few seconds, confused, disconcerted and feeling about as valuable as last week's toast.

Jay looked up and said, "Not gone, yet?"

"How will I get back in?"

Impatiently, "The outside door has three rows of bolts running across it. It's the bottom row, second from the right. Push the bolt head. The door will open. The green door has a row of vertical bolts. Pull the fifth from the top to the right." He spoke fast, "Hey, hurry it up, get out there and don't come back until you find those tools. I can't do this job without them."

He stood, knocking his chair over, and ran.

Good grief-are we eager or what?!

My friend still wouldn't look at me. I picked up my flashlight, grabbed the size too huge man's coat I'd found, took the .38 from its resting place on the floor beside her chair, and scurried back to the green door. Jay had already opened it, ordering, "Be quick!"

I gave him the angriest look I could muster, practically jumped through the opening and switched on my light just as the door shut behind me. I found the groove behind the ladder, slid a finger along it, and watched the entire wall slide away, leaving an opening wide enough for a large forklift to wheel through.

That's how they got all the loaded pallets and everything else into the cave.

I raced through that doorway. Jay was right. It shut hard and fast with no time to spare.

A passageway on the other side of the mammoth door curved up and away from me. I used my trusty little light. At first, I sprinted, hair flying, panting, until I said out loud, "This is ludicrous," and slowed to a walk.

About twenty feet ahead, the concrete tunnel changed direction, and as I came around a tight curve, the sunlight dazzled, warming the space. Smells of spruce and hemlock scented the rain freshened breeze. I stopped and looked around. My sense of confinement eased, and I drank in delicious air and clear, natural light. I'd never be a cave dweller.

Big H was parked. Someone had painted the sizable landing pad to appear like a tumble of rocks and cleverly fabricated a concrete wall to look like mountain boulders surrounding it. The art and skill of camouflage. Impressive. I began scanning the landing site for the bag Jay dropped. I combed over the entire area, taking my time, stalling, feeling miffed, not wanting to go back inside any sooner than necessary. I heard chickadees twittering in trees further down the mountainside. A dragon fly cruised lazily overhead. Long minutes passed. I opened the helicopter door, set my pistol on the pilot's seat, and bending almost double, slid my hand under it. The first thing I discovered was a plastic sandwich bag enclosing a toothbrush, toothpaste, and razor. I retrieved it, indignant. This was the bag of tools Jay needed? My second discovery? I was no longer alone.

"Don't move!"

I froze, bent over, half in and half out of the bubble-like cockpit. Not my most graceful pose.

Crap! Can't reach the gun.

"What are you doing here? Are you the pilot?" Words honked, as though the speaker was squeezing his nostrils shut, an inflamed adenoid, allergy encumbered voice. Someone poked my back. I started upright, but I was jabbed again. I bent over fast.

"Look," urgent sound, "I need a pilot, and I'm willing to pay. I don't want trouble. Are you the pilot?"

"You look, whoever you are," I said, pain and irritation sharpening my words, "My back hurts. You want information, move away and let me put my tail feathers down where they should be. I need to get my head out of this thing and stand upright."

"Ok, ok," came a muffled bleat.

I grabbed the gun, lunged to a standing position, turned with one movement, and leveled it at the voice -just as if I'd practiced.

I guess watching all those cop movies with my boys was worth something.

And there stood the frizzy-haired little man with the humongous mustache. He saw the revolver, shrieked, threw his hands in the air, tripped, lost his balance, and fell backward. He didn't appear to have a weapon. He waggled a broken branch. When he saw me examining him and his little stick, he reddened, flinging it away.

I loomed over him, fear constricting my vocal cords. My breath stuttered. He needed to believe pointing guns at people was how I made my living. I looked over my shoulder, attempting to see everywhere at once.

Is he alone?

My voice shrilled, "You need to tell me who you are and why you're here, and you need to do that right now." I cleared my throat, embarrassed, but he didn't seem to notice my screechy falsetto or my discomfiture.

Torn clothes, face scratched, plastered with dirt and organic detritus, he had fallen with one leg bent under him. The other stuck straight out like he was attempting a complicated ballerina pose. I noticed his footwear. That scrawny guy hiked up here wearing leather wingtips of all things. At one time, they must have been stylish or at least expensive, but now they were ripped and caked with mud. I imagined his poor feet didn't look much better. I saw a burnt spot near the end of his ferret-like nose; it looked as if someone had scoured part of his mustache and most of his hair off with an electric grinder. He removed his coat. I noticed raw sores dotting the backs of his hands and wrists; his tired brown eyes were smudged purple with bruises.

"I'm Duane Morgan. I work for Homeland Security. My creds are in my bag," he said, as he tried to get to his feet. "Have to talk to whoever's in charge. It's urgent." He was flushed, face glistening with sweat.

"Let's see some identification," I said, "Where's your bag?"

"Over there."

I stepped back, starting to feel foolish. I'd probably menaced enough for the moment. After looking him over, it didn't seem like the bedraggled man was going to be much of a threat. I motioned him to get his belongings. I almost laughed when I saw it was the same red duffle he'd unloaded from the helicopter. All ripped and dirty now, the piece of luggage lay squished and broken on the ground beside him. He pulled a disheveled mass of papers from inside and thrust them at me.

"I see," I said, without looking through them. I handed the stack to him and said, "Let's go talk to the guy who claims to know what this missile crisis is all about." I shoved Jay's items in my pocket, told Duane to walk, and kept the .38 aimed at his back as we headed into the tunnel. He put up no resistance. He watched, curious, while I stopped and went through the steps that got us through the complicated openings and closings and into the battery storage area. I shouted my hello in warning, hoping I had stayed outside long enough, and wasn't bursting in on something embarrassing, private, or both.

"People," I called, "I've brought you a visitor."

Jay showed up. Belle followed. Jay carried his pistol. He looked like he'd been cage fighting and gotten whipped. His shirt was sweat-soaked, hair trampled, his bloodshot eyes, sunken. Belle's face was blotchy, swollen. She'd been crying.

Something is going on. Are they trying to save the world, having a biology encounter, or what?

"He says his name is Duane Morgan," I said. "He's all yours, if you aren't too busy with personal stuff."

Jay gave me an odd look, as the frail newcomer clutched his crumpled bag to his chest. Duane stood drooping, defeated, and unkempt. Belle stepped forward, reaching for his luggage. It was apparent he didn't want to let go. A tug-of-war between them for a bit, but she persisted, pulling it out of his arms. She carried it a few feet away, dumping contents on the floor. We saw ripped and muddy papers, several thumb drives, a dented can of chili, four paper clips, and two plastic pieces that looked like old floppy disks, but no gun.

Jay patted Duane down. No weapons. Belle sat on the floor and sorted through his stuff. I wanted my coffee, even though it was cold by now and I also wanted to razz Belle a bit, because it seemed she was deliberately keeping me in the dark. As I passed her on my way to the kitchen, I whispered, "Remember what I said in the lodge about you two being soul mates? That poor guy comes up here, yes, indeedy, hikes all this way in his dress shoes, just think of it; miles and blisters, blood, sweat, and tears and more miles, carrying his special red bag, just to see you. And then," I paused, "He finds you've forgotten all about him. For shame."

"What?" Belle glanced at me, her upturned face tear-stained and haggard.

Ok, that fell flat.

Duane was conversing with Jay when I returned.

"…Yeah, I worked on these missile sites several years ago. That was all top secret, as you know. My assignment last year was to infiltrate Chametz's team. I came on as their computer security guy and passed intel back to…" He stopped talking when he noticed I was standing there. He shifted, then continued, "I found out about the missile deal by hacking their computers. Listen; this is an imminent threat."

"Where were you during the explosion at the lodge?" I asked, knowing my voice revealed my suspicion.

"Look, guys," Duane continued, ignoring my question, his face a mask of fatigue and worry, "This isn't just a Russian plot. They're running the show, that's for sure, but I'm almost positive a multi-country, terrorist group is helping carry out this missile take-over from eastern Europe. They plan to bomb Israel, using our missile, so we get blamed."

Turning to me, he said, "I'm not a terrorist. I almost got killed in those explosions. If I hadn't tripped and fallen behind that concrete wall just before the bombs, or whatever they were, detonated; well, I most likely wouldn't be here talking about it. During the shooting and confusion after, I hid, but they found me, pounded on me for a while, and gifted me these." He held out his arms.

I could now see cigarette burns had made the raw sores covering his hands.

"They knocked me on the head. They must have gotten bored because they stopped hitting me and stuck me in a shed. I got away around four this morning and headed for the missile site. I knew where it was because Homeland Security briefed me when I took this assignment. Two guys guarding me got drunk, and I overheard them talking. They don't know where this missile site is, but I think they're looking."

"Why didn't they kill you?" I questioned.

Jay said, his voice grim, "Because they thought they might use him a while longer."

"Duane, someone's hacked into the computer controlling this missile," Belle said.

CHAPTER 18

Jay broke in, his voice tight with stress, "We've been trying to override and destroy the hacker's program, but so far haven't been able to figure out how to do that. You think you could get into the computer and shut this sucker down before they fire it off?"

"Yes," Duane said, "If I have enough time and the right equipment. The explosion destroyed most of what I brought."

Jay said, "I want you to tell me what you know about the Chametz/Russian angle and who blew your cover, but right now, I've got to get back to work on this missile problem. I'd appreciate any help you can give."

Should I leave now?

I trailed after them.

Jay led Duane to the kitchen and the electronic equipment on the table.

"Here's what we were working on when you showed up, Duane. Hey, Loren, did Big H look ok, out there?"

Was he still perpetuating that fantasy?

"Far as I could tell, and here are the 'tools' for your job," I said, handing Jay his little sandwich bag, my voice cold.

Belle motioned, and I followed her to the food storage area. She said, "You have a right to know this. Jay asked you to look for his 'missing tools' to get you away from a missile meltdown. When we hacked into the missile's computer via satellite, we found the launch sequence code activated and counting."

My voice squeaked, "You mean it was counting down to an actual launch? Why didn't you tell me?"

"Yes. Someone broke into it via computer and programmed it to deploy. I didn't tell you because I knew you wouldn't leave, or you'd try to drag me out with you. It was minutes from a launch. And where would it have detonated? Duane says Israel. I don't know, Israel or where, but an hour ago, we believed our only option was to explode it here behind tons of rock, instead of letting it fly out there somewhere and kill thousands."

"Would any of us have survived that?"

"Doubtful," she said. "I mean, for sure Jay and I wouldn't. We were just trying to get you away to give you whatever chance there was."

And I felt jealous and left out, thinking they were trying to manipulate me for their self-interest. Do I have issues or what?

"Gulp," I said, feeling mortified and looking away as red suffused my face, "You didn't detonate it; we're all still here, so what happened?"

"We weren't able to shut anything down for good, but a minute or two before we were going to force detonation, we were able to change the countdown time frame." She saw my hopeful expression and interjected, "Not by much, you understand, but we added twenty-four hours."

"You're saying, unless someone figures out how to override the countdown, this missile will launch tomorrow?"

"And that was twenty minutes ago. We only have twenty-three hours and change."

"Why can't you go back in and override the countdown thingy, again?"

"Because they caught us. Someone is monitoring all the systems. Whoever hacked into the missile saw what we were doing via interconnected computers and locked the timeframe launch code so we can't change it anymore."

"Crap."

"Indeed. And as soon as Duane and Jay get that old hard drive turned on and operating, I need to help with whatever I can. My computer skills are rusty, but I might think of something."

Feeling useless, I followed her toward the kitchen just as Duane and Jay emerged from the battery room loaded with bulky computer components.

"This," Duane explained, red-faced and puffing as he set the dusty monitor down on the already crowded tabletop, "Had to be the original one used when the missile was first upgraded. They set it up to send and receive data from a satellite. It can't do that anymore; they've changed codes and everything else so many times, but I'm hoping I can turn it on, and these old floppy disks I've brought will work and show us a schematic of the inside of the missile."

Jay shoved more papers off the table and put the ancient tower next to the monitor.

And then I caught on.

If they can't use their computers to dismantle it, they're going to use the schematic to literally crawl inside and disconnect everything that way.

The men hunched over the table, laboring to get the obsolete computer running. To shut the missile down, they had to be able to study a diagram of its inner workings, so they'd know what to do to take it apart.

Belle gathered more freeze-dried meals, heated water, and poured it into the pouches, reconstituting the food. She handed the steaming containers to them. They gulped their meals, returning after to their work. I kept going back to the cave entryway, looking through the crack, watching for anyone moving toward us. Hours passed. Tension crackled through the room. Duane got the old computer to read his disks, and we watched as the entire shell of the missile unzipped, displaying the inside as a detailed diagram on the monitor. He said he wanted to spend the rest of the day using Jay's equipment to link into the main computer via satellite to stop the launch. If that wasn't successful, start tomorrow morning to begin the mechanical, hands-on, dismantling process.

"We don't know how long that'll take," Jay said wearily, in response to Duane's proposal. "We're not getting any closer to fixing the situation we've got, now. We still haven't found out who or what has hacked into the computer; we can't tell for sure if the launch time will happen when scheduled, and there's no reason to believe we'll have any better success, tomorrow." He paused, then said, "We all know what happens if we run out of time."

Belle had been making notes on scrap paper. She said, "My vote is we do whatever's necessary to shut this thing down as quickly as we can. We can go back to working on the computer/satellite communication angle after, but guys, we've got less than seventeen hours until this missile flies off somewhere and detonates."

My voice sounded extra loud in the sudden hush after her pronounce-ment. "I'm going to head off. I admire what's being attempted here; you're all true heroes. There doesn't seem to be anything I can contribute. So good luck, everybody. I really hope you're able to fix this."

Duane began pouring over the schematic once again, but Jay, searching my face, asked, "Off where?"

"I'm going to hike over past the lodge, take a boat, cross the Shelikof, and head for Kodiak Island."

I didn't want to interrupt their work any further, and I was unwilling to discuss my plans, so I rushed to the bunk room to grab my meager pack, not realizing Belle was behind me until she spoke.

"You know I'd go with you if I could."

"Yes, and I'd stay here and help if there was anything I could do. It's like this. You think you can help fix this missile problem; I know I can't. I have nothing to offer, and I'm doing nothing of value here."

"What do you mean? You saved my life yesterday."

I didn't look at her. She touched my arm and asked, "Could you listen for a minute?"

Without waiting for my response, she began, "You remember that class for girls at the missionary's house we attended in eighth grade and the story the lady told us about Queen Esther, a Jewess who saved her people? How the narcissistic villain, Hamon, came up with a scheme to kill all the Jews because Mordecai, Esther's uncle, wouldn't bow and scrape to him? You've got to remember because that was the day you stayed after and made me wait while you talked with the teacher about how you could help the town get a library," she said, smiling.

Seeing my expression, she sobered and hurried on, "Esther told Mordecai she was afraid to approach her husband, the king, and ask for help for her people because the king was known to have, shall we say, a mercurial tem-perament. He was one of those, 'off with your head,' rulers. Mordecai told his niece that perhaps God placed her in that very situation, at that time and place, to help save the Jews. So, after gathering her courage, Esther approached the king and asked for help to save her people, even though she was afraid he might kill her for doing no more than interrupting his day.

And, as we know, after a lot more details and drama, this story ended happily with the king granting her request, and her people, the Jews, survived."

"I remember." Impatient, I pulled on the heavy coat I'd grabbed from the supply closet. "Why are you bringing this up?"

"Could be God has us over here to do a job."

"We are not queens, last time I looked."

"Yes, but if this missile gets launched, depending on where it lands, it's most likely going to kill a lot of people, and all I'm saying is, possibly God has us here so we can help get that stopped."

"Great," I said, pushing past her, exasperated. "That's wonderful for you and the God-given direction for your life. You keep telling me you and God have a relationship, and unlike a lot of so-called Christians I've been around, it really seems you do. But what about me? God and I are not buds. There's no reason for me to be here, because I don't have any help to offer. So, what am I? the no-name extra in this crazy movie that needs to hang around, just to get killed off?"

"I've already told you, dozens of times," Belle said. "God loves you and has good intention for your life. Why don't you ask him about it? He says if we draw near to him, he'll draw near to us."

We'd had this, God, and his purpose for my life, discussion before. I didn't want to be in this cave; didn't want to think about an armed missile flying off and killing people, and I didn't believe God was particularly interested in me. I walked into the bunk room, pulled the curtain and sat.

A purpose for me. Of course, I remembered the girl's class at the missionary's house. Tearing home after, running through rooms, calling for my dad so I could tell him about my library idea. It turned out he was flying a load of hunters down the coast. At the kitchen table over lunch, with my brothers and mother listening, I made my announcement. I found my purpose, I said, and it was to start a fund drive for a community library. Right after lunch, I was going to go door to door around our town to ask for donations. Excitedly, I shared my plans; until my mother's derisive laughter shattered me.

"The only place you're going, young lady, is to the kitchen to do the dishes. Who gave you that stupid idea? Don't you dare start stringing around this hick town asking people for money."

Enough remembering, I picked up my pack and walked out the cave entrance.

Skidding down the mountain did not take as long as it had to climb. I arrived at the bottom prepared to skirt the dead wolves but saw nothing there. Eaten or dragged off.

I'd tried to plot my course back at the cave entrance while I could still see over the trees. The sunny day would help with visibility. Trekking into the spruce, I headed in the direction of the lodge. I planned to get within a quarter-mile, skirt around the buildings, and sneak my way to the smaller dock Howie had pointed out days ago. After years of fishing experience aboard my husband's boat, I felt confident in my ability to get an engine started on at least one of them.

Before leaving the missile site, I found a small cache of guns and took the .38 and a Ruger Mini 14. This rifle was lighter, not a weapon for bears, but I was now more concerned about bad guys than running into a brownie. With less weight to pack, I knew I could move much faster, and speed was critical. I picked up a branch and, using it as a walking stick, shoved through thick bracken and undergrowth. Less than three hours into my hike, my face and hands were already smarting from the ever-present devil's club. This aptly named bush has stubby branches and broad leaves covered in sharp thorns that break off at the slightest touch, penetrating the skin, causing swelling, itching, and burning after contact. I had a friend that swore salve made from its sap helped her eczema. I'd spent hours making paintings of this plant, entranced by the beautiful foliage.

Well, no more.

"My love affair with you is over," I stated aloud, swatting at a bush with my stick as I walked by.

I quieted, feeling foolish, not wanting to draw attention from anything in the woods.

Stepping across mud where water from recent rain trickled in a rivulet, something caught my eye as it lay glittering in the muck. A candy wrapper? I bent to pick it up and saw a boot track. Instantly wary, ready to run, scanning every direction. More tracks.

I slung the mini 14 across my back. Clawing my way through dense brush days earlier had convinced me I couldn't count on being able to whip a rifle down into firing position in time to defend myself if I suddenly came across a threat. I pulled the .38 from the pocket of the voluminous coat I'd found in the cave's storeroom and held it ready to fire as I moved further into the undergrowth.

Voices.

Men. I crept forward.

People coming to help us? The idea tantalized.

I edged closer.

Angry sounds. Still too far away to make out what they were saying, but loud enough to tell it wasn't English.

Now sneaking through soft moss, I dropped to my belly and crawled. Only a few trees between me and whoever stood there, so lying almost flat, I inched forward on my stomach, pulling myself to a wide, thick hemlock. Under its bottom boughs, I curled up as small as possible, waiting. They hadn't noticed. I peeked through the branches.

CHAPTER 19

Two men stood in a clearing, arguing. One was well over six feet, dressed in camo, unshaven, lardy pocked skin with squinting yellow eyes. He held a rectangular black device about the size of a pack of cigarettes above his head, moving it in circles. I heard a faint beeping sound and realized the repetitive noise was coming from it. The angry man was shorter, coffee colored, wore a curly black beard, and one bristly eyebrow which flourished above his bulbous nose and crowded his features. His clothes looked as if he'd stolen them from Fidel Castro in 1959. The tall guy had grown loud in his attempt to win the argument with Black Beard. He didn't appear to be getting satisfaction, because the shorter man gesticulated and stomped his foot, hollering the only word I could understand.

"No! No! No!" He then turned and marched straight toward me.

I shrank, gripping the revolver with clammy hands.

Stay still. Don't panic. Please, God, don't let him see me!

A milli-second wondering if I was praying, and then Black Beard was right in front of me. I waited, holding my breath, hoping I wouldn't have to shoot. The incensed man strode right past without noticing me, so close I could touch his boot. No time to relax, because Tall Guy chased after him, and both men stopped about twenty feet from my tree.

Their argument resumed. Although I couldn't catch everything said, it was obvious the tall one was once more attempting to appease the belligerent man standing in front of him.

In broken English I heard, "… Not blaming. Fedyor's fault… you smart; tracking… in coat still working… signal… heading for missile… follow. Not lost. Little traitor… die."

Another sizzling outburst from the swarthy man, and they headed rapidly into the brush.

Black beard and Tall Guy are tracking Duane. That's why he could slip away from the lodge. They found out he was working for our government and planned to use him to get to the missile site. If they catch him, they may try to force him to do something that allows them to control the missile, but regardless, they will kill him and whoever else is in their way to ensure the missile launches.

I sat, stunned, remembering Jay's comment about Duane "being used." A new wrinkle and a big one at that. But I had my plans. Take a boat, contact the Coast Guard, tell them about the explosion and drug runners, and ask for help for myself and my friend. To keep the missile top secret, I would mention nothing about Jay, Duane, or the Chametz/Russian business. But then another thought:

How do I get the Coast Guard's help without exposing information about the missile?

Also, Black Beard and Tall Guy discussed going to the site, and I knew they weren't going there to make friends. What was I supposed to do? Run up behind and try to intimidate them with my guns?

I'm not a soldier, not a cop. How can I physically stop these two, short of shooting them? Is this my business, my job, my purpose? Shouldn't I keep going, grab a boat and call the Coast Guard, explaining we need emergency help as soon as possible? But there's no way the Coast Guard can get here before those men locate the missile site. What am I responsible for, anyway?

I wriggled away from the tree, knowing, as much as I hated it, it was time to get back to the site and warn Belle and the others, and I must get there before Tall Guy and Black Beard showed up. They probably could walk faster than me, but I was more familiar with the terrain and this time knew where to go, so that evened the score a bit.

Back. I had to watch for bears, wolves and the two bad guys, but somehow get to the cave before they arrived. Jogging through every clearing, I struggled to find the quickest way around rock piles and fallen trees.

The men did not go directly toward the cave, so I surmised they were still trying to find their way. Maybe the tracking device they'd put in Duane's coat wasn't giving a steady signal.

On a moss-covered boulder, I rested, gulping water from my canteen. My clothes were becoming scratched and filthy, my hair hung in limp strands. Winded, I rubbed a sleeve over my damp face and tried to slow my breathing. A sudden swishing noise startled me. I stumbled to my feet. An eagle, clutching a still thrashing salmon, landed on a nearby slab of rock, and wings spread for balance, dug into it, bloody beak tearing off hunks of flesh. The raptor gazed at me, unblinking, impassive, and unafraid. I trudged into the trees. The bird's high-pitched call followed on the wind, and I wondered if it felt as alone as I.

I am so over fighting my way through this jungle. These tangled bushes and fallen trees are a nightmare. If I ever get myself out of here and feel the urge to hike, it will be on groomed trails and nothing else.

I had to retrace the same route followed when leaving the cave, only do it much quicker. Couldn't help anyone by getting lost. That anxiety-producing thought kept me alert.

Wonder where Black Beard and Tall Guy are, now?

Were they behind or ahead of me? I hoped they were fighting bears or each other, or at least so engrossed in tracking Duane they wouldn't notice anything else.

I dragged off again, tired, wincing, my legs unsteady. Tripping over a root, I fell, scraping my hands and knees. The piquant scent of high bush cranberries reminded me of berry picking outings with my boys on sunny fall days; I missed those happy times. Tears stung my eyes.

"If you're there, God, and this is my job, my purpose," I mumbled, looking up through the trees toward the sky, "You must know I'm not going to be any good at this. There's no way for me to help fix this missile situation. I'm only going back there to warn my friend. I'm pretty sure I'll end up failing again, like I failed my baby girl."

I pulled myself to my feet and slogged on, making my way through a field of sharp-edged boulders. The bright day dimmed behind oppressive clouds. A sudden damp breeze cuffed me. Cumbersome boots I'd found in the cave made me clumsy and uncertain as I fought through nature's debris.

The world around me slid into soft shades of twilight. I hid in brush at the base of the mountain, listening and watching for movement.

Where were the two men tracking Duane?

Minutes passed. It was now so dark there was no way to see the ledge or the jagged crack that showed the cave's opening. A field mouse squeaked, and the wind murmured and sighed, sounding tired. I hadn't seen the two men tracking Duane, so it was time to get up into the cave and warn them. I also sighed, muscles aching, then began struggling up the steep slope. Like the last time, the climb seemed to go on, forever. Finally, I located the ledge, after smacking my head against it.

I explored my repertoire of unhappy noises, crawled over the lip of the rock, pulled myself upright, ran my hands over the vertical stone face, found the narrow opening, and slipped inside. Feeling safer, I switched on my tiny flashlight and located the camouflaged door opener. As I pressed the button, the rock panel slid back, and I walked through.

To my right stood Jay, facing the door; arms extended, pistol aimed straight at me. He balanced on widespread legs, his eyes sparked fire, his jaw steel. I resolved to play it just as cool as he had when he'd entered earlier through the green door.

"Something's up. We need to talk. Where's Belle?"

"Decided to come back, huh?" he said, recovering his composure and lowering the weapon. "Missed me, didn't you?"

"For certain sure. Where's Belle?"

"In the bunk area, I think. What do we need to talk about?"

"Let me find her, first."

Belle came out of the curtained sleeping area as I got to the kitchen. She limped over, giving me a ghost of a smile.

"I'm so glad you're back," she said, grabbing my hand.

"We've got to talk," I said.

Duane was still bent over the old computer, studying the missile's schematics and making notes on paper.

"Two guys are coming after Duane," I jabbered, my shaking voice betraying my fear. "I hid and listened to them. They put a tracking device in his coat."

Duane croaked, "My coat?"

134

"Not surprised," Jay said.

Belle asked, "Can you give us more details?"

I related how boot tracks and angry voices led me to the two men. I described Tall Guy and Black Beard.

"The man you're calling Black Beard sounds like one of the two guarding me," Duane said. "He called the other guard, Fyodor. Guess they weren't as out of it as I thought," he finished.

We were silent.

Jay asked, "Where's your coat?"

Duane paused, trying to remember.

"I was kinda freaked," he said finally. "That pretty lady kept waving her gun at me, and I couldn't think."

"Come on, Duane, 'that pretty lady' is standing in front of you and her name is Loren," Jay said, amused.

Belle grinned at me, jiggling her eyebrows up and down. I turned away, pouring myself a coffee. I felt about as pretty as I had right after being blown out of the boat, Monday night.

"My coat is here, somewhere. Right now, I'm on my way to the john, then I'll find it," Duane said, as he left the kitchen.

Jay took in my disheveled appearance, grinned and remarked, "Glad you're back. We're getting ready to open the missile and disconnect it from anything computer related. We'll then take pieces off it and shut it down so it cannot be launched without a major overhaul and lots of new parts."

"How many hours away from launch time?"

"Less than twelve," Belle answered.

"You've figured out how to get into it?"

Jay, looking and sounding much less stressed, answered. "It's a complicated older model with certain upgrades. The schematics are difficult to read, but fortunately, Duane really knows his stuff. Now that the plans have shown us where the warhead, as it's called, is located, we're ready to pull off some metal skin and get to work. I'm too big to get in there, so Duane will do the honors. I'll give him step-by-step instructions, and we'll work together."

About that time, we heard a faint yell and realized Duane hadn't returned. Belle grabbed the .38 I'd set on the counter; I picked up the mini-14, and Jay pulled his pistol.

I ended up in the lead, running through the battery room. Jay caught up, putting a light hand on my shoulder as he whispered, "Keep the gun, but get back to the bunk area. Stay down and stay hidden. Don't shoot unless you have to."

Belle limped after him. Dismissed. I didn't know whether to feel insulted or relieved. I crouched behind a loaded pallet. Right before the doors closed, I heard shots. I ran back to a bunk and wriggled under. It was dark. There was no way to tell what was happening. Shouldn't I help? I slid out, remembered Jay's instructions, and lay down again, trying to figure how I'd be able to shoot my weapon at someone while I lay stuffed under a bed. Time dragged. I could hear nothing. Then, footsteps. I aimed the gun. Someone was going to get their toes blown off.

"Loren, it's me." Belle walked into the bunk area. I scooted from under, dragging the rifle.

Jay and Belle stood quiet; eyes somber. My friend nervously fingered the .38. I noticed the long scratches on her throat again. Her face drooped with fatigue. Jay set down a satchel, brimming with tools.

"Where's Duane?" My voice cracked.

"One of the guys you told us about, the tall one, shot him. Duane didn't make it." Jay said.

"Shot him? Where was he? I mean, what?" I stammered. "What happened?"

"He went outside looking for his coat," Jay said, as he held out a round object about the size of a large marble. "Here's the tracking device." He threw it onto the concrete floor and smashed down with his foot. The electronic gadget splintered.

"I should have remembered Duane dropping his coat. The entire time I worried I'd mishandle the situation, and that's what happened. I got the poor man killed." Tears blurred my vision.

"It's not your fault," Belle said.

Jay said, face grim, "We neutralized the tall one. Let's go talk by the ladder; I have an idea."

Why are we going back there?

As we walked toward the green door, I asked, "Where's the guy with the beard?"

"We climbed all over the rocks out there, looking, but we only saw one man," Belle said.

"Well, unless Black Beard died out in the woods, which would be great, he's still alive and dangerous, somewhere," I said, feeling skittish as the door shut us into the concrete room with the tall, tall ladder.

"I don't think he can get in, now; so, we don't need to worry about him," Belle assured me, aiming her light up the rungs.

"What we still have to do," Jay said, running his hand distractedly through his hair, "Is get inside the missile and deactivate it." No longer at ease, he tapped his watch. "We're fast running out of time, and we're going to need your help." He was looking fixedly at me, and this time he wasn't smiling.

I felt my core muscles tighten.

Me? Why is he looking at me?

"My help? I don't know anything about missiles, nix, nada, zilch," I babbled.

"That doesn't matter," Jay said.

"What do you mean, 'that doesn't matter?' This is a bomb we're talking about." My voice wavered high and thin. I wanted to pound on something. I was so angry my brain felt fuzzy.

CHAPTER 20

Inside my head, I mewled like a lost kitten. Desperation flooded me. I slapped at the ladder angrily, feeling half inclined to slap Jay.

No way can I take this on. I'll fail. I know I'll fail. This is not my responsibility. I don't know anything about working on a missile. Is he crazy?

Even though it was pitch dark, and rain poured like a demented giant's car wash, I wanted to race out and leap down that rocky slope, crash through brush loaded with bears and wolves and bad guys and grab a boat, any boat. I was even willing to brave Shelikof Strait with its screaming winds just to get away and never have to think or remember this horrible place again.

"Look," I began, holding Jay's eyes, forcing my quavering voice down a couple octaves. I was a mature, full-fledged woman after all, and didn't need to lose my dignity sounding like a panicked teenager.

"I only came back here to warn my friend Belle, and yes, ok, you and Duane. I don't plan on staying, and yes, I've used weapons for hunting and helped repair engines, so I know a little about guns and a little about machinery and motors, but I don't have training for this military action, gunplay stuff; let alone am I qualified to work with bombs."

They both stood there, silent, pensive, watching me, worry tightening their features. I felt asinine and defensive for my outburst, but confident in the assertion I was not the right person for this job.

Whatever they think, I'm not lying; I don't have any idea how to defuse a bomb.

"I know this is probably a bit outside your comfort level," Belle said gently, touching my sleeve.

I jerked away and shrieked. "A bit outside my comfort level, Belle? My comfort level? Are you for real? This is as far away from my comfort level as it would be if you were locked in a house full of uncaged snakes for a month."

"All right, all right, I get it, but I'm too big to fit in the missile," she said. "And we know Jay won't fit. Duane was to be the inside guy, and even that was going to be iffy. You're smaller than Duane," she continued. "So, I know you could climb in there, and I also know you were pretty handy helping Brad work on that old diesel and other machinery on your fish boats."

"Mostly, I handed him tools," I argued, "And it seemed like I often got that wrong."

Why is Belle doing this to me? She's supposed to be my friend. She, of all people, knows I'm not qualified to mess around with a bomb.

"I feel sick about Duane and all the other killings for that matter, but is trying to shut down a missile my responsibility? I would help if I knew how to do the job, but I know nothing about this. What if I made the problem worse somehow, or set the bomb off?" Distress made my voice strident, high-pitched.

I need to simmer down; I sound like an overloaded wash machine on spin cycle.

"All any of us have is what we have, and that's all we can offer. We're just asking you to try with what you have," Belle said.

"All you need to do is follow my instructions," Jay said. "I'll be right there with you, I promise, guiding you through every step."

Crap.

And there I was, going up the ladder again. Belle ahead of me, and Jay several steps below, bringing a bag, loaded with tools.

At least I'm not climbing alone this time.

We reached the landing and clambered out. I felt a little better when I saw my usually confident friend clutch the railing with both hands.

We waited until Jay arrived and took the lead. He shined his light around the cramped space, illuminating the levers and ominous launch button I'd seen the last time. I noticed another ladder that led even higher.

"Go up that," he instructed, pointing, "Climb out on the first platform you come to and wait for me."

Life keeps getting better.

"Where are you going to be?" I asked Belle, stalling.

"I'm going to de-activate the launch button," she answered, whispering. She seemed very tense. "See you two, later."

I clipped on my miniature flashlight and climbed until I reached the steel deck and framework, which was smaller than the one below us. It quivered and shook as I stepped out onto it, and I quivered and shook, just plain scared, my hands cold, my face hot, and my heart tripping.

Jay was right behind me.

"This is where we get inside," he said, quietly. "Haven't been able to get the lights working in this part of the complex; I'll need you to hold this for me." He handed me an LED lantern and opened his pouch.

Unfolding a sketch-covered paper, he held it up to the glow. He ran his hands over the missile's metal exterior and, within a few minutes, found what he was looking for, picked up a tool, and began working to remove the panel.

"After I get this off, it'll be time for you to climb in, and we'll get started."

I held the light for him in one hand, gripped the railing with my other, and wished I was anywhere but here.

Jay worked methodically. He removed screws and popped rivets until he had the panel loosened, pulled free, and leaning against the railing. I handed him the lantern, and he shined it into the opening. All I could see were wires running in every direction.

"Your turn," he said.

I shuffled over, not wanting to make the platform shake.

How high are we, anyway?

"You have to take off those big boots," he said. "They won't be any help inside this thing."

At last, a responsibility I can handle.

Boots removed, I asked, "How do I pull myself up into it?"

"One of my jobs," he answered, lifting me high enough to get my feet and legs in through the hole. He smelled like mud and sweat and oily tools and man.

"Wait," I pleaded, grabbing at him. "Don't let me go! What will I stand on in there?"

With his arms still tight around me, he said, "As I slide you down, you'll feel a flat piece of metal bracing under your feet. That'll be your floor. By the way, Loren, you can trust me. There isn't any way to fall through in this section. Stand on that brace; you'll be able to work from there."

Moving slowly, he tipped me in. I stood, afraid to breathe, muscles tight, my face shoved in the jungle of wires.

Jay's voice was slow, pleasant, no hint of anxiety. With only the skin of steel separating us, I almost thought I could feel the heat of his body, inches from mine.

The first part of the job involved cutting wires. To find each section he wanted to take apart, I had to trace every wire with my fingers from where it began up in front of my face to a location below my knees where it fastened into a metal container he called the war head's, "brainbox" or "motherboard." All this without being able to bend forward from the waist or see what I was doing. That was the simple part. The process became more complicated. I forced myself to focus on his voice and nothing else. I cut and stripped away wires connected to timers and heat sensors and various pressure gauges and more, according to what Jay said they were, anyway. Removing these created a portal big enough to get my head and arms inside a cone-shaped aluminum housing directly in front of my face. I was using a light Jay had given me, one of those headband gadgets that left my hands free, but when it quit, I had to slip my pencil-sized flashlight from a pocket and aim the beam by holding it between my teeth.

After I described everything in exacting detail, Jay told me step by tedious step what to cut, squeeze, pull, pinch, and loosen and handed me the tool he thought would do the job.

I had removed what seemed an insignificant triangular-shaped metal piece and handed it back to him when a light on a panel about four feet below me came to life and began blinking. From somewhere deep in the missile's innards, a fizzing noise started. It sounded like an electrical relay that went belly up on my boiler last winter, only many times louder.

Wedged into this cramped space, teeth clenched around my light, drooling because I couldn't close my mouth, I couldn't move any part of my body except my arms and hands.

Pulling the penlight from between my lips, I squalled, "Can't you hear that? Something's happening in here."

A metallic hammering behind me, then Jay's voice, "Yeah, hold on a sec."

Buzzing, loud, irritating; like one thousand, turbocharged, cranky bees now filled the surrounding space, roared through my ears, stalled my thoughts.

The yellow light was blinking faster, the fizzing becoming a snapping staccato pop, pop, pop.

I could've been halfway to Kodiak by now. This missile's going to explode. Will my sons ever know what happened to me?

"Jay, come on!"

"Here. You need to put this back on," he said, pressing something that felt familiar into my waiting hand.

I was holding the triangular piece he'd had me remove.

Below me, more lights now blinking, and the buzzing had turned into a muted roar.

I snapped the metal piece back into its slot. I twisted the wires I'd snipped back together, and tightened the screws holding the piece in place, but the lights kept blinking, and the noise grew louder.

"It's not working."

"Take it off again and make sure none of the small electronic attachment points are bent. If they're bent, they won't connect."

The roar turned into a deep throbbing sound, vibrating through every bone in my body, shaking my soul loose. Impossible to concentrate.

O, God, help me.

There was no doubt I was praying at that point.

I untwisted the two wires, loosened the screws, and pulled the piece from the slot. My fingers felt like clubs.

Two tiny pins were bent.

Pouring tears, I could barely see. I forgot Jay, forgot everything except reattaching the piece. I managed to straighten the delicate slips of metal and pushed them back into place, twisting the wires yet again and tightening the screws. The roaring stopped; the electronic popping sound ceased, lights blinked off—quiet, blessed silence. Honestly don't know how long I stood there frozen; it seemed an eternity, but it couldn't have been more than a lifetime. I was crying, screaming, singing and I never made a sound.

"Minor setback," Jay said, his voice calm, "My fault, but you fixed it. You did well. We've got this. Let's go on. We're almost finished."

I didn't care if he was cheering me on or trying to encourage himself; I drank it in like spring water—next challenge. I couldn't get a rusty part to come loose, no matter how I twisted the thing. Frenetic, I worked it back and forth, slicing my palm in the process on something that was thin metal and razor sharp. Jay heard my whimper and began singing a funny song about a frog on a yellow yacht off to learn yodeling in Swizerhop. My fingers slipped with blood. Stuck in the cone of a live missile, twisting on a rusted nut, and the guy giving me step-by-step directions clapped and yodeled behind me. Too much. I started laughing and almost dropped my light. Here I was, cozied up to a live bomb, trying to play mechanic and save the world, or a part of it. Bizarre. I must have been slightly hysterical because once I got the giggles, I could not stop, until next thing I was crying, and then the whole soggy episode ended with a few hiccups. I was glad no one could see me.

I felt better after, even though I knew my world could end with an explosion that would make the blast at the lodge last Monday night look no more impressive than a guppy's sneeze in a fishbowl.

No more lights blinked on, no more scary noises. I got that nut loosened and, after a while, all the others and just like that, finished. Jay lifted me back out and held me, big warm hands pulling me close as he touched his forehead to mine and breathed, "Thank you, lovely lady. You did it. She's shut down, can't launch, and you did it. You're gutsy, know that?" I enjoyed hearing his deep voice up close and personal and enjoyed feeling the firm, warm muscles in his chest and arms as he held me and set me on my feet. I slipped my boots back on, woozy from the emotional roller coaster ride. I couldn't stop smiling. Our success glazed me with happiness.

We're still alive, and we shut it down, and he called me, 'gutsy.' Well, why not? I just shut down a missile. I just deactivated a bomb.

Jay said, "You can go ahead down the ladder. I want to dismantle switches up one deck higher, then I'll be right behind you, and we can get out of this place, and I'll fly you two home."

I stood there, giddy, wanting to celebrate. Should I dance? Burst into song? Shouldn't I look different, like a super-hero in a movie or something?

That super-hero bit probably isn't going to happen. But for now, I feel good, and that's enough.

I thrust my fist into the darkness above my head and whispered, "Yes!"

Truth? Belle and Jay practically had to drag me up here, and more truth: Jay and I shut it down together; I couldn't have done it on my own, and yes, I asked, uh, begged God for help.

"Jay," I said, feeling as awkward as a twelve-year-old with her first crush, "Thanks, you were great. There's no way I could have done that without you."

"It was the yodeling," he said, grinning. "Works every time."

I think I might have swaggered a little, walking to the ladder, but it could have been the metal scaffold, shaky as before. Going home? I tasted hope.

"And thank you, God," I murmured, feeling grateful and wanting to be polite.

I started down the ladder. That is, until I heard it.

Guttural panting.

CHAPTER 21

I stopped. Belle's lantern, knocked sideways on the scaffold below, gave the tableau an eerie luminescence, like a Rembrandt painting, only scary.

I couldn't see her upper body or head, but she'd curled her legs around a rung above her. She was upside down, clinging to the ladder. Shaken, I moved down a few more steps and saw her arms wrapped tight around bars behind her. The man had his back to me. He couldn't lean over far enough to reach her body but was punching and yanking on her feet. His voice, low, inarticulate, angry, muttered something in a language I didn't understand.

I saw his bulbous nose and thick black beard just as he pulled one of her legs loose.

I didn't think. I jumped down the last few rungs and raced at Black Beard. My arms out, I hit him in the back, shoving his thick, stubby body as hard as I could, at the same time, screaming, "Hold on, Belle!"

I knocked him off the platform, but somehow, he twisted around as he fell and now looked up at me. He was holding onto a pipe just below the metal stage, flailing his legs and feet, moving sideways, kicking savagely at my friend, and about to get his legs around the ladder. I didn't hesitate. I clasped the rail with my left hand. With my big, American-made boot, I kicked him square in the face, seeing his eyes, cold as a frozen snake. Hatred stared at me.

He bellowed, incoherent rage.

I kicked him again and again. Blood spurted, and his nose collapsed. Eyes shining with fear, he slipped, dangled for an instant, lost hold and fell, screaming and flailing into the shaft. His cry ended as he slapped onto the concrete below.

Jay charged over, and together we lifted Belle to the platform.

"I didn't know you could kick like that," She croaked, retying her boot.

"Me, neither."

"What happened?" I asked, when I could get my breath.

"I set the revolver down to work on destroying the launch button, so when he jumped me, I was unarmed. We fought all over the scaffold. I knocked his gun off the platform and thought I could keep him at bay until you and Jay were finished. So glad you showed up when you did, 'cuz I was almost done for.

"Why didn't you call for help?" I asked.

"Getting the missile disarmed was the primary objective."

She continued, "I was able to smash the launch button just before he got to me. You told us two guys were looking for Duane and the missile site, and we knew one had to be around here, somewhere. We left the doors open in our hurry to go out and help Duane. We hadn't seen the bearded guy come into the complex ahead of us. I didn't think he had. It turns out he did sneak inside, so it's a good thing Jay asked me to keep watch."

Jay said, "Fantastic job keeping that guy off us, Belle. We shut down the missile. It's not only disconnected from any computer interaction; no one will be able to re-activate it without showing up here, bringing parts and doing a lot of mechanics."

Using his light, he found the gun Belle dropped and brought it back to her. "And now," he said, "It's time to get us gone."

"By the way," I announced to Belle, as we descended the ladder, "I'm starting to rethink what you said about purpose. I mean, baby, we defused a bomb up there."

I tried to sound casual, but she laughed. "Way too cool for your socks right now, aren't you?"

"Just about."

Jay called me gutsy, but Belle was the brave one, protecting us and keeping watch, and fighting Black Beard. She wanted me to concentrate on working with Jay, so she said nothing about the possibility of the terrorist being in the complex.

My voice sounded small and choked. "Thanks again, my friend, for looking out for us like that. You're amazing."

"Swut friends are for," she replied.

I was relieved Black Beard's body was not right at the bottom of the ladder. Instead, it lay crumpled against the concrete wall. I did not go over to get a closer look. We walked into the living area, where we gathered our belongings.

We bundled Duane's paperwork into his bag and set it on a bunk. Jay said he needed to get gas for Big H, so he planned to fly us to the cabin he'd camped in, pick up fuel and staying clear of the lodge, head for Kodiak.

"Soon as we get away from this airspace, at the very latest landed in Kodiak, I'll get the right people notified," he said.

I'd lost track of time. I squinted, seeing the first glimmer of daylight as we emerged from the tunnel and onto the landing pad. Jay covered the bodies with tarps, and tears filled my eyes as I thought again about Arthur Cook, Duane, and Howie.

What a waste.

The wind became combative, and the morning sun shot timid rays from behind glowering clouds as Belle and I climbed into the cockpit and fastened our seatbelts. We sat silent and exhausted after our adrenaline rush. Jay, careful as ever, checked the helicopter's mechanical systems, looking for sabotage from the two men who had tracked and killed the plucky little computer expert. Nothing touched, he assured us, strapping himself in, saying, "They were most likely too fixated with getting their hands on Duane."

We lifted off. The wind sent an angry message, bashing into the little chopper so hard it slammed us sideways. However, Jay's fast work at the controls kept us clear of the slope, and we flew away, keeping below the tops of the mountains.

"It's going to be bumpy," he said. "I've got to stay low and as close to the mountains as I can, to stay hidden. Sick bags under your seat."

And now we get to do this.

As the little craft jumped and swayed in the breeze, I thought again of a tiny balloon bouncing alone in a big sky. The first wave of nausea slid over me. I reached for a bag.

We flew over Arthur Cook's burned-out cabin and on along the beach, then Jay turned Big H, and we climbed high over the bay heading toward his camp site. I knew good pilots always flew higher over open water. After my one sick episode, I was feeling better, watching clouds rush by. The wind didn't seem as violent at this altitude, and I relaxed, getting drowsy when Belle said, "Jay."

Just one word, but the strain in her voice brought me wide awake. She pointed down and off to our right. I saw a boat.

Jay dove the helicopter and sheered left. I looked at the skiff, far below. Did I glimpse a flash? Our small chopper swayed and wobbled.

Jay yelled, "Hang on!"

We spun twice, dropped with sickening speed, then roared upward again, veering back and forth as Jay tried to elude gunfire. With a loud crack, Big H shook and slewed sideways.

Jay shouted, "Anyone hurt?"

Belle yelled, "Not yet."

The helicopter rotated; it enveloped us in howling, screaming racket and the stink of fuel and smoke. Big H was going down.

Jay fought the controls, his feet and hands coaxing every bit of flight left in the broken machine. I heard him say, "Come on now; you can do it; take us down easy."

As we fell, the swells grew bigger and bigger. I could imagine sea water pouring over me. We had flotation devices strapped onto us, but the waves loomed like mountains, and all I could feel was dread.

About fifty feet above the bay, the engine caught and began running again. Rotors turned, and somehow, we flew forward, a gust of wind pushing us, or I don't know what, but we surged away from the wild ocean for several minutes. I thought we're ok; we're going to make it, but the helicopter collapsed, shuddering, shivering, cracking, rotors moving in long arcing sweeps as we plummeted.

Belle screamed, "Dear God, for what we are about to receive...!"

I'm not ready to die. I'm not ready...to die.

I tried to brace myself; there wasn't much to hold on to, grabbed the edge of my seat as we bounced, skidded, flopped, bounced again, slid, and settled.

Our landing was a lot less violent than I expected.

Quiet except for a steady ticking. The smell of fuel and something else. Something rotting, like moldy leaves in stagnant water.

Will Big H burn?

We've got to get out. I ripped at my seatbelt, calling Belle's name.

Jay groaned. I could see blood, a lot of blood; his hand dripped as he gripped his left leg.

I felt wet on my face and realized water was running through the cracked acrylic bubble surrounding us, then the primordial stink, like something dead, oozed in. Greenish water poured through the shattered windshield.

Trapped, we'll suffocate!

Gasping, I reached for the door handle; need air, can't breathe. My fears abated somewhat as I peered through the mud splattered plastic. We weren't sinking; we had crashed into a shallow, spongy swamp.

Take slow breaths.

I wondered if I would ever forget our tearing, shuttering fall through space, and then I remembered my father's plane plummeting into the ocean, grinding onto rocks and surf, wings breaking off, me screaming and screaming and running down the beach. Into the water, Belle towing me back, holding me. The panic, confusion of noise and boats, and no one to rescue, no one left alive. And the horrendous silence as people walked past, shoulders drooping, averting their eyes.

Belle plucked at her seatbelt.

Jay called, "Ladies, I could use your help."

His voice shook me from paralysis, and I crawled to him. Hunched in his seat, shoulder harness snarled, he was trying to free himself, to reach his leg—where a thin piece of metal strut or landing gear broken loose from under the helicopter shoved up through the cockpit during the wreck, and the tip of it now protruded from his thigh. Blood seeped from the puncture. He struggled to maintain pressure on his injury, but the way his seat had broken, he was tangled in his harness and couldn't reach far enough.

Belle and I removed his belt and used it to apply a tourniquet right above the injury.

"You'll have to pull me off that broken piece of gear," he said.

He was gritting his teeth. Belle and I looked at each other. I knew she was hoping the same as I, that Jay hadn't nicked or torn into his femoral artery, or he was likely going to bleed out, despite our efforts. I held up three fingers. She nodded, as I mouthed, "One, two, three," and together, we pulled his leg free. Blood gushed. He groaned. His face lost color. He leaned back against the broken seat and closed his eyes. His mouth bled and I could see he had a split lip and chipped front tooth. We applied pressure to the gash on his leg and the bleeding slowed, a good sign. Belle rummaged in her survival bag and pulled out bandage material which we used to wrap his injury. We removed the tourniquet. We were bloody by the time we finished. As we extricated ourselves from the wreckage, the overwhelming smell of death rankled the air.

Belle grabbed her survival bag, climbed out, slipped, and fell. She wobbled upright and began struggling through something grayish-green and as viscous as cold honey.

"Thank you, Lord, for saving our lives," she sang, her fluting warble fading as she sloshed her way to higher ground. How she could feel like singing, I didn't know. I grabbed my pack, crawled out next, and gagging, fell into a slimy mess of moss, dank pond water, and rotting plants. Jay, carrying his bag, splashed behind me. We half crawled and slogged through greasy gunk onto dry grass at the edge of the bog.

Belle said, "Look what we almost landed on."

I turned back to the wreckage. Big H sprawled over the swamp, one twisted rotor resting right above a bull moose. A very bloated and putrid dead moose. No wonder the stench was overwhelming. Jay sat on a log, shaking his head sadly as he peered at the wrecked machine. He grimaced. "Daley and his boys will not be happy about Big H." He opened his bag and pulled out his "discombobulation" machine, in three separate pieces. Both it and his laptop were smashed. "And I'm not happy about this, either," he said, looking at his wrecked electronics.

"Let's change your bandage before we head off," I suggested, pointing at his muddy compress. "We have more first aid materials. There's no need to let it get infected."

While Belle set about cleaning and re-bandaging Jay's injury, I retraced my steps to the helicopter where I pulled out two rifles, the mini 14 and a 30-06, both undamaged. I scrounged around and found Jay's pack and three, crunched up, freeze-dried meals. As usual, my friend refused to let me carry her red bag, much lighter now, but still containing supplies. Jay had a small pack and the '06. I brought the mini-14, crammed the packaged meals in the bag I'd taken from Arthur's cabin, and stuffed the .38 deep in my coat pocket along with extra bandage material. We walked into the trees, trying to put distance between ourselves and the downed chopper.

Jay hid his broken equipment. He limped but declined Belle's pain pills. He said, "Yes," his leg hurt, but he wanted to be clear-headed. He made a joke about a flesh wound and the need to walk it off. Belle was favoring her side again, and I wondered if the crash had re-injured her ribs. I seemed to have escaped unscathed for the most part, although, somehow, I'd ended up with a ripped sleeve and a deep stinging scratch down my left arm. Almost every muscle in my body felt kicked, sore, and ill-used.

"Anyone care to guess who shot us down?" Belle asked. She picked a handful of leaves, scrubbing them against her boots and pants, trying to remove thick grey mud.

"Guessing either the drug runners or the Chametz/Russian/terrorist group," I said.

"Or a boozed hunter going after what he thought was one of those giant Alaska mosquitoes," Jay said.

"Yeah, that's it," Belle said.

Jay grinned, "Trying to be a good soldier and lighten things a bit. Service booklet seven, page fifteen, paragraph B: 'Use creativity and appropriate jokes to lift troop's spirits.'"

I asked, "Do we know where we are?"

CHAPTER 22

"Yeah, I remember flying over this swamp," Jay said, serious again. "We're about five miles from the cabin I stayed in. There's a creek, well, more like a river, that runs by the place and empties into the bay. The owner keeps his boat anchored there all summer. Tide's low, so there won't be enough water to float it right now. Later, when it's dark, and tide's in, we'll take it and head for Kodiak. We need to get ourselves to the cabin, lie low and wait."

Great. More tramping through the brush. And this time, swamp to wade around in, too. At least, with all this wind, there aren't many mosquitoes.

I hoped Jay knew where he was leading us. I didn't know which direction to go. He limped ahead, and I admired how swiftly he covered ground, even with his injury. I watched him pick up a long smooth stick and use it for balance as he plowed his way, loaded with rifle and rucksack, through thick clumps of swamp grass and scrub.

We arrived at the cabin in early evening, wet, hungry, weary, and smelling like muskeg. The tide was flooding in; the boat would soon be afloat, only about an hour more to wait.

I think Jay noticed them first.

Two men carrying packs walked toward us, weapons raised. I heard a sound, turned, and saw a teenager with curly hair, mahogany skin, another large pack, and a mean-looking rifle coming up behind us.

"Put your hoods up, now," Jay said.

I glanced at Belle in surprise and saw her pull the hood of the man's coat over her hair. I followed suit.

"Stay behind me, look down, and don't speak unless they ask you something, directly," he said, voice urgent. "If I order you to do something, do it as fast as you can."

152

Order?

By now, the men were close enough for us to see their features. The teenager, rifle still raised, joined his comrades. The curly-haired youth and a man who looked to be in his late forties with a prominent hooked nose, black hair, deep-set brown eyes, and coffee-colored skin stared at us. Hostility pulsated from them. They exchanged a few words, not English.

Wonder what these unfriendly guys are doing up here?

The third man, probably late thirties, blond, bland, beady-eyed, small flat nose with slitted nostrils and cheeks like an Egyptian cobra, was costumed as a wealthy European tourist. I guessed he was Russian.

Although not sure why, I was glad Belle and I were swathed in the extra-large men's winter parkas we had found and taken from the missile site. The poofy coats hung to our knees. The hoods enveloped us, covering half our face.

Jay took my rifle and held both guns, barrels down, in a relaxed fashion. I still had the .38 in my coat pocket.

"Hello," he said.

No smiles, no friendly greetings. Long awkward pause, then the older man with the hooked nose and eyes like coal chips spoke.

"What doing?" he asked Jay.

"Hunting," Jay replied. "Fall, time to hunt moose."

"Your women?" The hook-nosed man asked, gesturing to Belle and me.

"My wife and my sister," Jay replied, pointing to Belle when he said wife.

The blond man said something in a foreign language to Hooknose, then stepped forward. Sunburned, face oddly smooth except for a wispy mustache, he wore leather pants, a long-barreled revolver on his belt, a fussy scarf, and camouflage trench coat. I was still guessing he was Russian, and affluent. I wondered if he had some association with the lodge. After sucking on his smoke and exhaling a gray cloud, he removed the thin cigar from his lips and held it, pinched between a thumb and finger. Everything he did seemed calculated to draw attention to himself. He again said something to the two other men. They lowered their rifles.

"Allow me," he intoned regally, thrusting out his right hand. "Sergei Ignatius Velichko."

Jay, with no trace of sarcasm, said, "John Paul Jones," and they shook hands.

Was this the Sergei that Jim Daumier double crossed?

"We're stay my uncle's lodge," Sergei said. "We're hope to do fishing while here. You tell where fishing good, no?"

Right. If these guys are on a fishing trip, I'm a Hungarian noodle maker.

Jay said, "If you hike past a creek about four miles back in the direction you came and follow it away from the beach about two miles, you'll come to a lake. That's a great place for dollies."

"What is this doolies?"

"Trout, good eating."

"My friends not like this hiking," Sergei said. "We hike two day so far. Also supposed meet man at cabin, my friend, name Daumier, Jim Daumier. He wear cowboy hat. Perhaps, you know this his cabin?"

"No, this place belongs to Jason Kent."

I kept my head down, not daring to look at Belle.

Great. Jim Daumier, Cody's friend. The drug runner.

Jay said, still in that easy conversational tone, "Sorry, man, can't help you there, never met Jim Daumier."

The three strangers began talking among themselves. The language wasn't Russian. Sergei unscrewed the lid from a large, ornate flask and gulped. He said, turning to Jay, "We decide we hunt, and we hire you be our guide."

Jay said, "I'm not authorized to guide. Also, non-Alaska residents must buy a special permit, a license to hunt. It costs quite a lot of money. Closest place you could pick that up would be Kodiak."

Sergei translated. More talking.

"Then you be our guide for finding, no hunting."

"I'm afraid you've misunderstood," Jay said, "I don't guide; I'm just out here hunting moose for our winter's meat supply."

Sergei took a slow, sucking drag on his cigar. He blew another cloud of smoke, looked off into the distance, and said, "No, no, Mr. USA, you misunderstand; you will guide us, or I kill her, and he pointed his revolver at Belle.

She and I yelped and jumped back at the same time.

Hooknose and Sergei sniggered.

The men's guns raised once more. Hooknose came back over to Jay and took our rifles.

Sergei pulled his flask out again and drank. He said, "See, if you no have rifles, no one say you are hunting guide." He translated this to the men, and they laughed as if he'd said something witty.

Jay said, "How can I help?"

Sergei translated Jay's question to his two cohorts. They brayed again, and Sergei, voice dripping with hauteur, said, "You Americans, always sure you have something to offer rest of world."

"We're happy to go on our way and get our hunting done," Jay said.

"Not so fast, big hunter, you will guide us where we need to go."

"Sure," Jay said in a conciliatory manner, "Let's leave the slow women at this cabin; that way we can go faster."

"Ah, but if we leave them here, perhaps you miss them so much you forget to guide us and keep trying to come back to them, and that is no good. They come too with us, and we will be," Sergei stopped and considered, an ugly smirk spreading across his ophidian features, "Yes, one big happy family of not related peoples."

Jay said, as if speaking to a good friend, "How would you like to travel?" He hunched over his walking stick, portraying nonchalance, keeping his expression neutral, but I saw anger flickering in his shadowed eyes. The torn leg of his jeans was stained dark from his puncture wound.

Sergei conferred with his comrades, returned to us, and pointed at the boat, as yet untouched by the rising tide. "Take us across to other side."

Jay said, "The tide's coming in, as you can see, but we need to wait until the boat is floating before we can leave."

"What are you say? You want to trick me? What excuse you make? We do not wait. We go now."

Sergei snapped the barrel of his .44 against the top of Jay's shoulder. A muffled whap! Jay's eyes almost shut, and his jaw clenched, but he made no sound.

Sergei said again, "We go now."

They herded us toward the boat. When we reached the grassy edge of the bank, Jay tried again. "You can see the boat is sitting on rocks because the tide hasn't reached it. If we wait a bit, incoming water will float it, and we can go."

"We are men," Sergei said, flexing his scrawny arms, "My ancestor, Petr the Great, would not wait; we will not wait. We will push it into the water."

Peter the Great? Terrific, this guy is an egotistical fruitcake.

Uneasy, Hooknose and the teenager shuffled on the bank. I wondered if they understood Sergei's directive. They didn't look at all eager to wade into the mud.

Sergei talked to them, with much hand waving, apparently explaining what he wanted. I could tell they were unsure by the way they looked back and forth from him to the boat.

Belle and I stood close together, trying to be invisible.

Jay squelched through the sticky gray sludge to the stern end of the fishing vessel. Fresh muck covered his short hiking boots. He didn't seem to notice.

"I'm ready," he called. "Let's go."

Making a production, Sergei removed his silk scarf and backpack, the tailored trench coat, and draped everything over a nearby bush. He had on a short-sleeved black turtleneck.

"I think that's a Ralph Lauren," Belle whispered, "Of all the things to bring to this place."

Geeze, Louise. Even at a time like this, she notices designer clothes.

Sergei walked several yards away behind tall salmonberry bushes. I watched him swig from his flask as he disappeared.

Hooknose berated his companion, the curly-haired youth with high cheekbones and angry gray eyes. The handsome young man, using his rifle, pointed back the way they had come and started striding away, indignant. As Sergei emerged from the brush, he noticed the argument and ran toward them, shouting. Their heated conversation cut off; the boy turned back. They dropped their packs and rifles on the grass, stepped off the creek bank, and began wading towards the boat through the goop. I wondered what hold Sergei had over his two companions. He splashed out behind them, still carrying his revolver, returning to the bank when they began pushing. He stood, pumping his arms and yelling as if he expected the craft to slide obediently across the slough and into the water. Jay, positioned where they couldn't see him, was doing nothing. He glanced over at us and grinned. We watched the two, red-faced and beginning to sweat, trying to shove a twenty-eight-foot fiberglass boat about fifteen feet across barnacle-covered rocks and sticky goo. It wasn't about to budge.

Sergei called, "Stop," in Russian. Hooknose and the younger guy turned and hurried back toward solid ground.

"Waits!" Sergei called, then he shrieked, "Stoi!"

"Sounds like he said, 'halt,' in Russian," Belle whispered.

The two, unhappy, stopped and looked at Sergei.

"I have better plan," he shouted. "You women's come here, now."

Should I pull the .38?

I glanced over at Jay. As if reading my thoughts, he shook his head, a definite no, and motioned for us to come out to the boat.

Not the first time I'd sloshed through Alaska silt. Commercial fishing, a regular baptism of fish slime, mud, and salt spray combined with diesel's pervasive scent, filled my summers for years.

Belle and I plodded to Sergei, keeping our heads lowered. Jay stepped around from the stern and waited, looking unconcerned.

Sergei announced, "You, all you, move boat into water. I will hold gun and engineer procedure."

I wasn't sure how much Hooknose and the teenager understood, but I could tell they did not want to wade around in the creek, nor did they like Sergei standing behind them bellowing orders while they labored like farm animals. Sergei slogged to the bank, where he waved his revolver, playing general. He fired a shot toward the sky and yelled in English, "Work, monkeys!"

Belle and I crowded close to Jay near the stern. He spoke low and fast, "Copy what I do, pretend you're trying. We'll get away as soon as we can." Then he raised his voice and shouted, "Push!"

The boat did not move. Sergei chugged from his flask again. He marched toward us, calling to his companions, "Go other side boat, I have new plan." He demonstrated, then called to Jay, "You and women's press on your side this way. It will slide boat forth and back, and boat will move."

Hooknose and the younger man were now throwing Sergei angry looks. Sticky gray mire covered their boots and pants, and they fought to stay on their feet. They trudged to the downhill side of the boat, near the bow. We could not see them, and they couldn't see us.

"That's a bad idea," Belle muttered, watching the men move to the lower side.

CHAPTER 23

Sergei hollered again.

"He's saying, 'Get busy,'" she translated, and we pretended to.

Meanwhile, the incoming tide was doing what incoming tides do, flooding higher and higher, now up to the vessel's other side.

The heavy craft shifted. Hooknose came splashing around the stern, flapping his hands, yelling, distraught.

We waded to the other side, following him. The youth had apparently put himself right against the downhill side of the boat, pushing. As the water loosened the gluey mud, the heavy prow slid over on him. Stuck on his belly, thrashing, head in and out of the water, he howled. Sergei appeared from the bank, watched the young man struggle, and stood there, nonchalant, sipping his drink, offering nothing.

I said to Jay, "The tide will be in far enough to float the boat off him in a little while, but he's going to drown before that."

"Yep," was all Jay said. He waded to the front of the bow and grabbed the anchor line, yelling at Sergei and Hooknose to help. I knew he would try to rock the front of the boat off the frightened, screaming boy, and I ran to add my weight to the line as Belle held onto the boy's shoulders, working to keep his head above the rising water. We finally got the boat off him. He stopped screaming and floated on his back, limp as a dead fish. Belle stood in the creek, holding his head above the incoming tide. Hooknose picked up the unconscious young man and waded back to the bank, depositing him on the grass. His right leg and right arm, both pinned and smashed under the boat's weight, flopped limp and bloody. He was soaked, muddy, and most likely in shock. Sergei, who had stayed on the bank, took another long pull on his flask and announced it was time to load up and go find Daumier. He yelled and gestured at Hooknose, who had picked up the disabled boy again and was trying to get to the boat, faltering with the youth's dead weight. Sergei ran over and, arguing, pulled at his sleeve, almost knocking the staggering man down.

After a prolonged and angry exchange, Sergei backed off. He stared out over the bay, petulant. Jay walked the boat, now afloat, over to the short pier and tied it off. We climbed aboard. Hooknose made two trips, carrying the young man first and placing him on a bunk next to the galley. He climbed off the craft and came back with their packs. The youth was still unconscious. He looked vulnerable, pathetic, and very young, splayed on the bed. I wondered if the argument was because Sergei was trying to talk Hooknose into abandoning the boy. His chances for survival seemed slim. I wondered if Belle, Jay, and I would survive.

Jay climbed onto the bridge and fired up the diesel. After a few uncertain coughs, the engine took off and Belle untied the line. Sergei disappeared down into the cabin. Soon after, I heard thumps and smashing noises. Next time I looked; he was slouching in the cabin doorway. He began a running commentary of lewd comments as well as guzzling from his oversized flask. Tired of his loud insults and rude antics, I considered how to get close enough to push him off the boat. My great aunt Sherry, advised kicking inappropriate males on 'a fragile area of their anatomy where they receive no benefit of solar illumination.'

Even if I could knock Sergei into the ocean, Hooknose was once again brandishing his rifle, prowling between the deck and the unconscious teenager. I wondered if Jay had any get-away plans as I climbed to the bridge. I watched him calmly guide the boat along the flooding creek toward the ocean.

Why is he so passive? Sergei will kill us. Jay isn't doing anything to help get us out of this situation.

I whispered urgently, "So, big brother John Paul Jones, remember what your 'wife' and I told you at the missile site about Daumier stealing drugs? Daumier double crossed Sergei, so they are now enemies. We need to manipulate this situation and come up with a plan for our escape, right away. Being in the middle of a conflict between Sergei and Daumier is not something I'm looking forward to, and once we transport Sergei to Daumier, there's no further reason for him to let us live."

"All kinds of ways to fight a battle," he murmured, voice grim. "Belle says you're good at creative invention. This is going to be, a fly by the seat of our pants operation, for sure. Right now, I need you and her to find something to hang on to. We're about five minutes from taking back control. You both be ready."

Sergei staggered to the stern and half fell a moment later, trying to seat himself on an upturned bucket. He kept yanking his revolver from its holster like he was doing wild west quick draw, except he dropped it twice. He was drunk. Belle was nowhere in sight. I slipped inside and found her in the galley, sitting in a booth, contents of her survival bag spread out on the small table in front of her, her right cheek a purple welt of bruise.

"What happened?"

"I was trying to find pain medication for the boy in the bunk. That older guy was sure I was up to no good, so he smacked me, took my bag, dumped everything, and pawed through it," she said, irritably. "But I'm sure I've got some pain pills in here. The young man in the bunk has bone sticking out of his arm, and his leg looks smashed."

"He hit you?"

"Yeah, after he kicked me, but the boat rocked and he fell hard; seemed to twist his ankle, so he limped off, cussing," Belle said.

"Is the young guy, conscious?"

"No. Good thing, too."

"Yes, but you're going to give him pain pills?"

"He for sure can't hurt anyone, now, and he may not even survive." Her tone was thoughtful as she murmured, "Wonder where he came from and how he got involved in all this, whatever 'this' is. He looks like an adolescent."

"Still," I hissed angrily, "These guys are vermin. That kid held a gun on us, he's our enemy, and we might need the pills. You should take a couple for your injuries, and Jay's leg has got to be hurting."

"Oh, I've got enough to share. Besides, enemy or not, at some point in our lives, each of us needs a little mercy, don't you think?"

No answer for that. I knew Belle's credo, and I also knew she would not hesitate to pick up a weapon to defend herself or others, but she believed in showing compassion, even to an adversary.

"Jay said we're going to take back control, soon. I'm supposed to tell you to be ready for anything. I know his first trick will be with the boat, because he said we need to find something to hold on to."

She put the pills into her pocket. We jammed everything back into her survival bag, and I helped her fold and stow the galley table, securing it into place.

"Tell Jay, Sergei destroyed the radio," Belle said, her voice low and worried as she leaned close. "I also saw him tap his revolver on that teenager's forehead when the other man wasn't watching."

"Yeah, I was pretty sure he was trying to get the older man I'm calling Hooknose, to abandon the young guy back there on the grass."

Belle said she would stay in the galley. I saw Hooknose sitting on a bunk near the helpless youth, and turning, I climbed the short set of stairs leading to the deck.

Sergei leaned against the cabin door, sighting along the barrel of his gun. Couldn't stand the thought of having to squeeze by him and worried he'd find my weapon, so I waited for him to move, but he continued to skulk there, his knowing eyes looking me up and down. If only I could knock that sneering smirk from his face.

I said, "Excuse me, please," and attempted to move past, trying not to touch him, but he pushed his body against mine, pulled my hood back, and ran his tongue up my neck. His breath, stinking of booze, scummy teeth, and stale cigar, choked me. My muscles tightened; stomach roiled. He jerked my pack off and threw it overboard, then grabbed my sleeve with one hand and pushed the barrel of his gun between my breasts. As I fought to get past, he shoved his hand under my coat, his hairy knuckled fingers grabbing at me, thrusting and squeezing.

"Gopnik," I sneered, putting as much venom into the word as I could. I grabbed at his face, raking his cheek with my nails.

Sergei, startled, took a step back, and I darted past him.

I only knew a few Russian words. "Gopnik," or thug, was one.

Furious, disgusted, scrubbing my neck with a sleeve, I scrambled up the ladder as he grabbed at me, again. By the time I reached the bridge, the boat was rocking at the mouth of the creek. Sergei swayed below in the cabin doorway. Too drunk to climb after me, he waved his pistol and heckled.

I can't kick him where the sun doesn't shine, but I can shoot the doughy sewer rat.

Turning so he couldn't see; I pulled the .38 from my coat pocket. Jay looked at the pistol, then his eyes moved to my outraged face. He touched my trembling hands.

"We'll fix this, one way or another, but let's go with my plan, first," he said.

I turned on him, spitting, "What plan? You seem more submissive than anything else."

"In this case it's compliance first, confusion next, then we conquer. Turn anything and everything into an opportunity to take back control," he whispered. "If that doesn't work, it'll be your turn."

The dying sun lit the lacy tops of huge ocean breakers tumbling to our left or port side. About thirty feet ahead of us, but off our starboard, I could see a cut bank with calmer water indicating the channel and the passage that would typically be followed when piloting a boat into a bay; but he said we weren't going for typical.

Jay said, "Is Belle ready?"

"We're both ready."

"Brace yourself."

He gunned the powerful diesel and headed straight into the rolling waves. I clutched the safety railing and held on. I realized what he was attempting and knew Belle would understand because of her time on commercial fishing vessels, even if she couldn't see much from the galley. The first breaker hit us hard, washing over the outside of the boat and crashing onto the deck with spectacular force. The Plexiglass cover above the cabin protected Jay and me, although the ocean found its way through cracks and sprayed us with mist. I tasted salt. Below us on deck and unprepared for the deluge, Sergei was thrown, carried up and along by the wave like a forgotten toy. I saw him flailing, grabbing for a handhold, anything to keep from being flushed over the side. No longer arrogant, face putty-colored and distorted with panic, he washed across the deck like a blob of tangled seaweed. He was halfway over the stern before he saved himself by grabbing onto a downrigger used for trolling salmon. I turned toward the bow as the boat rolled away from the wave, then bobbed back, shivering, pushed under another swell. It shook like an animal desperate to free itself, like something fighting to escape. Jay, face set, yanked the steering wheel violently to port. The boat slipped sideways into the oncoming wave.

We'll roll, the boat can't recover, he's taking us in too far; he's going to sink us, and Belle will be trapped in the cabin.

It was all I could do to hang on.

I could hear a gravelly, scraping, gurgling noise under the craft and realized a breaker had knocked us into shallows. Another wave hit, and it sucked us back into deeper water. I hung on and forgot to breathe. I could see the boat's lights, all misty underwater, and nothing but foam and splash and churning blue-green ocean. This was what any fishing vessel tried to avoid; an experienced captain knew the danger. Get your boat in shallow water with giant breakers pushed by high winds, and she'll go over; you'll swamp her for sure.

The engine moaned like a wounded beast, then shifted to a low rumbling; followed by a gritty, grinding noise. The boat reversed. I looked back, no salvation for Sergei, the outrigger ripped away.

Jay fought to back us off the killer breakers and into the channel. The boat felt ungainly, as sluggish as a loaded scow. Our engine coughed again, then died. Water splashed in the hold.

I wiped salty water from my face with my sleeve as I rushed inside, looking for Belle. She used a long bungee cord and had strapped herself to the sturdy wooden seatback. She now sat, clutching a seat cushion.

"You, alright?" I mouthed.

She motioned toward the fo'c's'le. The teenager had fallen out of the bunk and rolled underneath, still unconscious.

"Sergei got washed overboard," I whispered. "Hurry and find something you can use for a weapon. We need to take control of Hooknose. Where is he?"

Belle pointed to the john as wild bellowing, crashing and clatter erupted. I pulled the .38, raced up on deck and crouched beside the open cabin door, waiting. It didn't take long. Hooknose burst from the head, breaking the top of the door off its hinge, and lurched out the galley entrance. He waved his rifle, yelling. Blood from a deep, ugly gash on his forehead ran into his eyes and colored his face and neck. I couldn't tell whether he was angry, scared or both, but being knocked around in that tiny room while pounded by breakers couldn't have done anything for his sense of wellbeing. I'd have exited, hollering, too. He saw me and turned, snarling, just as Jay leaned from halfway down the bridge ladder and conked him with a short solid club used to dispatch big halibut. Hooknose quieted a lot quicker than a wacked fish. He lay on his back, unconscious.

My son, Matt, on U-Tube listening to someone half singing, half yelling, nothing but clamor and dissonance: 'Out light a light, out like a light.' Long minutes of that same phrase repeating, until I finally hollered, "Turn it off!" His juvenile annoyance, "M-om, I'm listening to mu-sic." I was remembering and laughing as I grabbed Hooknose's gun. Belle emerged from the galley with her weapon, a cast-iron, frying pan.

"Rats," she said, "I'm too late. I wanted to help fry this big fish."

"He's out like a light," I said.

The ominous gurgling of the too-full bilge worried me. Nothing musical there, either. Jay, already back at the controls, started the engine and flipped switches, sounding stymied.

He yelled, "How do I get the bloody bilge pump started on this thing?"

CHAPTER 24

The boat wallowed. We were carrying way too much water, and I knew Jay was trying to get the pumps running to get it sucked out of the hold so we could stay afloat. Remembering my grandfather and his boat, 'My Dizzy Tin Lizzy,' a vessel very similar to this old craft, never mind the name, gave me an idea. I recalled Gramps working on a broken pump in the bilge one sunny afternoon when I was about six. I picked up a wrench and climbed down to work with him. He hugged me and asked me to stay up on the bridge with Grammie and help her by flipping 'an important lever,' a bilge pump lever, he called it.

Back to the here and now. Stepping over an unconscious Hooknose, I climbed up on the bridge again, reached past where Jay sat in the captain's chair exploring the instrument panel, found I had to practically stretch out across his lap, felt around under the edge of polished wood, discovered what I was looking for and flipped the unobtrusive little switch. The pumps hummed. A moment later, water shot from the hull.

"Nice," he said as I stood back up. I figured it was my turn, so I gave him a big, triumphant wink.

We tied Hooknose. There was plenty of rope on board, and Belle and I used yards and yards of it, competing, with knots we'd learned during our commercial fishing days, wrapping him around and around with half hitches, an anchor bend, bowlines, and a few sheep shanks. We finished by fastening him to a cleat on the deck, back near the stern. He came to, groaning. We gave him a deflated orange buoy as a pillow, tucked him in with two smelly old gunnysacks for blankets, and left him to think about his life choices. Jay helped us lift the unconscious young man back into the bunk. We taped his arm and tied him there to keep him from falling out again. Sergei never reappeared. Belle was sure he decided to swim back to Russia.

The wind quieted. We kept the boat idling in the slow-moving current and let the pumps do their job.

It was dark when the last of the seawater spewed from the bilge. The boat was much lighter, buoyed up, ready to go, and bouncing on the waves.

Jay said he wanted to discuss a plan for getting to Kodiak Island.

"It's obvious," he began, throwing us a sideways grin, "There are people who want to keep us from getting out of here."

"You think?" This from Belle. "Problem is, we don't know who our enemies are or what their agenda is."

"We don't have the option of using the radio, so I guess we use this boat and make a run for it?" I asked, looking from Jay to her.

Jay said, "I think we should head across the fiord, now. We'll travel with no light, so it'll be slow. Once outside the bay, check out the wind and wave action before heading across Shelikof Strait. Don't know how you two feel about, but I don't want to try crossing Shelikof in seas higher than about twelve feet in this boat.

Belle asked, "How do you know anything about the Shelikof?"

"Location research before I'm sent on assignment is part of every job. That's how I knew the names of all the little towns flying over here. Shelikof Strait has quite the reputation."

"We got caught in a storm crossing it," I volunteered. "Something I'll never forget and never want to repeat. We were in a fifty-eight-footer, much longer and wider than this boat, but the gigantic waves tossed us like a kid throwing a toy around a bathtub. The guy I was married to, broke his arm on that ride. One deckhand sprained an ankle; another ended up in the hospital with a concussion."

"What I've read is about three close calls per season and a couple boats missing in the last five years," Jay said.

Belle said nothing. With a crew of four, her cousin and uncle had gone down with their boat in the Strait one stormy September six years ago.

Both she and I grew up in large, extended, fishing families. We'd worked on boats as deckhands, cooks, and everything in between. We knew commercial fishing is one of the most dangerous occupations in the world. I lost my first boyfriend, Jimmy, one winter when the boat he was on became covered in ice, grew top-heavy, and flipped over near Sand Point. He was sixteen. Every year there were men and women full of anticipation, hope for a strong season ahead of them, running the waves on the bright shining water. Some didn't make it back home. Capricious, the sea might stir turbulence so quick it caught the fishermen before they knew where the wind had blown from. Sometimes the waves swallowed boats and people, everything gone and the ocean, dark with secrets, never told.

Emptied of so much weight, our little boat frolicked across the bay. A sliver of moon rose and peeped from wooly clouds. Angry noises now and then from Hooknose. But besides that, the evening was almost peaceful.

Belle left to check on the young man in the bunk, leaving Jay and me alone on the bridge.

I started to follow her, feeling self-conscious about being alone with him, but told myself to get a grip and grow up.

So, I stayed and watched the moon flirting with the waves, trying not to think how small the space was between us. After Belle left, it seemed Jay's presence filled the bridge. The water lay down, peaceful. I wished the quiet could go on and on.

Hooknose let out a loud, gargling snore. Startled, I jumped. Jay looked over at me, and we began laughing like kids out of school. He was steering with his right arm, but when he reached out with his left and pulled me to him, holding me warm and close to his heart, I didn't pull away; instead, slowly, I relaxed. When I rested my head on his shoulder for just a moment, it seemed as if the moon tipped sideways, too, smiling at us.

So close to the mouth of the fiord. We'd almost made it. Even running with no lights and slow traveling, we were within fifty feet of the opposite shore. Jay planned to follow the faint line of beach, staying far enough off rocks to avoid chewing the prop or going aground as we motored toward Shelikof Strait. I climbed down in the galley to find something we could eat. Belle talked to the young man tied in the bunk. He didn't seem to understand any English and only a few words of Russian. There wasn't much she could do besides giving him a drink and offering him food and pain capsules. He took water and a couple pills and appeared to be sleeping.

I passed around chicken noodle soup, and we crunched pilot bread and drank instant coffee. Jay drove from inside the cabin. We were doing our best to glide through the waves as unobtrusively as possible. Our get-away plan worked for a while, almost sufficient to slip out of the bay and into the open sea. It wasn't enough.

The boat roared toward us, its spotlight perforating the darkness, so fast there was no way we could outrun it.

Jay said, "Listen, ladies; I'm sure there are more of them than there are of us. If we try to outshoot them, we'll be killed. Follow my lead. Think on your feet and watch for any opportunity to escape. Don't help me if I get attacked. Act compliant but look for ways to become valuable to them; keep planning to live."

We watched him pull a pair of spectacles with extra-thick black frames from his pack and put them on. He loosened his belt, pulling his shirt out so it bagged, and then hiked his jeans high on his belly much as an old man would wear. He looked around, grabbed a baseball cap from a nail on the galley wall, and jammed it down far enough on his head, so the edges made his ears stick out. The effect was startling. He held his eyes in a squint, pursed his lips, pushed his belly out, and let his shoulders stoop. He looked much older, a passive, nearsighted nerd.

The bigger craft was upon us with crushing force; the pilot cracking our hull with his steel bow. I saw the name as it crashed into us, *ViKing Revenge*. The men swarmed us like swamp flies, like rabid wolverines, like the pirates they were.

Belle, Jay, and I became prisoners. They hauled us aboard their boat and pushed us down into a smoky galley that reeked of rancid grease and cigarettes. Jay shambled, limped, squinted, and didn't put up any kind of fight. Three men sat silently around a bottle-crowded table in the squalid compartment. More Russian's, I presumed. One was gray-haired, early fifties, built like a fireplug with a green eye patch and vivid scar running diagonally across his left cheek. Another, much older, sallow, puffy eyed with a cadaverous physique and pencil line of mustache, coughed almost continuously. Crouched next to them sat a miserable-looking, bearded man wearing tinted glasses.

Why doesn't anyone know these guys are sneaking into our country?

I still had the .38 hidden in my coat pocket. No one touched Belle or me at first, instead concentrating their energies on Jay. Four men thundered into the galley, looking eager to take him down, but stepped back, surprised when they saw how decrepit he looked. While everyone watched, two of them shoved and slapped him around, found his pistol in his coat pocket, took it, punched him, and bloodied his nose. Jay kept up his bewildered, clumsy, duffer act; using the nose injury to his advantage, coughing, choking, and spitting blood, after which he slumped to the floor, head bowed.

What if they find my gun?

They pawed through Belle's pockets and pulled a pair of wool socks from one and a tube of ointment, bandages, and pain pills from another. Someone was going through her red bag, dumping her stuff on the galley floor. I could tell that annoyed her. She wasn't carrying any weapons, but the revolver in my pocket seemed to expand in size, and I was sure it would soon drop onto the floor, announcing itself. One man grabbed my arm and, twisting my wrist, began searching me. He removed two cans of tuna, then reached into the pocket that hid the .38 and pulled out the box of gauze I had shoved on top of it after the helicopter crash. Before he could go further, I recalled Jay's advice and dropped to the floor, rolling on top of the little sidearm.

My heart pounded. I clenched my fingers to stop my hands from shaking. The tears running down my face were one hundred percent real. I felt sure we wouldn't be getting out of this alive. Our meet and greet ended with someone tying Belle and me together. Restraining us had to be for intimidation as there was no place to run. Once again, our ultra-thick coats helped keep us from injury, although I knew Belle's ribs had to be hurting. She remained silent, but her eyes were dull with pain. We hunkered on the galley deck near the bunks where they dragged us. They hauled Jay off to another part of the boat, loaded Hooknose and the injured youth aboard, and headed up the fiord toward the lodge. Someone dragged Hooknose into the galley, and we heard him jabbering as they untied his restraints. Although we couldn't understand what they were saying, it was evident they were making fun of him. They carried the unconscious teenager into our room and dumped him on a bunk.

The men at the table smoked and passed a bottle. They began talking as soon as they hustled us from the room. The small compartment, or fo'c's'le, where we huddled was located right next to the galley. I'm sure they didn't realize we could hear them. Their voices carried through the ventilation ductwork installed directly above the floorboards.

They knew we were Americans. They began questioning Hooknose. The hairy sunglasses guy sitting at the table between the two Russians translated his words into English. We guessed the language was Arabic.

Hooknose said he and his two companions were hunting moose with Jay as their guide. He told a whopper of a tale saying a gigantic wave hit the boat, sent Sergei overboard, and caused his nephew to get injured when he fell off the bridge.

Hooknose said there was a disagreement, and Belle and I tied him up at gunpoint because Jay thought he was making a pass at Belle. The story seemed to confuse the men at the table and led to a long, intense discussion, most of which we couldn't understand. The two Russians seemed unsure whether Jay, Belle, and I were running a guiding business, somehow connected in an operational capacity with our government, or both. They questioned Hooknose in Russian, their voices becoming harsher and more and more suspicious. They used the word helicopter more than once, but Hooknose insisted he knew nothing about it. After Hairy Sunglass Guy berated him, they took him off somewhere, still their prisoner. Conversation continued around the table. Belle and I perked up when one of the Russian men said the word 'missile.' It surprised us that they spoke so often in English. They seemed most interested in Jay. We heard "Jay" and "scientist" several times. We surmised we were being taken to the lodge. Why, we could only guess.

Noise entered the galley, interrupting their conversation. A voice too low to understand, then a scream, choked off. The new arrival spoke in a frightened rush, his words firing like gunshots from an ancient mitrailleuse. He blustered, speaking English, talking on and on, as if the barrage would convince his listeners.

"I shot 'em down," he bragged. "Right out of my skiff. Told you I'd get 'em. Shot their helicopter down. I'm telling you, these guys you just picked up are CIA operatives and they were in that helicopter. Two women, one man; CIA operatives," he said again, louder.

More noises from the galley and the man talking let out a shrill cry, then swore, his tone strangled, "Get your hands off me. He cut me. Tell him get that knife away from me; I delivered like I said I would. They control the missile. I delivered them to you, like I said."

His voice rose higher, faster. He cursed, fear rushing out of him in gasps. "I said you could count on me. That 'Nif' Cody talked to them earlier, a few days ago, when they ambushed him in that old man's cabin. Cody says they know where the stuff is; they're planning to sell it. We can make them tell us where they hid it, get it back. That's a lot of money hanging out there, but we can get it back. Whatever it takes, I can handle them," he stammered. "I'll make them tell us where the goods are right now, long as we don't kill them, we're ok, then we deliver them to Rafenski, let him deal with making them bring the missile online."

Another man spoke. I thought it sounded like one of the Russian men sitting at the table. The accent was there. "You lie, Daumier. You lie always."

CHAPTER 25

Raw terror in the voice, "But I shot their chopper down, I found the operatives. They know where our stuff is, and I delivered them to you. I said I would, and I did. I kept my word. That was a long shot, too."

"Daumier, it's you of which I grow tired. Too much cheating, ingratitude, stealing from you. Your lies pile up—too many. You sink a boat near Sitka with four million American dollar worth of top-quality product on board, a total loss of boat and my inventory. I was going to overlook, but now this. Twelve million dollars of my product you say is lost somewhere in the wild forest. Then I find out you stole all of it. This Vlodir Rafenski you speak of. We are business partners. He wants this trouble now ended."

The voice, Daumier's, pleading, groveling, shrieking, "But sir, wait, stop sir, please, listen, please... please," ending in a wet, gurgling sigh. A thud, a scrabbling, scratching noise, then silence.

Belle and I looked at each other. She shuddered, and I closed my eyes, trying to erase those awful sounds. I was sure he was going to be fish food. Moments later, a splash confirmed it.

Does this mean Belle's brother is back in our lives, again? Is he on this boat?

A minute later, answers. The door burst open, and they shoved a man with his ankles bound, into our room, where he flailed about, toppling onto the floor. Cocaine Cody ...*crap.*

He rolled over, sat up, and stared at his sister. He stank of feces and puke. His right hand, wrapped with a dirty rag, oozed blood. He was battered and bruised and sober. He grabbed Belle's arm, sobbing, and hung on, a penitent pleading for preservation.

"They killed Jim." Cody trembled, his voice choked into a gravelly monotone, his face was the greenish white of a dead halibut. "They cut his throat and threw him overboard, and I'm next." He began repeating part of the story he'd told us at Arthur's cabin. "We were taking drugs to Seattle, and we got drunk and hit some rocks and there was a fire and we sunk their boat down near Sitka; and me and Jim stole the drugs and hid them in a life raft. He said I have to help him because I owed him money. Jim made a deal with that Russian guy Sergei, whose uncle owns the lodge, or used to own it, but Jim, he double-crossed Sergei and keeps the drugs. We hid most of them in the woods late last winter, then put them in the generator building the night they blew everything up. Two months ago, Daumier decided to run off to Albania with the red hair girl at the lodge, and he said he gonna need a lot of money, so he waited and steal the last drug shipment that came through. We hide that in the old troublemaker's cabin, and we can't get away and sell the stuff like we planned because we couldn't find the old man or our stash and that mob boss, Androv, that mean Russian guy with the eye patch who took the lodge over from Sergei's uncle in the poker game, just now killed Jim. Jim tried to make a trade with them, but it didn't work, and they cut his throat." Cody wound down like a cheap alarm clock. He curled on the floor, sobbing.

And in the middle of all this drama, stress and our impending doom, all I could think right then was:

Albania?

"Jim Daumier said you told him that Loren and I ambushed you at the cabin; we know where the drugs are, and we're trying to sell them out from under you. It's pretty clear when Jim showed up at the old man's cabin that morning, and you hadn't found the drugs, you were afraid he was going to kill you, so you made up a story. You, my dear brother, were willing to betray Loren and me to save your own hide." Belle's steely voice cut through the silence.

Cody, you are such a greasy little rat.

173

"Jim and those two guys he hired were gonna' kill me, Sis. They said they were going to chop me up in pieces, and they started cutting on my fingers, see?"

Cody sat up, pulling the dirty cloth away and waved his mutilated hand in front of her face. Dried blood crusted his swollen palm. His pinky finger was missing, and his ring finger to the first knuckle was sliced away.

I gagged.

"Didn't tell him you're my sister, though," Cody whimpered. "Only said I knew the old man had told you where the drugs were, and you two ran off."

Belle looked at him. Her face showed no anger, just pity.

"I had to say something, Sis. Jim was going to keep cutting on me. I had to buy time."

"You threw us under the bus to buy time; did you do yourself any good with it?"

"They're going to kill me, Sis," his voice barely a murmur. "They're like for sure going to kill me. You know I'm scared to die, Sis. I don't think I'm ready."

"I don't think you are, either," was all Belle said.

Cody sank back onto the floor.

She whispered into my ear, "You know I've got to try to save him."

Should I pity him? I don't.

I shifted, trying to find something to look at besides his doomed, pound pet expression. We're staring death in the face ourselves, and she's still trying to rescue that worthless turd.

"How?" My response was an indignant bark.

"I'm going to tell the guys in the other room we know where their drugs are and that we'll take them to the locations in trade for Cody's life. They might let Cody go if we deliver. I'm gambling they won't kill us, because someone back at the lodge thinks we might be CIA and wants us brought there. I'm going to tell the truth."

"The whole truth?"

She shook her head, "I'm not stupid. Just the part about the drugs."

Before we could continue planning, the door opened again. Two men entered, each grabbed one of Cody's flailing arms and began pulling him from the small room as he twisted and thrashed. He looked back at his sister in the dim light, eyes haunted. His features convulsed in terror, and he moaned feebly, "O, God, help me, God save me." As he sagged between them, the front of his jeans darkened.

"He's my brother, Lor; they're going to kill him. I've got to try help him," she said, one second before she yelled, "Wait, wait!" in Russian at the top of her voice.

Loud voices from the next room and a man stood in the doorway.

"I know where the drugs are," Belle said in English, her voice ringing. "I must talk to someone about the drugs."

The cords binding our hands and feet cut; they brought us, blinking, out into the light.

The three men still sat. I noticed a slick of blood smeared across the floorboards. Cody was on his hands and knees in a corner, sniffling.

I recognized the man who had spoken to Daumier when I heard him address Belle. It must be Androv. He was sitting, relaxed, shelling and eating peanuts.

"Tell me." His face was a map of hard lines, his mouth pinched and cruel. He wore a green patch tight over one eye. The other glittered, cold as glacier ice.

Belle started, "I work as a realtor, out of Homer. This is my friend, Loren, an artist. We were at the lodge to show it to prospective buyers. People began fighting. The boat we hid in, blew up and we were injured." Here she pointed to her scabbed-over scalp and missing hair. "We got to the lodge's generator building and found drugs. Next day we hiked to a cabin and found a wounded old man who told us Jim Daumier shot him. He said Daumier took over his cabin and hid drugs there. The old man took the drugs to another location to hide them from Daumier. We stayed with him, and that night he died. Before that old man passed, he told us where he hid those drugs. I will show you where the drugs are, if you let Cody live. Cody was a pawn of Jim Daumier; yeah, he's pretty stupid. He got himself in trouble and wasn't smart enough to figure Daumier out, but he was not in charge of what happened to the drugs; he was just a dumb flunky being used because he's addicted."

The icy blue eye stared. Shivering, my hands stiff with cold, I felt I was standing in an arctic blast and wondered if it was coming straight from the man's soul. I willed myself to be still, to appear in control of my body. Cold sweat trickled under my shirt: no pity, no understanding, no warmth from this man. I wanted to put my hand in my coat pocket and pull out the revolver but knew I wouldn't get one shot off before we were both blown away like the peanut hulls on the galley table.

The man spoke, "Yes, we found some inventory in machine building, already. Now, warning. You must not lie to me. I do not care, man or woman, whoever, I kill anyone who lie to me."

My friend's face was pale, her eyes dark in her waxen face. Her lips trembled. "I am not lying. I keep my word. Do you keep your word? True strength is not in fists or guns or bombs or threats. True strength is in our character, how we act when we have power, how we act when we have none. Our character shows who we are."

"Who this crying baby, to you, woman?" he asked, pointing at Cody. "Why to save his life, you risk yours?"

That's something that puzzles me, too.

Belle stood straight. The dignity enveloping her seemed to quiet the room. I thought again of the ancient story of Queen Esther standing in front of unpredictable king, what's his face, pleading for the safety and lives of her people, her family, knowing it might mean her own death. Belle's bravery made my heart swell.

Ok, Androv, and whoever else you bullies are, I'm not backing down, either.

I slid closer and linked my arm through hers. I was proud to be her friend.

Cody is not worth all this, Belle, but I'll stick with you, anyway.

She said, "This silly boy is my brother. Our mother died when he was young, and he didn't grow up right. My father has passed also. Cody is foolish and broken, but he is my family."

The man came to his feet. He stepped over to Belle and stood staring down, his body almost touching hers, a tower of frozen steel. His presence frosted the air with suspicion and animosity. She looked up at him, eyes wide with trepidation, but she did not back up or blink. She waited. My legs shook so hard I banged against the galley wall. I found I was chewing the inside of my cheek. The man looked from Belle to me and back. He leaned close, his lips brushing her ear, and said, "You speak like my grandmother.

176

I loved her, my babushka, so I will believe you in her memory. I keep my word, and this weak, pissing boy-man crying in corner will live if you show drug's location. We will keep this person, this boy Cody," his voice was loud and scornful as he said Cody's name, "Your little baby brother, tied in room until you show us drugs."

"Yes," was all she said.

Do they believe her?

They took us up to the bridge. We told the Russian piloting the boat the cabin was about five miles south of the channel marker. He said he knew where that was, slowed the blocky craft, turned it around, and we headed back the way we had come.

What if someone found the drugs, and they were no longer there? I wouldn't let myself think about that as they escorted us back to the smoke-filled room. The boat sped toward the burned cabin. I wanted to tell Jay, but knew, even though they untied us, we were still prisoners and wouldn't be allowed to leave the galley. We passed the marker, the boat's lights reflecting its numbers, and continued south.

Although the tide was in, the water was too shallow for the deep hulled vessel to go to the beach without running aground. The crew anchored her and brought a small, but sturdy inflatable off the deck. Once in the water, Belle, the two Russians from the galley, and I climbed down into it. The rubber raft had a motor attached to its stern, but neither Androv nor the other man could get it started. The men in the boat above us were quiet. No one made a sound.

Why isn't someone on the boat coming down to get the engine going? I answered my thought: *They're afraid of what Androv might do to them if they try and fail.*

Realizing those half-savage men above us in the boat were scared, somehow made me feel braver, so I said, my voice small and scratchy, "I think I can start it."

There was a long silence. I felt eyes boring through me in the darkness, but I persisted, "I used to run one of these for my husband."

Someone on the big boat snickered, but a sharp command silenced him.

Androv motioned to me, and we maneuvered around each other on the unsteady watercraft. I positioned myself in front of the cranky machine.

"I need to see," I said, louder, more confidently, and someone shone a light onto the motor.

Got to remember these fussy little engines have that touchy thing that happens with the choke and the carburetor and the problem of it becoming flooded. Must not get it flooded.

Brad, face red, yelling, "You've flooded it again. How many times do I have to show you how to run this (expletives deleted) thing? It'll be at least two hours before we can get it to start, and you know the fish won't wait."

I worked at running that motor like my life depended on it back then, trying to avoid Brad's anger, trying to merit his admiration. Now, ironically, my life and Belle's might depend on my efforts from so long ago.

Muscle memory, or something in my brain took over, and I coaxed life out of the persnickety outboard. The low chug, chug, sound as it ran made beautiful music.

Belle patted my arm. "Good job. I prayed you'd remember how," she breathed. "I never ran one of those, but the guys on our boat used to say they're not at all fun to deal with."

They handed us lights, someone turned us loose, and I steered toward the beach. We clambered out of the raft. Belle and I pulled it up on shore and tied it to a rock so it wouldn't drift off. As the second raft landed, she and I made our way up over the sand with Androv and the other Russians following. She told them we were looking for the old man's running line, and about the time the four guys secured their inflatable, we found the rope, still tied to the snag. The trail was right beside it. We started up, the men crowding us, almost stepping on our heels. The four guys from the second raft wore enormous packs. We could hear them stumbling behind Androv and the older Russian. We smelled sour rot, well before we reached the cabin, or what was left of it: nothing but crumbled pieces of charred log. The fire had burned hot. I was glad for the dark. I didn't want to see what had become of the old man's body. There was still a lump of partially eaten and rotting bear, the stench assaulting us as we darted around it. We surprised a small animal with glowing eyes, a scavenging mink, I guessed. Belle and I slowed and crept past the ruined building. The trail ended, but we continued, pushing uphill into thick, tangled brush.

The two older men from the galley seemed uneasy. They stopped and began talking in Russian, their voices rising in open displeasure. Belle walked over to them.

"Please," she said, using the Russian word, "I know the way." She was using her 'soothe the savage' voice again. The disgruntled men frowned down at her.

They do not trust us.

"Why no trail?" Androv asked. He looked angry.

"That old man liked his secrets," she replied, "But I know where your inventory is. Follow me, please. We'll be there, soon."

Let the drugs still be there. Dear God, please help us. Am I praying again? Does God answer prayers about drugs?

CHAPTER 26

The men thrashed through the undergrowth behind Belle and me. The older Russian had a hard time keeping up. His breath grew labored, ragged, with long pauses for coughing. I worried he'd keel over, and they'd blame us. He insisted on stopping halfway up the hill for a smoke. I wondered if he'd ever connected his breathing difficulties to his cigarette consumption.

We climbed higher, up over the natural rock barrier, and pushed through the intertwined hemlocks around Arthur's steam bath. Much muttering and complaints as the men fought their way through the tangled branches. The door was ajar, and Belle slipped inside, returning a moment later carrying three packages which she handed to Androv. His companion protested, thinking, I suppose, this was all she had to offer, but we led them around the side of the hut and under the tree to where we'd last seen the stash. It was still there, the tarp-covered box piled and overflowing with stacks of plastic-wrapped bundles. The mood among the men changed in an instant. Laughter, back slaps, high fives. The lead Russian, Androv, the mob boss, ole glacier eye himself, stood apart, silent. The older man, I guessed second in command, ordered the underlings to load up their packs. We all began hiking toward the beach. We motored back to the bigger boat with Androv. They brought us into the galley. He snapped orders at a flunky, and the grimy guy brought us mugs of steaming tea.

It took over three hours to get all the drugs transported to the boat, stow the inflatables, and head toward the lodge once again. The mood was celebratory. Alcohol flowed.

They kept us in the overheated galley, sandwiched between the Russians and their interpreter who, looking more and more seasick, finally fled.

It was late by this time; the galley clock said 2:30 am. Androv and the other man, called Max, drank vodka and bit off chunks of sausage dripping with fat. They became more loquacious as the night wore on, talking, laughing, offering us greasy hunks of meat. They handed us a shot glass brimming with vodka. I left my drink on the table until Belle poked me, whispering, "One sip, just take one sip, look grateful and say spasibo."

I watched in surprise; Belle hated booze.

She clinked her glass with mine, said something in Russian, raised her drink ceremoniously, turned to me, said, "Adapt," like it was a toast, laughed, and swallowed a gulp.

Ok, I get the message.

I followed suit, hating the burning fire shooting down the back of my throat. My eyes watered, but I affixed a smile on my face and made sure I said, "Thank you." My mom started drinking that stuff after my dad died, and what followed hadn't been pretty.

After Belle made her toast, she took the rest of her drink, lifted her pants leg, pulled away torn bandage, and slowly poured the shot glass contents over the ripped flesh. Max leaned toward her, staring at the jagged cut.

"What happen?" he slurred.

"Explosion at the lodge," was all she said. She picked up the ointment and gauze package the men had taken from us earlier and pulled the edges of her wound together, replacing dirty bandages with clean and tying everything around her calf. The men's gaze never left her, watching every move as if fascinated.

Is that male admiration I see in their eyes, or is it the vodka?

We arrived at the dock about twenty minutes later. The structure had been more than half destroyed.

Belle and I gathered her scattered belongings, repacking her survival bag, but when she attempted to bring it with her, Androv said one word, "No."

They tied the boat to one of the undamaged pilings and led by Androv; Jay, Belle, and I, with three mean-looking guys behind us, climbed up the one unbroken ladder and onto the remains of what had once been an impressive pier. We threaded our way across broken planks and garbage; and went up stairs now quivering under our tread. Max had stayed aboard, ostensibly to keep the men curtailed, but in truth because he was too drunk to climb out of his chair, let alone negotiate a ladder. The deck outside the lodge was strewn with shrapnel, wood, twisted metal, broken parts and pieces of engines and machinery, and who knew what else.

They took us through the hand-carved doors, now scarred and marked from the fury of the blast. No lights, but we could see shattered windows. Dangerous, trying to walk inside on splintered glass. Saying nothing, Androv left us and vanished up the wide plank stairs. We entered the room where we first met Howie. I saw his office chair upended and felt sad all over again. After being led through a narrow door in one corner and down a steep stairway into a dank room smelling of mildew, we were left in the dark. The room was rectangular, a damp cold cellar with a dirt floor. The men headed up the stairs, closing the door behind them. It was tar black.

"Everybody all right?" Jay asked.

Belle began filling Jay in, this time including details about her brother and how we'd shown Androv the drug stash location to save Cody's life. Jay said very little while she talked. He interrupted her when she first began and told us the room could be bugged, so we should speak as quietly as possible. As we moved into a tight circle, him on one side and Bell on my other, Jay gently pulled my fingers into his.

Can't remember the last time I held hands. Does this mean he's, my boyfriend? Are they still called "boyfriends," at our age? I stood there, shivering. Only part of me warm was the hand entwined with his.

How did I go from living my life and painting for an art show, to being held prisoner in a dingy basement, miles from anyone, holding the hand of a government agent? And standing here, feeling my fingers snug in his, I'm almost happy right now... or... I might be losing my mind.

Belle's recitation ended, and Jay said, "We need to do everything we can to get ourselves out of here as quickly as possible."

The tender, reflective moment had ended. It was time for action again, so I pulled my hand away and asked, "How are we going to do that?"

"First, we find the perimeters of this room," Jay said. "Explore the walls. Feel your way around whatever you come to. Pay attention to anything you find on the floor and whether you feel a draft."

Belle said, "When Howie showed me the water system, he took me down a set of stairs. The room we went into had concrete walls, washers and dryers, huge water tanks, and odds and ends of machinery on a concrete floor. I wonder if this room connects to that one?"

We began exploring. I moved cautiously, not wanting to crack my toes on something. When I reached a barrier, I slid my feet beside it, feeling my way along the edge, looking for anything that merited attention. Stacks of concrete blocks formed walls higher than I could reach. The floor appeared to be nothing but packed dirt.

Can we dig our way out of here?

Coming down the stairs, I had seen concrete pads and vertical steel pilings that stuck up into the bottom of the floor above us, forming part of the structural skeleton for the lodge. I continued feeling my way but found nothing. Jay called us back together, and we described everything we'd touched. We knew there was nothing further we could do for the time being, so we sat together against the concrete and slept. Sometime later, the door opened, and the same three guys shuffled down. One of them carried a tray and another a bucket. All looked hungover—definitely the worse for wear. The tray held a loaf of bread, two cans of tuna, probably the cans they'd grabbed from my pocket on the boat, and a block of yellow cheese. The guy carrying the tray set it down and opened the tuna. They brought three plastic bottles of water. The men said nothing but sat and waited while we ate. Belle, Jay, and I used the light from the flashlight they set on the floor to surreptitiously examine the room without looking as if we were doing anything but moving around a bit, stretching, and eating. Our guards sat on the steps; one had his head in his hands, one fiddled with the can opener, and one removed his boot and socks, examining a toe. They'd left us alone for several hours, and we thought it was because the men guarding us had been sleeping their celebration off. I also understood what the bucket was for, and while that did not fill my heart with joy, at least we wouldn't have to take care of our business on the floor.

Sudden loud banging above. Our guards left the light, tray, and bucket, raced up the stairs, slammed the door, and charged across the floor overhead. Jay grabbed the flashlight and hurried around the cellar, shining it carefully over every surface. There wasn't a lot to see. Pretty much what we'd discovered already. Floor was dirt, walls about nine or ten feet high, concrete. Massive beams crossed the space forming the foundation for the main floor one level up. We followed Jay around the large room, hoping we could find a way out. We all saw it at the same time—a rectangular hole about seven feet high on the wall in front of us.

A vent?

We stood below it, our faces turned toward the opening, trying to feel a breeze. I felt nothing.

"That could be it," Jay said, "Our way out of here. Only problem is, we'll have to wait until tonight when it's dark." He hid the flashlight under the bottom step where, if remembered, it would seem forgotten in the confusion of the men racing upward.

"No way I'll fit through that," Belle whispered to me.

We carried the bucket to a corner and took turns, grateful for the privacy of darkness.

The door opened, a gruff voice called, "All come up."

After climbing the stairs, we passed through the narrow opening and stood, not knowing what to expect.

A man entered the room wearing rumpled wool trousers and a short military-type jacket. He was stout, late middle age with no facial hair and thick, liver-colored lips. A pair of pistols on a wide leather belt girdled his middle. His manner was brisk, authoritative. Our nervous guards shuffled back against a wall and lined up at attention. I remembered him, one of the men who had flown to the lodge in the first helicopter the night of the explosion. Closer, I noticed what Belle had described at the missile site, an ugly, protruding growth near the top of his bulbous forehead, rumored to be the "devil horn" that he wouldn't have removed because it frightened subordinates. Belle had told me he was Vlodir Rafenski, third in command over the entire Russian military. He paused, appraising us. I didn't think we appeared prepossessing. The last few days left us bedraggled, dirty, cut, and scraped. Torn clothing and muddy boots, hair straggling. I didn't know how Jay and Belle were holding up, but as my Irish grammie used to say, I felt like I'd been drug through a knothole backwards. The thick-bodied man spoke American English. There was no need for an interpreter, and I suspected he had several other languages at his command.

"You are Jay Carrel," he said, with no preamble. "You work undercover in various capacities for US government. We are not yet sure of your names," he continued, pointing at Belle and me. "But we will be. Soon enough. Regardless, we know you shut our missile down, and we want it back online, reinstated, I think is how you might say it. We want it operational."

"Your missile?" This from Jay.

"Yes, your very own esteemed Speaker of House traded it to us." His eyes held all the warmth of nail heads on an outhouse in January.

"It wasn't hers to trade," Belle burst out.

"I did not address you," the Russian blared, "Quiet!"

Jay's eyes flashed a warning at Belle and me.

"It seems you now can call her a traitor," Vlodir mocked, changing the "d" in trader to the "t" sound.

"We've been calling her a traitor for some time," Jay replied.

"The missile is ours until we finish with it. Then you may have it back."

He stepped closer, his laughter matching the sounds of broken glass crunching under his boots as he walked.

"We have computers, satellites for you to interface, and all the necessary equipment. Our computer programmers are missing. One killed in the explosion, and the one Chametz brought to us, that little man with red bag supposed to be hacking genius, has disappeared with two of his guards. We are still looking, and we will find them."

He fondled a pistol. "The explosion hampered us. The never-ending storms have slowed us. We've already changed our deadline twice. I see now why we sold Alaska to you. The unpredictable weather. Our window is closing. We must have the missile operational within the next forty-eight hours."

He doesn't know we tore pieces and parts off the thing. He thinks we can sit in front of a computer and do tricks and launch it for him. What's he going to do when he finds out there's no way to get it operational?

I felt sure I knew the answer.

Crap.

"I think we can do this," Jay said.

"No. No thinking or almost. You will get the missile back online by tomorrow afternoon."

CHAPTER 27

"We'll do our best," Jay said. "But we're going to need sleep tonight and food. We can't work fast when we're exhausted."

"That is your problem," Vlodir shot back. "Get the job done, you live, fail, you and companions die. Perhaps," he continued, voice sly, "I will help you understand my meaning by getting rid of this one, now."

He grabbed the front of my coat, lifting me off the floor.

"Pretty rabbit," he said, his grin predaceous.

His sudden attack shocked the fight right out of me. I couldn't seem to move. I dangled, quivering. His "horn" grazed my sweaty face. Something metal scraped my neck, and I smelled gun oil and his body odor. Belle gasped.

I knew someone else had entered the room.

Jay's voice, blasé, as if finding this tedious, "You can get rid of her, but they've trained the three of us as a team. You'll be deleting our main missile engineer right there. She is the one that knows the mechanical systems. She is the one who climbs inside it."

"She does seem to know the mechanical business," came a familiar voice near the open door. It was Androv.

The bulky Russian, his hot breath on my face, shook me like a dog with a toy, then opened his hand. As I dropped, the .38 fell from my pocket and clattered onto the floor. There was a long silence.

A guard raced over and picked up the little gun. I expected Vlodir to attack me again, shoot me, but he turned on his underlings and began castigating them in Russian. It didn't take a linguist to understand they were being read out for not searching us thoroughly. They pushed Jay and Belle against a wall and ran rough hands over them. A burly guard jerked me to my feet and seemed to have fun poking and prodding me. Belle and I had to remove our heavy coats. They sliced the linings in several places before handing them back to us. Another guard yelled at Belle and me to remove our clothes. The room was filled with dark and scummy anticipation. The burly guard closest to me plucked at my shirt, and reacting with no coherent thought, I smashed my bony fist into his groin. He doubled over. The men guffawed.

"Enough," Vlodir shouted. "To work!" He and Androv left the room.

They pushed us through the doorway again and onto the stairs. They locked the door behind us. We felt our way down, and I collapsed onto the dirt floor, trying not to hyperventilate.

Jay touched my shoulder. "That had to be tough," he said. "But you did very well up there."

Belle hugged me. "Good aim."

"They'll be fetching us again, soon, and expecting us to get the missile running." Without waiting for anything from us, Jay continued, "We pretend to be computer experts doing what they want. I'm going to attempt to get a message to my contact via satellite phone if I can get my hands on one. Only five other people are aware of our missile being compromised and what I'm trying to accomplish up here in Alaska. None of them will be easy to contact. Look, I realize neither of you know me very well, but I'm asking you to follow my lead, stay clear headed, and keep thinking about how to survive even when things get weird."

Vlodir's assault gave me a nasty headache. I said, "You might say I'm overreacting, but I think we already broke through the "weird" barrier, days ago." No one said anything for a few minutes then Jay,

"I'll make up a few jobs for you, Loren, but I've already established that you're more of a hands-on mechanic, so they won't expect you to do much with computers. We'll pretend to do what they want and figure how to react as we go. Another flying by the seat of our pants situation, this. Belle and I can fake like we're running into problems, which might help confuse the issue."

"They're going to kill us, aren't they?" I said, "As soon as they realize we can't get the missile back online."

"Yes. Regardless, they would never let us live. So, we've got to get ourselves out of here because as soon as they realize we're not fixing the missile problem, they'll get rid of us," Belle said.

Jay said, "Our job is to play dumb, but not too dumb, or they'll see through the pretense. We'll act compliant, as if we're ready to kiss their rings to save ourselves. If they give us food, try to hide some. We escape tonight or die trying, because there's no way we can keep the subterfuge going for more than today."

Androv didn't get this far by being stupid. He is quick and cunning, and he doesn't trust us. How long before he catches on?

Belle said, "Hoping I can remember enough about programming to come up with something that makes them think we're getting closer to what they want."

About two hours passed before the door opened. A guard summoned us again, and we stumbled up into the room. Wind whistled through a crack in the wall.

They took us through Howie's office, up the same wide, wooden stairs, wet now with rain coming through broken windows, down a carpeted hall into one of the luxurious suites we'd seen the day we arrived. The room, no longer pristine, stunk like mold and dirty sheets. The door to the bathroom hung open. With no toilets flushing anymore, the raw, outhouse reek dominated the space. A round table brought from the dining area was set up with three laptops and other electronic devices. Battery packs to run the specialized computers were stacked on the carpet. Jay examined everything, telling us the computers were similar to the electronic equipment he had brought to the missile site and in all probability could send and receive information directly from at least one satellite. He began tracing wires from the laptops to the batteries. He unplugged connections, then plugged them in again. Belle seated herself in front of one and hit a key. It came to life. I sat heavily at the table, head down, eyes bleary, feeling numb. I was sure our ruse would end in a few hours, in the only way it could. We'd be found out and shot.

One guard stood at the closed door. He held a pistol in both hands. Another guard hovered behind us, and the third walked the perimeter of the room. No broken windows in this suite, thankfully, as outside, gelid torrents streamed down the glass.

Jay began giving me minor tasks. I sat up, did my best to look alert, and tried to act as if we three were legit.

He asked for food and water, saying the words in Russian. The guards conferred for a few minutes. One left, returning much later with an unopened box of crackers, more cheese, and two open cans of spam. The young Russian placed the food on the unmade bed. After grabbing a few crackers, Jay asked again for water. The same guard, aggrieved, brought three bottles. More time passed while Jay and Belle clicked around on the computers, doing their best to look busy. A notepad laying on the table became Jay's main prop. He wrote on it every few seconds, passing it to Belle and me. At first, the guards tried to read his notes, but his penmanship was deliberately messy. He combined obscure words and numbers. The men lost interest. His latest message was a set of instructions. It read: hide note after reading argue loudly stay by table until I'm in toilet leave table keep talking get food, stand by window argue take sat phone.

As soon as we read his note, Jay made loud retching sounds, jumped up, and scrambled toward the bathroom. Belle and I, following his instructions, stood, waving our hands, arguing loudly, and moved from the table. I crumpled and tore the note, shoving it under the bed. We picked up crackers and cheese and, still quarreling vigorously, hurried to the window. A guard lunged at Jay, grabbed and almost caught him, but Jay pulled loose. He reached the bathroom just ahead of the Russian, shut the door in the man's face, and clicked the lock. The infuriated guard pounded on the door.

Inside the bathroom, he created a cacophony. Raucous grating noise, metal upon metal. Sounded like he was ripping the commode off the wall with his bare hands. The guard reacted by hollering at his startled companions and yanking at the doorknob. While Jay distracted the men, Belle and I stowed crackers, cheese, and spam in our pockets. Just as the Russians reached the area and began pulling at the door, Jay rammed into it from the other side. It flew open. The unfortunate guards were slammed back into the room where they crashed into each other and caromed onto the table, knocking it sideways, spilling laptops, wires, writing implements, and three satellite phones onto the rug. Jay acted as though he merely stumbled and fell out the door. He picked himself up and shuffled over to the electronic jumble on the floor where he knelt, expression puzzled. Belle and I hurried over and began sorting through the computers, tangling wires and making more of a mess. The angry guards surrounded Jay, jerking him to his feet. He did his clumsy geek routine, hitching his pants and blinking.

"Noise?" a guard yelled in his face, pointing toward the bathroom, "What noise?"

Another guard joined in, yelling, "Noise you make?"

Jay mumbled, "Was trying to fix the toilet; it won't flush."

The Russians were furious. I could tell they wanted to throttle Jay, but were too afraid of Vlodir. I saw them casting furtive looks toward the door. With a great deal of fuss, we picked up the computers and plugged everything back in. The men grew more uneasy when we showed them a laptop with a smashed screen.

Using the confusion, Belle shoved a satellite phone into her pocket.

The hours dragged. Once Vlodir came to the door and looked in. The guards, ill at ease, made a show of hovering over us while he was there. We pretended to be hard at work, and Belle delivered a quick burst of computer gibberish as if she was explaining some complex process to Jay and me. Jay kept trying to get up and go back into the bathroom, but a guard stayed close, shoving him into his chair.

The interminable day passed, darkness descended, it finally grew late. Someone came to the door and called us. We followed the messenger from the room into a much cleaner suite with no cracked windows. Vlodir Rafenski, looking tired and tense, sat stiffly upright in an overstuffed red chair behind a curved wooden desk. His eyes, almost swallowed by mottled flesh, glittered like black beads.

He tapped his fingers on the polished desktop, removed a fat cigar from a box and barked, "Your progress, now."

Jay began spinning a story. I could sense he was careful not to become expressive or fantastical. He droned on, salting his monologue with technical terms, saying we had a few difficulties, as the missile's computer did not want to recognize the laptops, but the missile could be up and active again by sometime next day.

"The missile must be ready to launch by two p.m. tomorrow, Alaska time," Vlodir said.

"One minute, if you would allow, General Rafenski," Jay said politely.

Jay turned toward Belle and me, his expression contemplative. He peered over his glasses, tapping his chin with one forefinger, as if deep in thought. Belle pursed her lips and wrote numbers on a notepad. I looked at the tablet, frowning, and poked at the page, nodding at them. Belle and Jay flipped through their notes, mumbled together for a few seconds, then Jay turned back to Vlodir.

"We estimate, General," here he paused, looked at some notes again, and continued, "We will be ahead of schedule. We should be up and running five hours earlier than two p.m., tomorrow."

Vlodir's face seemed to relax. He sat back, crossed his legs, and lit his cigar. His thick lips closing around it looked like curled strips of raw seal meat. I looked down, trying not to shiver. Dried mud painted his boots.

"You should then keep working and get finished, tonight."

I took a chance and eased down onto the floor, where I curled as small as I could.

"General, Rafinski, sir," strong emphasis on the sir. I paused, opening my eyes very wide. "We're tired. We led Androv and your men to your lost supplies early yesterday morning. Without help from Belle and me, it would still be lost. Earlier, we also overpowered Sergei and two others who were attempting to steal your inventory." I gazed up at him. For some reason, his horn looked bigger from that angle.

Ok, do not overplay this, I reminded myself, *do not use the word "drugs," and do not complain about being kidnapped.*

"Before that, someone attacked and shot us down in our helicopter. An exhausting two days. We don't want to be so tired we make mistakes. You said there is a forty-eight-hour window. Charlene Chametz did not trade a missile with the latest technology, no matter what she told you. This missile has been out of commission for years. Although, yes, it is still in working condition, it is a touchy beast, and we must complete each part of the setup with careful precision and total accuracy."

I was gambling on Vlodir being desperate for our help to bring the missile on-line because he had lost his own computer experts and had no one else.

I continued, feigning confidence. "We can have no missed steps and not even one mistake. We are very close to achieving success, and we will achieve success, but the last part of the setup is the trickiest. It will require our complete concentration. The stakes are very high, of course. I'm sure you cannot afford failure. I ask you, General, sir, please let us rest for a few hours to ensure everything will go as you want it."

From my subservient position on the floor, wide-eyed, I hoped I looked a bit like the pitiful cat from that old Disney movie, *Shrek*.

Thoughtfully, Vlodir stood, exhaling a cloud. His features distorted through the noxious smoke resembled a carved gargoyle.

An American missile takeover and launch from US soil had to be the biggest happening in his career by far, a coup of unbelievable proportions. Failure of this mission would mean disgrace and death and perhaps the death of his entire family.

As if bequeathing an exceptional, undeserved favor, Vlodir said, "Sleep for three hours."

He dismissed us with an impatient wave, spat an order at our guards, strode to the window, and stood, staring out into the night, his shoulders rigid with his own importance.

They returned us to the dark, clammy cellar.

As soon as a guard locked the door, Jay picked up the flashlight from behind the stair and motioned us to follow him as he walked to the vent we'd located earlier.

We stood close as he whispered, "I'm going to climb into that and see where it goes."

He scaled the concrete wall, his fingers and feet somehow finding holds I couldn't even see. He disappeared inside, carrying our only light, but we could hear faint scraping sounds as the cellar darkened. Minutes dragged by.

CHAPTER 28

Belle said, "Nice acting with Vlodir. I think you made him consider what he'll lose if this missile launch fails."

"And I thought it was my big-eyed, pitiful kitty routine that saved the day."

"Normally, my dear, you're a real cutie, but have you looked in a mirror lately?"

"I'm going to ignore your last crack, for the most part, but ok, so I haven't polished my nails this week, and lost my lipstick and artsy earrings. Probably even have a few split ends, but I can still work my charm thing, baby.

Another subject. Can you believe Jay? I thought those spy guys were all about fierce fighting, amazing tricks, death-defying stunts, and magical multipurpose tools."

Belle sighed. "Always the idealist, you are, my friend; real life does not work that way. It seems to me you kinda like him, anyway, geek or not."

A minute later, she said, "I won't be going out of here with you and Jay."

"What're you talking about?"

"I've been wandering through buildings selling real estate for eight years, and I've never seen a vent that was big enough to crawl through. For sure, there's no way I can squeeze through there. I'm way too fat."

"Take another look, Toots," I said, using her grade school nickname. "Looks to me like you've lost weight without even trying."

Jay's feet appeared at the vent opening as he backed out and down the wall, the flashlight illuminating a circle around us.

"That was a dumb idea," he said. "I got stuck. That vent gradually narrows and is not nearly big enough for us to use as our escape route."

We stared at each other, dismayed. We knew we had to get away from here, and right now. They were going to kill us tomorrow.

"Let's look around, again," Jay said. There was a ragged edge to his voice. We feverishly combed over the room.

The flashlight threw shadows from the support beams and stairs. These distorted geometric shapes stretched and shrank on the walls as we searched the gloomy basement. It was then I noticed a slightly darker patch high on the concrete block wall behind the stairs. The beam shining through each step created rectangular silhouettes that had hidden an opening with a similar shape. Excitedly, I grabbed the light from Jay and shined it directly up onto the wall revealing a gap in the concrete.

Jay said, "Wait here," stuck the flashlight into his pocket, climbed the wall with astonishing speed, scraped through the opening, and disappeared.

We waited. Anxious, I shuffled from one foot to another. After a time, I said into the darkness, "I've been praying."

"Yeah? Why?"

"Well, we've needed help. I mean, I've been really scared, crap, I'm scared right now, so I guess because I feel desperate."

"And you didn't pray before because you didn't feel you needed anything from God?"

"A few times, but I've spent a lot of my life up until now, thinking I could handle situations by myself. For the last week, it's like any minute we might die, and I guess I'm kinda like Cody."

I couldn't believe I admitted that out loud. "I mean, I'm not sure I'm ready to die. To be honest, I'm petrified. I remember my dad talking to me about six months before he crashed his plane. Waiting for the weather to clear for a bear-viewing flight, he and a tourist had a conversation about God. Anyway, the tourist told him that Jesus is God, and it's only through belief in him we can go to heaven. He said Jesus' death paid for our sins, which means we can have the gift of eternal life. Dad said later he'd asked Jesus to forgive his sins and be his savior. I remember feeling confused and saying, "Dad, you're a nice guy. You're no sinner."

He said, "Honey, everybody sins."

"I didn't understand everything he said, but he seemed so peaceful after that. Mom wasn't. She was angry. She said he got religion, and religion is stupid, but Dad didn't act religious at all; he just seemed more patient, more kind. When we were kids, Mom would say ugly things about church people being hypocrites."

"Sad truth, some are fakes," Belle said. "But was your dad a hypocrite?"

"No. I was just a kid, but I could see a big change in him."

"That's the thing. When it's real, we will change."

"After Dad died, I became afraid and angry. I mean, if God loves us, why do bad things happen, especially to good people like my father? Mom started boozing. My grandparents were in Arizona by then, and Mom sent my brothers to live with them. It was just her and me, and she was in her bedroom drinking most of the time. God seemed very far away as we grew up. You left for the military; it was college for me, then marriage and Brad's two boys that came along with it. Life was pretty good, that is, until I lost my baby girl and found out Brad was running around on me."

I couldn't talk, anymore. My throat squeezed down until I thought I would strangle. My heart felt cold and as hard as a frozen dirt clod.

Belle said, "God's still here, and he still loves you. What your dad said is right."

Jay reappeared.

"Some good news and some not so good. Good news, the hole in the concrete wall goes directly into the laundry and water storage room. Not so good news: there's a door in that room leading to what I think is the outside, but it has a heavy padlock on it, and I can't find anything to help us get it open."

Belle radiated. "Wait here." She walked out of the circle of light and came back less than a minute later, holding her handyman gadget.

She gave it to him. "Try this."

He looked it over, started to say something, shook his head, thanked her, scaled the wall again, and slipped headfirst through the opening.

As soon as he was gone, I asked, "Where were you hiding that? They searched you twice."

"I found underwear at the missile site."

"Yeah, men's briefs. You gave me a pair."

"But these were different."

"How different?"

"They have pockets. Anyway," Belle said, evident pride in her voice, "I hid my handyman helper in one of them."

"I'm glad you did, but it doesn't sound like it was one of the more comfortable accessories you've worn."

"What part of this trip has been comfortable for either of us?"

Jay climbed back into the room, whispering, "It's past time we got ourselves out of here. Belle, first, Loren, second, and I'll be last. That hole is about three feet off the other room's floor, and I put laundry under it which will make your landing's a lot softer. I hope the rain is loud enough to cover our noise."

Belle said, "I can't climb the concrete wall, and I'm too big to get myself through that opening."

"You both need to take your coats off, first, but I can help lift you up. It was tight on my shoulders, but you saw me. I managed it, and I'm betting you can, too."

She looked at him a moment longer, still dubious.

"We've got to go, ladies," Jay said, "We're running through our allotted three hours."

Jay hoisted Belle toward the hole. It wasn't easy, she couldn't get a handhold, and her boots slipped down the concrete. Her face was red and sweaty with the effort, and in the dim light, I saw the cords on Jay's neck standing out as he wrenched upward on her from behind.

Finally, she had her head and shoulders inside. Jay pulled her boots off, then continued to push on her feet. Groaning, she managed to pull her body up and halfway through the horizontal opening.

Would she make it? I rocked back and forth, hands balled into fists, waiting, wondering what we'd do if she got stuck. Finally, she was through. Jay bent forward, flushed, hands on knees, breathing hard.

It was my turn. He lifted me in front of him, bending so I could place my feet on his thighs, an awkward position for both of us, and I worked as hard as I could to climb the wall, grabbing, clutching, and clawing at anything that would give me purchase on the concrete. Scrabbling upward, I seized the rough edge and, wheezing with the effort, wrenched myself through. The room I was entering was dark as arctic night, but I heard a faint sound from Belle, which reassured me.

I slid over the opening and, without meaning to, somersaulted into an enormous tangle of cloth, scraping my back on the concrete wall as I fell.

The fabric felt damp against my face and smelled of mildew. I rolled over, wallowing in the pile, trying to extricate myself and get out of Jay's way, glad he'd piled the laundry below us.

Jay led us to the door he'd described, saying, "Wasn't able to open it, yet, but I'll get it soon." He hadn't returned Belle's handyman gadget, so he began working on the lock while I held the light. Minutes passed.

Belle said, "No offense, Jay, but I'd like to try. Loren and I spent a long time sawing a lock apart to get a bear rifle, and when I realized later, the gadget I'd been carrying around all that time has amazing lock picker tools, I've hoped for a lock to try it out on."

"Are you saying all that sawing was unnecessary?" I asked, incredulous.

"I didn't want to tell you because I knew you'd make a big deal out of it," Belle said.

"What do you mean, a big deal? I sawed through most of it. That lock was awful. My shoulder was killing me, and I took some of your turns, too, and now you tell me…"

"Hey," Jay said, interrupting my whispered rant, "Could we just get the lock opened and save the replay until we've gotten away from here?"

Belle had it picked in about twenty seconds. She kissed her handy helper tool triumphantly and opened the door. We were at the back of the lodge where trees crowded up against the walls. We emerged, single file; I waited until Belle disappeared into the brush. I looked to my right and saw the gravel path she and I had taken on our way to Howie's cabin all those nights ago.

There were no lights. Rain all around us, splashing and pinging on metal. I tried to be invisible and fast, moving until I slipped behind dripping branches. Belle stood hidden there, waiting.

She grabbed my hand and, in a hushed but exultant tone, said, "I made it through the opening and didn't get stuck. I really must have lost weight. I want to do a happy dance. I want to sing."

"I'm excited for you, but please, please don't sing, and I already said you lost weight. Besides, I'm still mad about your handyman lock picker."

"Fine," she said. "Fine." A whisper, "God, this adventure is kind of a weird way to answer my prayer to lose weight, but I'll take it, so thank you I got some pounds off."

And remembering my worry that she might get stuck, I murmured a heartfelt, "Amen!"

Jay showed up, saying, "Let's get further into the trees. First thing I need to do is disable tracking on the sat phone Belle grabbed."

We moved from the lodge, stopping for a quick second to discuss our escape route. Hike through the forest about an eighth of a mile, then walk parallel to the fiord on the lookout for the small dock Howie had described. Once there, take a boat and head toward Kodiak Island. We decided we'd stay off the radio until well away from the fiord, because the *ViKing Revenge*, the boat we'd been Androv's prisoners on, was somewhere close.

How long before they missed us?

We stumbled through clots of grass and bushes along the edge of the bay. There was no beach. Sharp rocks jutted every direction. We didn't dare use the light and there was no moon, so we had to feel our way over saw-toothed boulders. Miserable and slow going. We knew they had discovered our escape when the *ViKing Revenge* turned on megawatt floodlights, sweeping the water's edge and the rocks and brush behind. Lights flickered through trees around the lodge. We slipped, slid, and ran when we could, single file, scrambling over the rugged scumble of boulders.

Jay, ahead of Belle and me, slowed. We found ourselves above a creek which flattened out on our left and emptied into the fiord. Without a word, he jumped in and began wading upstream. Belle and I were panting like my cousin's sled dogs after a race. I cut my knee on a boulder right before she stuck her hand in my face, showing a slice across her palm.

"Sharp rocks," she hissed.

I knew Jay hoped that the ground upstream would widen with fewer obstacles and make for faster and easier going.

Shouts from the guys following us, but their lights and sounds faded away as we hiked around a copse of tangled bracken near the creek. Had we lost them? The ground seemed to flatten for a few hundred yards then showed a steep rise. The creek narrowed, gushing, forced between enormous, piled boulders. Noise from the surging water intensified. Jay motioned for us to wait, ran ahead, then silently returned. He said, "Pretty sure we're close to a large waterfall. From what I can tell, the mountain goes nearly straight up next to it, and that isn't the direction we want to go."

We paused, wet, bedraggled. I couldn't stop shivering and was so tired I wobbled. I wondered if Belle and Jay felt as beaten as I. The rain and wind were relentless. In the dark, water running into my eyes, I tripped over a log, sat hard on the ragged edge of glacier shattered stone, and silently cried.

From somewhere above me, Belle whispered, "There they are, again."

Through my tears and the rain running down my face, I saw bobbing lights heading our way.

Belle said, "Jay, did you watch that movie, *Last of the Mohicans*?"

I didn't hear what else she said, but Jay replied, "We can try it."

Belle tugged on my arm, pulling me to my feet, saying, "We can't outrun 'em, so we're going to hide behind the waterfall."

It was a crazy plan. It was a desperate plan, likely a hopeless plan, but what else was there?

CHAPTER 29

We worked our way up close beside the stream. We couldn't tell what size it was, or much of anything about it, except that water was falling in heavy sheets over the edge of rocks higher up, making a tremendous racket. Between spray from the tumbling cascade and heavy rain, it felt like we were swamp creatures, breathing mist.

We clung to each other, clutching arms, hands, or whatever we could keep hold, helping to drag ourselves up and over the slippery moss and stones next to the foam and splash.

Jay said, "Think we've gone high enough; I'm going to try to get behind the falls. Stay here, ok?"

What if he doesn't come back out?

We waited, shaking with nerves and cold, clinging to the rocks like two misplaced barnacles. Water in my ears, sinuses, and running down my neck. I sneezed, burying my face in my coat.

I will not panic.

Jay touched my shoulder. Startled, I croaked like a stepped-on frog. The flashlights were now about 50 feet away, but the thick, wet blanket of night hid us.

We followed him, sliding into the deeper darkness right beside the flow. Drenched already, I expected the tremendous wash to grab and send me down the gully of the falls, submerge and drown me. To prepare for this imagined disaster, my body began trying to hyperventilate, my lungs felt compressed.

With all that water pouring over my face, I won't be able to breathe. I know I'll drown just like those passengers in my dad's plane. My thoughts raced; my heart pounded against my chest.

I can't do this. I can't do this.

Belle moaned, startling me from my terrified reverie.

"You, ok?" This from Jay.

"Yes," was all she said.

"Now," he said, face inches from ours. "Grab onto my jacket, Loren. Shuffle your feet right behind mine. You hold on to Loren's coat, Belle, and do the same."

We did as he said, and after a brief time, found ourselves behind the falls in a water-carved recession of solid rock. Crowding into it, we pasted ourselves against the damp stone wall, our bodies pressed together. I couldn't believe it had been that easy.

The rushing curtain of pounding water filled our ears with sound. I was thankful it was fall. Even with autumn rains starting, the water was much lower than in spring. I was sure there wouldn't have been any room to hide back here during late May with heavy snowmelt.

Squeezed between Jay and Belle, I stopped shivering.

Minutes ticked by. Jay put his lips against my ear. "I think they've gone. Let's head out and take a boat before it gets light. I'll be able to call using the satellite phone once, then I've got to chuck it, because what I did to the phone to disable its tracking device only works until a call is being made."

I relayed his words to Belle, and we shuffled out from behind the streaming sheet of crystal-clear water.

As we clambered back down and away from the noise and plash, Belle said, "That was the falls I told you about before we flew to the lodge, Lor. I wanted you to see it in daylight. It's supposed to be especially scenic around here."

"Well, I experienced more of it a whole lot closer than I ever planned on," I growled, limping into the brush.

The first hints of dawn striped the sky. We tried to hurry; we tried to stay hidden, and we tried not to let each other know how tired and drained we felt.

There was no sign of our captors, no appearance of activity. The world was still, no rain, no wind, no sound of anything at all. More disappointment:

Jay attempted a call on the satellite phone, but got no response, so he threw it into the creek.

And more wrestling our way through heavy growth; devil's club sticking us. Our choice, getting poked with thorns or hiking next to the fiord with the genuine possibility of being seen and shot by someone on the *ViKing Revenge*.

We voted. It was unanimous; we all felt stickers were going to be much easier to remove than bullets.

It didn't take long to get there. Far below, we saw a sliver of inlet and a section of dock through the spruce.

Jay motioned us close, keeping his voice low, "Don't know who's down there, hiding in a boat or stationed around the water waiting for us. I want to go first and check it out. I'm asking you two to stay up here and keep watch. You might see someone coming before I do. Those guys don't want us getting away. Let's be careful, and let's be lucky."

He looked at me, smiled, then turned, disappearing behind the trees.

The thick forest made it impossible to see distance, even though we were not that far from the dock.

How am I supposed to let Jay know someone is coming?

"I can't tell what's happening through all this brush. I'm going to climb a tree and see if that helps," I said, peeling off my wet coat and walking over to a spreading old hemlock. Thick fog was sneaking in. Anxiety prickled my skin. Tired as I was, I couldn't stay still. There were too many variables here; our plan was sketchy. We had no weapons.

Belle removed her coat, wrung it out, and sprawled near the base of a birch.

She groaned, "My leg is killing me. Hope my cut isn't infected. I'm going to stay here and wait while you climb up there and tell me what you see. Just so sore I don't want to move."

I hadn't climbed a tree in years, not since my boys got a kite stuck one summer afternoon. This one had branches close together, curving out and upward into a natural ladder. Also, the needles wouldn't be poky and sharp like spruce.

Climbing and finding a perch, I crouched, holding onto the trunk. Surrounded by foliage, I felt invisible and a little bit proud of myself. I was also glad the weather had warmed, less danger of hypothermia in our damp clothes.

If only my boys could see me.

Through the branches, I now had a sweeping view of the fiord and the dock. It wasn't as Howie had described.

What I saw was the burned hulls of two boats, one almost filled with water and sunk, the other still floating, but a scorched wreck, unusable.

My heart fell into my boots.

I glimpsed movement. A man clambered over boulders and waded out into water far to the right of the dock. Jay. Trees jumbled on a granite outcropping obscured my view, but as I looked closer, I could see a mast. There was another boat.

I clung to the tree, feeling suddenly dizzy, exhausted, and overwhelmed by the danger I knew was all around us. Soon it would be light, and unless it remained foggy, we were going to become easy pickings for the bad guys.

Jay, swimming. Long minutes later, a Kodiak gillnetter floated silently around the rocks and drifted toward the pier. I watched him pole it forward. Just as the boat touched the dock, I noticed two guys running down the beach.

Echo of gunshots and through thickening fog, Jay disappeared into the boat's cabin, the men racing toward him.

Scuffing noises and looking down, …I realized Belle was below me, climbing up.

She stage-whispered, "Can't see anything up there; where are you?"

I started to answer; I started to tell her about the two men on the dock going after Jay.

From the corner of my eye, I saw movement. Someone walked out of the trees below us—no time to say anything. The same, sadistic-looking guy who dragged Cody away on the *ViKing Revenge* appeared in the clearing. The very same guard who tried to force Belle and me to remove our clothing at the lodge. He pointed a gun at my friend. My heart hiccupped.

"Down," he commanded, waving his pistol.

Belle, startled by his appearance, lost her grip and screeched, then curled around to the back of the trunk just as he shot. She slid slowly at first, then faster, grabbing for branches that broke off and fell with her as she almost circled the tree, falling down and down. I scrabbled after her, reacting, not thinking. She landed with a shriek and a shower of broken branches near the base of the hemlock. The man crossed the distance, and I shrank back as he loomed over her. Belle made considerable commotion and noise flailing, bumping and smashing through branches as she plummeted, which is why the armed man hadn't noticed me. I slid further down and clung to a broad, bushy branch about fifteen feet above him.

She lay still, eyes closed. I had no gun, no weapon of any kind.

Four more shots from somewhere near the dock, and the man cursed and stepped away, investigating. He rushed back. He was going to shoot Belle.

With no creative strategy or game plan, I jumped, landing kind of on all fours low on the guy's back with my hands reaching for his neck. Got his hair, instead. We both sprawled. His arms and hands flailed and spread out wide to protect himself, but with my sudden weight knocking him off balance, he had no time to stabilize. He crashed hard into a lichen-covered boulder. I'm sure I would have broken a leg or worse if he hadn't been under me, cushioning the impact.

I staggered to my feet, expecting him to get up and shoot me, but he lay there, unmoving.

He'd dropped his pistol; it glinted from the moss. I snatched it up and approached. He lay spread like a dried starfish, eyes half-open. I held the gun in my sweaty hands, leaning over him, smelling stale booze. He didn't move. I did not want to touch him, but needed to see if he was alive, so reached out one finger, ready to yank my hand back and shoot if he so much as twitched. Felt a pulse. He must have bonked his head when he fell and was unconscious or pretending to be.

"Hey," I called, moving to Belle. I was still holding the pistol aimed at the man on the ground. I brushed my hand across her forehead, "You ok, Toots?"

She opened one eye, wincing, "I feel like I just fell out of a tree." A second later, "I might've fainted or something. Why aren't I dead? An ugly guy pointed a gun at me."

"Yep," I replied, working to keep my voice steady, "That guy is now unconscious. He's not interested in you, anymore. However, he could wake up any time and start up again."

I babbled, fueled by adrenaline, close to tears. My friend looked up at me, concerned, but I wouldn't meet her gaze. My eyes burned.

Belle sat up, her breath coming in noisy snuffles, her face pale with the effort.

"We'll just have to help him calm down," she said, reaching into her coat pocket. She pulled out a roll of silver duct tape and handed it to me.

Attempting to stand, she wobbled and nearly fell. She leaned against the hemlock, wincing.

"First that gash on my left leg from the explosion, now something's messed up with the right one, too. Ollymon!" she exclaimed, an expression from her village.

I noticed a rip in her jeans below her knee.

"Hold still." I pulled the cuff of her raggedy pants up and examined her calf. I saw a small puncture and a bigger tear on the other side.

"He shot you. Falling out of that tree didn't do this."

"Get that guy secured, quick," she said, "I don't want that kind of attention from any man."

"Where did you get duct tape, of all things?"

"On the bed near the food they brought us in the hotel room. Thought it might come in handy. I took it when Jay was ramming his way out of the bathroom. You can do almost anything if you have enough duct tape."

Scared he'd regain consciousness, I handed the pistol to Belle, pulled the guy's arms behind his back, wrapped tape around his wrists, and covered his hands. I removed his boots and socks, almost retching from the smell, wrapped more tape around his ankles, and covered his feet. I traveled up his legs to his knees, wrapping and wrapping. The roll had been almost full. I wasn't sure where to stop, so I just kept putting on more. I covered his mouth and eyes and left him there, taped and unconscious, and began working on Belle's gunshot wound.

There wasn't as much blood as I expected. The bullet tunneled through muscle but must have missed major vessels. I tore the tail off my shirt and made a messy bandage, of sorts, using more duct tape, but unlike my application to the guy on the ground, I was careful not to stick it against her bare skin.

A twig broke. I grabbed and aimed the pistol just as Jay emerged from the bracken.

He glanced at the fallen man, then at us, then back at the package the unconscious man had become, due to my zealous taping job.

"Where you plan on mailing him, to?" he asked, with the barest hint of a smile.

"He shot me," Belle said weakly, "But Loren took care of him; she jumped on his back and rodeoed him. That cowgirl saved my life, again."

Crap. I thought she had fainted.

"Is it safe to go down to the dock, now?" I asked, my voice unsteady. I wanted to howl, "Get me out of here," to the universe.

I remembered the two guys I saw running at Jay and wondered how he'd handled them. Jay now carried a pistol and had two rifles slung over his shoulder. He was soaked from his swim. I noticed a blood streak across his shirt.

"What happened down there?" I asked, trying to compose myself by forcing an unruffled tone.

"Pretty close to what happened here, except no need for duct tape," he replied, looking at the man who still lay unmoving. "And I ended up with some weapons. We can talk about it when we have more time, but, yeah," he said, running his eyes over Belle's bandaged leg, "I got rid of some of the opposition, so we should get moving."

Hmm, two guys against him, and he had no gun. Starting to believe he IS one of those tough, trained, fighter dudes.

CHAPTER 30

"I'd like to help," he said to Belle.

"That would be very nice," she replied. He handed me the rifles, saying, "Climb on," as he bent in front of her. I helped Belle get situated piggyback style on Jay's back. She was sweating and glaring and rosy and embarrassed as she clung to his shoulders.

Jay took off through the soupy fog with surprising speed and agility, climbing down through trees and brush. I wondered if his injured leg was bothering him as he pushed between branches and climbed over deadfall.

Suspense mounted as we neared the dock. My mouth went dry, and I turned in circles, scanning. How could we possibly check behind every tree and rock? I knew armed enemies might appear at any moment.

We got ourselves onto the fish boat. I saw bloodstains across the deck. I wondered who anchored the craft there and who owned it, but my desperation to escape pushed those questions away as I helped Belle into the cabin. I untied the rope securing it to the dock while Jay started a miniature trolling motor hanging off the stern.

As we drove away from the pier, I was thankful for thick fog surrounding us. We headed toward Kodiak.

Jay turned the piloting over to me as we moved closer to the mouth of the fiord. Judging we couldn't be heard once we reached the ocean entrance, I started the diesel engine. Jay lifted the trolling motor up and out of the way, and we edged into the Shelikof.

The earlier quiet had given us hope for calm weather conditions. Although it was now daylight, calm was not happening. The fog covering the fiord behind us began melting away. Waves rose in front of us, Shelikof Strait showing its unpredictable nature.

Jay stood near the wheel as I maneuvered the boat.

Heavy dark clouds scurried by, and now outside the warmth and shelter of that narrow bay, rain and wind pummeled, another storm was fast approaching.

"I don't think it's a good idea to head out into the Strait, right now," I said.

"Any ideas?" he asked.

"You know how much fuel we've got on board?"

I gripped the wheel as the boat rocked. I pointed at the instrument panel. "The fuel gauge says the tank's full, but I'm hoping for extra, just in case we have to go further than we thought. If there's more stashed away, it'll be in the hold or the cabin somewhere."

"So busy trying to get us away, I didn't think to check," he replied. "I'll go look."

"I'm going to turn back out of the Strait and run along the outer beach. I'll use the radio to call the Coast Guard and find a cove where we can hide from wind and the bad actors back there. The incoming tide is causing rough wave action, so if we can hunker down somewhere until high water slack, we may have a better chance getting across this."

I was busy turning the boat and running before the storm for several minutes, getting as close to the rocky shore as I dared. I flipped the radio's "on" switch; it wouldn't come to life. Rain and spray splashed against the windshield. I turned on the wipers; they refused to budge. I opened a small side window and stuck my head out, trying to see through the downpour.

Jay climbed to the bridge, saying, "We've got two, five-gallon containers full of diesel fuel, at least that's what the labels are calling it."

"Better than nothing." Pointing at the instrument panel, I said, "The batteries that run the plotter, radar, wipers, and radio must be dead; would you check and see if there's a chart somewhere in the cabin we can use, and also see how Belle's doing?"

The wind increased. The sky was now stained a metallic ochre and rain thrashed us.

Jay reappeared and handed me a chart. "Belle's in a bunk. She said she's ok."

"Thanks. Could you take the wheel while I look at the map?"

The marine chart he handed me was grease spotted, worn, and illegible in places, but I could see three inlets that we might run into for shelter while we waited.

Enormous rocks crowded the entrance of the first bay we tried. I wasn't confident enough in my piloting skills to risk it with blustery wind gusts; chances of being slammed by a wave onto one of the mammoth boulders was frightening high. I drove on. The second cove was little more than a sticky mud hole. Much too shallow; I was afraid of running aground and getting trapped in there.

Finally, the third seemed promising. It was long and wide, almost as big as the fiord we just left. I motored in. Happily, the wind and waves were calmer in this bay because of the mountains protecting it. As I eased the boat up the inlet, Jay and I looked for somewhere to tie up or anchor out, so we could remain hidden while we rode out the weather.

The rain stopped, but fog lay heavy on the trees, so when I first saw wisps of gray in brush near a jagged granite peninsula, I dismissed it until floating further in, Jay and I said together, "Smoke."

Coming closer, we saw a cabin through the brush.

A blackened chimney cocked at a rakish angle above a tattered tarpaper roof emitted bluish-gray puffs.

I slowed the boat to an idle as the cabin door burst open and a raga-muffin woman hurried out, waving a blue cloth above her head like a flag as she raced toward us.

Closer, we could see she had a thick curtain of long gray hair covered with faded strips of disheveled ribbon that hung down her front like matted seaweed. She'd lined her eyes in black. Her skin was burnt leather brown. Barefoot, she wore a long, bright orange skirt that billowed and flapped like a parachute around her spindly legs. She carried a pipe in one hand and whipped her flag back and forth with the other.

"Halloo," she called, jumping on the rocks above us. She puffed on a pipe and, "Halloo, halloo," she shouted again, still waving the banner. "You're here, you've arrived!"

"This is totally weird," Jay said, quietly.

"Totally," I agreed.

"Should we ask if she's selling magic mushrooms?" Belle spoke from behind us. I turned and saw her bracing herself against the cabin door.

"How are you feeling?" I asked.

"Been better, been worse, but who is this lady?" she whispered.

Jay looked up at the elderly woman. "We're waiting until the seas lie down so we can get across the Shelikof. I'm John Paul. My friends and I had some bad luck getting to Kodiak, with the storms and all."

"Your name isn't John Paul," the beribboned old woman said, correcting him. "I recognize you from another life. "You are now entering the ambiguous, the oracular epoch of Eden Song; but we can set all that straight, soon enough." She began turning in slow circles as she waved her banner and puffed on her pipe.

"Right," I said quietly. "Methinks the lady is quite mad, and I don't want to wait here for high tide. Sometimes, Jay, people go into remote parts of Alaska alone, and stay too long and become complicated and strange. I know a few like that. Conversations can be interesting, if you can get away when you want, but I think in this case, we should wave, put the boat in reverse and anchor out somewhere else."

"She may have a working radio," Jay said.

"This is the day," the woman announced, as she stopped spinning and pointed her pipe at me, "Hurry. You can tie up there and come with me to inspect my prisoners."

I gaped up at her, "Prisoners? You mean human prisoners?"

"Yes, prisoners. Not sure what they will be tomorrow, but I will show you what they are today. They could be star beings from that moon by Jupiter, or they could be reptilian shapeshifters from middle earth, but one of them laid an egg yesterday."

Is she messing with us?

Jay looked at me. I looked at Belle. Belle looked at the old woman.

Jay spoke quietly, "She seems crazy, maybe even real crazy, but we need a radio, and before we leave, I'm going to have to check out what she means by her 'prisoners.'"

Crap a doodle doo.

We left the boat idling, and Jay found a half-buried piece of rusted keel to tie to. He and I climbed off the stern and up the rocks to where the woman waited. Belle said her injured legs were hurting, so she stayed aboard. Jay had a pistol hidden in a pocket. He left the rest of the guns with Belle.

"I'm Wind Dancer," the old woman said, smiling. Her nose was straight and prominent. Her large, slanting eyes were sea green with soft lines radiating from their corners. It was easy to tell she had once been beautiful. Her features were still elegant. She reminded me of someone.

"Greetings, Wind Dancer," Jay answered, keeping a straight face. I wanted to say, "And I am She who Jumps from Trees," but I smiled, said, "I'm Loren," and offered my hand. She lowered her banner and touched each tip of my fingers with a pinky, counting, "One, two, three, four, and five," as she reached my thumb.

Jay said, "I'd like to inspect the prisoners."

"Follow on," she sang, "Follow on, follow on." Her voice was high and piping and hazy with smoke. She moved as light-footed and agile as a young girl. As she skipped ahead, I noticed she appeared to be wearing nothing above her skirt, while her blanket of hair covered her front, her back was naked. She led us up a winding path past her cabin and onto a grassy area. I could see four miniature stick huts and, beside them, a fenced-off area with tall, lush green plants.

Jay said, "That's a marijuana crop."

Why am I not surprised?

"Stay behind me," she ordered, flourishing her flag. "This could get dangerous."

She pulled away a branch covering the first hut. We bent forward, peeking through a tangle of driftwood. A chicken stood in the middle of the stick cage, pecking at something in the dirt.

Jay chuckled, then covered it with a cough.

"Do all your prisoners look like this?" he asked.

"Oh, no, I should say not. You must see."

"Thank you for showing us, but we should get going, Miz Wind Dancer," I interjected.

She's a complete loon.

"Oh, no, no, no, follow on," she breathed, "Cosmic design meant you to arrive here and now."

Jay looked at me; I rolled my eyes and mouthed, "Let's go."

"Won't take long," he said, and continued after her.

The next held two rabbits.

The third hut was much larger. Four, half-grown, beady-eyed, white feathered turkeys stared suspiciously back at us.

"I know for sure that one flew in here from another planet. He's an alien," the old woman cried, pointing at the largest bird.

I resisted the temptation to say what I was thinking; instead, asking, "How long have you been out here?"

"Times and times and times," she replied.

"Do you have a working radio?" Jay asked.

"I did," she said.

She meandered back to her cabin. Jay and I trailed after.

"We'll have tea," she announced over her shoulder, "Come inside, now."

Jay shrugged. We followed her into the small cottage and stopped, staring.

She'd gathered and covered the walls in what looked like viny tree roots, peeled and knitted into twisting, twining decoration with carved driftwood leaves and flowers and fruit. Barest traces of color illustrated tendrils and petals. The interior felt as if we were standing inside a skillfully woven, upturned basket. A table fashioned from a single piece of driftwood; a trundle type bed and furniture put together with bits of wood and handmade pegs. The building looked as if it had grown, fantastically, plant-like, from the earth.

Wooden bells fashioned into intricate shapes and hung by an open window rang in soft, muted tones as the breeze moved through.

It was one of the most exquisite rooms I'd ever been in. Wind Dancer, or whatever her name, was an artist and one of considerable ingenuity.

The woman took a steaming kettle from a cracked and rusted wood-stove and poured hot water into pint canning jars. It relieved me to see the tea was in ordinary bags from an ordinary brand you could get at any grocery. As she handed me the hot drink, I thanked her and said, "We left our engine running because the battery that powers the radio is dead, and we aren't sure the other battery is holding a charge. If we shut our engine off, we might not get it started again. We need to make a call to Kodiak. My friend Belle is injured, and we need the Coast Guard. We also need to use your radio."

"That's a lot of need," she said, "But, no."

"No?"

"I left all that. I gave up radio."

What does she think of computers and cell phones?

Jay asked, "How do you get food or fuel or take care of getting necessities?"

I broke in with, "What if you need medical aid?"

"What is need? We don't need, we want, and the more we want, the more we want."

"Does someone come by and bring you supplies?"

"Yes."

"Do you stay here, year around?" I asked.

She dropped her flag on the floor and sagged onto her bed.

"I've been waiting here more than thirty years," she said.

CHAPTER 31

"May I ask what you've been waiting for?"

"For Saint Thomas to return."

"Who is Saint Thomas?" Jay asked.

"My husband." She sat on her bed, and clutching her tea, spoke slowly at first, almost as if talking in her sleep. "He left with my boys, and they never came back."

"Were they in an accident?"

"No, no, no. Saint Thomas said we needed a change, so we drove to Alaska from Colorado. Moved over here after living in Seldovia. We had a toddler. Awhile after we got here, I got pregnant and had the baby in Kodiak. A healthy boy, but something happened to me; I never felt right after that. My thoughts became jumbled. So many voices, and I saw shadow people. I couldn't stop crying, I couldn't sleep, and I couldn't take care of my babies very well. When our youngest was almost two months old, Saint Thomas said I was very sick and needed medicine. He kept trying to talk me into going away with him and leaving this place, but I was so afraid, I couldn't step outside our house without a cage covering me. I made my cage from what grows in nature, twigs, and roots. That way, shadow people couldn't see me. He didn't believe what I saw. One day, he said he couldn't live here, anymore. He took my babies, because I told him we were visited by things that whispered in the night. He left. After three months, I felt safe going outside without my cage. Twice, I tried to move away from here, but the voices screamed at me, so I came back and built this cage." She pointed at the carved and woven vines twisted upon the walls around us.

Whoa. This poor lady has had her share.

"Thomas set it up. Someone brings me supplies every three months. First by Gregory, then fourteen years ago, his son, Rick, started, and five years ago, it was Gregory's nephew. I don't know where Saint Thomas is, and I don't know where my boys are, or what happened to them."

She stood and pointed a bony finger at Jay. "You look like my grandpa looked when I was a little girl," she said. "Are you?"

Jay glanced at me; eyebrows raised. He tried to smile, but his features looked troubled.

"No," he said, "I am not." The woman's story had affected me, too, but Jay seemed more than a little upset. He set his jar down with a thump and left.

"Do you have other relatives or siblings?"

"I lived with my grandfather until he died when I was six. I ended up in an orphanage in Tennessee." She set her tea on the table and began slapping her hands together. "I was told I had no other relatives. The orphanage was rough. They hurt me." Her hands slapped faster, and her voice became childlike. "I didn't like that place."

Wonder if she has ever been treated? Her issues seem to involve a lot more than running off into the wilderness and going whoo-hoo. Bet she got worse after her family left. Has she been alone all this time? We've got to try to get her help.

"Where's your radio?" I asked, changing the subject. I set my tea on the table.

"You're not the ones I saw in my dream, so, let's go to the big house."

We left the cabin, and I followed her up another winding trail through dense spruce. Jay stayed several feet behind us. I noticed her stride falter and drag to something stiff and plodding and become even slower as we arrived at what was once a yard, now overgrown. A dilapidated, log building squatted in the scrub, no sign of life. The door was gone. She hesitated on the threshold for over a minute, finally moving inside. We followed her. Obviously, a family had lived here; I saw dirt-covered toys on the floor and a small kitchen with shelves, sink and a counter built into one wall. A broken crib sat deserted, desolate, and tiny animal tracks spattered dust on the floor beside it. A ladder led to a loft, presumably a bedroom. She led us through another door into a crowded area lined with shelves slumping under stacks of books. I wanted to go over and read titles. The place smelled of damp and rotting wood. Something had nested in a corner. I could see a broken window covered with grimy cloth; cobwebs hung everywhere. She pulled the drapery from the cracked glass and, as more light penetrated, pointed at an object on a sagging desk. Jay uncovered an antique machine. I could see the dull shine of glass tubes and old brass.

"That's your radio?" I questioned, surprised.

"It's an old ham set up," Jay said.

"He used to talk to people all over the world," the old woman mumbled. "He would crank it up to get the battery charged and sit there by the hour, in the winter."

I walked over and picked up a book, pages damp and stuck together. The title, *"Retro Hypnosis in Therapy,"* intrigued me. The moldering library covered a range of topics: psychology, psychiatry, and much more.

"Are these books, yours?" I asked.

"Used them in my profession," she said, her voice flat. "I was a hypno-therapist in Detroit, until they fired me. We moved to Colorado, but they let me go, there, too. I helped people retrieve ancient memories, memories from before they were born, memories from another time when they were star children."

Good grief.

My foot grazed something as I stepped away from the shelves. Looking down, I saw a fabric-covered, pink box, an old-style, cosmetic container woman used to carry when they traveled. Back in the day, my grandmother traveled with a case like this. I picked it up.

"You may look," Wind Dancer said, "It will reveal the forgotten."

Inside, I saw a pile of old photographs. Some taken with a 35 millimeter; others were Polaroid. The pictures were remarkably well preserved. I guessed the quality seal had kept them from water damage, unlike every other thing in this chaotic ruin. There were photos of a truck pulling a trailer loaded with house-hold goods, an old double-ender boat they must have used to ferry supplies, felled trees, and peeled logs. A new house was shown taking shape in several stages, which I recognized as the broken-down wreck we were now standing in. I saw a smiling and pregnant Wind Dancer, although the name on the back of that photograph said, "Gili Maureen." I saw a toddler sitting on a chair with a newborn in his arms, supported by the hands of a man whose head wasn't in the picture. Feeling uncomfortable with the domestic intimacy of these images, I handed the case to the old woman. She looked at a few pictures, snapped it shut, and set it in the exact spot I had first seen it.

I walked over and stood behind Jay, watching him turn a brass crank on the old radio.

"You tried to move away and live somewhere else after Saint Thomas took your children and left?" I asked.

"Year after year, I tried, and then twice more after, but it's the voices," she answered. "The voices are quieter here."

I won't ask her anything else.

"Does anyone use ham radio, anymore?" I wondered aloud.

"People form radio clubs," Jay said. "It's become a hobby pastime, mostly, except for some third world situations."

"Did you learn Morse code?"

"Believe it or not, I had a choice; take a class in Morse code or government statistics, so guess which one I chose," he said, adjusting a rusty dial.

Glass tubes glowed and crackled, and static spat from the speaker. Jay rotated the few knobs on the front of the radio, trying to pick up a signal.

The old woman burst into song—more of a high-pitched keening, not a pleasant sound.

"I feel for her, but I can't concentrate; could you get her away from here?" Jay asked.

I asked, "Miz Wind Dancer, will you come outside with me?"

She grabbed my hand and pulled me out the door, saying, "Sometimes we have to grieve, Loren. Sometimes, it's necessary to empty our soul before we can fill it again. Those pictures made me think about what was, and that man in there made me remember what used to be. He reminds me of my grandfather, his nose and forehead, and the way he walks. And when I remember all the before, I get so sad. I get so lonely and sad." Still holding my hand, she ran with me down a hill away from the cabin toward the sea. We walked through a half circle of trees into an open area covered in wildflowers, edged by a cliff of rocks that spilled into the bay. The fog had vanished.

She sang, "It's all right now, here comes the sun."

The ocean below us gleamed like silver satin, and the warm meadow bloomed with wild geraniums, iris, forget-me-not, and lemon-yellow paintbrush plants, unusual flowers for this late in summer. She dropped my hand, ran to the cliff's edge, and danced. I watched, entranced, as she jumped and twirled, her billowing skirt dipping and rising, floating around her like blowing petals. When she turned away from me, she was a lithe young woman, when I saw her face, she was old. And she cried, how she cried. Transfixed, I could not look away. I rubbed my hand across my wet face. I was crying, too.

"Come with us on the boat," I called, when she stilled. "Come with me."

"I cannot," she cried, "For I am the solitary keeper in this beautifully haunted silence. What if they return and I'm not here? Now, I must see to my precious prisoners." Without another word, she took off down the path.

I met Jay as he stepped outside the decaying building.

"Were you able to call anyone?"

"Got a Morse code message to some guy in Perth, Australia. I gave him information to send to a number in DC and another to send to the Coast Guard, anywhere he could get through, but asked him to try up here in Alaska."

"I hope the messages get to the right people."

"I kept sending Morse code until two tubes on that antiquated set got hot and shattered, so that ended that."

As we got closer to the old woman's hut, I whispered, "She needs help. I asked her to come with me to Homer, but she said she can't. How did she put it? She said she's the keeper in this haunted silence, or something like that."

"Sad and strange," Jay said. "If we weren't in the fix, we're in, I'd work very hard to get her to come with us, right now." He paused, then, looking at me, said, "I don't know why; something seems familiar about her, as if I know parts of her story already, but that isn't possible." He shook his head and continued, "When we get back to civilization, I'm going to do my best to track this Saint Thomas guy or his sons, and we're going to have a serious conversation. She needs to be brought out of here and cared for. I don't remember my mother. My stepmother said she died in a fire when I was a baby. My father would not talk about it, and there weren't any pictures of her. My brother and I used to make up stories about what she looked like and what kind of person she might have been. Once, as a kid, I watched a documentary about Amelia Earhart and decided she was my mom, until my brother told me Miss Earhart crashed her airplane decades before I was born. All my life I've wished I could've known my mother. I can't imagine anyone abandoning their family like this, especially if they aren't well." He spoke evenly, but his eyes glinted with anger.

It struck me that the three of us, Belle, Jay, and I, lost a parent as children. Odd coincidence.

I put my hand on his chest, near his heart. "I'm sorry you lost your mother. It's hard to grow up and feel ok, with a parent missing. I feel sad for Wind Dancer, too, and just as soon as we get ourselves away from the people hunting us, I'll be glad to be a part of getting help for her."

By now the water in the cove across the bay was almost to the high tide mark, a natural line made along the shore by what the waves carried in.

"We should get going," I said, "It's high water. Time to head across Shelikof Strait."

We saw Wind Dancer bent beneath a handmade wooden yoke, carrying pails toward her home.

Jay hurried up to her, saying, "Thank you for the tea and letting us use your radio. Pointing at her buckets, he said, "I'll be glad to help you."

"I'm doing ok, Jay," she said, stopping and smiling up at him. "You do what you need to do with your friends, then come back."

He turned and ran toward the boat.

"I'm going to check the batteries," he said, as he hurried past. His face was ashen.

How does she know his name?

"Miz Wind Dancer," I said, walking up beside her, "Thank you for the tea. Your house is lovely. A work of art. We have to go now, but I'm already planning another visit with you, again."

"He loves you, Loren," the old woman said.

"Why did you call him, Jay?" My voice sounded tremulous.

She set her buckets down, slipped off the yoke, and reached out both hands. I hugged her. Pressed against me, her bones were fragile. Muscles in her arms felt like rubber bands. She smelled of spruce pitch and fireweed, smoke, and ocean air. We stood, wrapped around each other for longer than I had hugged anyone in years. She stepped back and said, "I used to call him Jay Bird."

"What are you saying?"

She smiled at me. Heartbreaking. It was one of the saddest I've ever seen.

"You go, now," she said, "Get help, and remember to work on releasing your anger and grief. I'll keep here, waiting."

"Take care," I breathed. I untied the boat and saw her waving her flag as we pulled away.

"I think I can get the radio going," Jay said. Belle was asleep in a bunk.

How and when do I tell Jay what the old woman said about him?

I pushed on the throttle, and the boat bounded ahead.

Time to make a run for it.

Once I got her up to speed, we zipped out of the bay and into the Shelikof. The windstorm had calmed with the tide. We headed across the Strait.

CHAPTER 32

I gillnetted with my husband for five years on a thirty-two-foot boat, like this one, so I felt confident in my ability to pilot it. I glanced over my shoulder, seeing the large reel loaded with what I guessed was about one hundred fifty fathoms, or 900 feet of fully hung, operational salmon net, and wondered again who this boat belonged to. Had the owner anchored it in the fiord and gone hunting, or had someone stolen it from Kodiak? Had anyone reported it missing?

After studying the chart and using the magnetic compass mounted beside the instrument panel, I headed toward Kodiak Island.

Trouble started when we were almost to the midway point. The breeze blustered, but the waves were manageable. No worry there, yet.

Jay poked his head out the cabin door and called, "Something's starting to smell like overheating down here. Check the temperature gauge for the engine, would you?"

Startled, I looked. There was no indication from the gauge that anything was malfunctioning. I tapped on the glass. No change.

"Nothing showing up here," I called back. "You want to come up and take the wheel while I check down there?"

"I'll keep watching down here for a bit. It might be nothing. Try the radio. I think I fixed that problem. If it works, call the Coast Guard. Also, we might be getting company."

"Company? Where?" My throat tightened. Looking around, I saw nothing but miles of rolling sea. Slowing the boat, I clicked the radio's "on" switch. A muted, scratchy noise, and it hummed to life. I picked up the microphone and found the boat's registration on the instrument panel.

A faded call list was stapled under a plastic sleeve near the steering wheel with a Coast Guard number near the top.

Hurrah, it works.

A crisp, female voice answered my call. I gave her our location, saying we urgently needed help; we were being hunted by pirates and dealing with mechanical problems. Jay vaulted up the short ladder, grabbed the mike from my hand, and hollered, "May Day, May Day," into it.

About then, I smelled smoke. Leaving him to transmit details, I scuttled down the ladder into the cabin. Belle stood spraying a fire extinguisher at flames in the hold near the bow. A wave shifted the boat sideways, taking her with it. She stumbled and fell. Coughing, I grabbed the extinguisher and raced forward, squeezing the lever. Fire retardant shot from the can. I moved closer and aimed at the blaze as black smoke roiled. The air in the narrow space was dense with chemicals, fumes, and smut. Belle was up and beside me with a blanket from a bunk clutched in her hands. She beat at the conflagration. My extinguisher emptied, but I could still see flames. Frenzied, I dropped it and spun around, looking for a bucket or any kind of container that would hold water. Jay jumped the three steps down into the cabin with another extinguisher.

"Get back," he yelled. I grabbed Belle, pulling her out of the way into the bunk area. Jay released the powdery contents. The fire died. The entire incident couldn't have taken five minutes, but as Belle and I emerged from the cabin, blackened and choking from the fumes and smoke, I felt like I'd been trying to hold my breath for an hour. She slumped to the deck. The boat had drifted crossways to the current and was being punished by the swell. Turning the wheel, I got the craft headed into the waves and used the compass to aim us toward Kodiak once more.

I tried the radio—no surprise when it wouldn't respond. Jay climbed to the bridge, and Belle moved back into the cabin to lie down.

"I sighted that boat off the stern again. Too far to see what it is, but you and Belle need to know there's something out there."

I sucked in my breath, but before I could say anything, he said, "An electrical short caused our fire, I think. Anyway, a lot of nasty smoke, but not a tremendous amount of damage. Nothing that'll sink us before we reach

Kodiak. Burnt the wires I used to hook up the radio, and wrecked wiring for the depth finder and radar. Could've been a disaster, but we're still afloat, and the Coast Guard know we need help, so that's something."

"Wonder how long it'll be until help gets here?" I cleared my throat; my voice sounded pinched. I turned, staring back over the stern.

Was there a boat back there? Was it coming after us?

Crap.

Something else I didn't want to think about, the weather: wind was picking up, waves were climbing higher, and as raindrops splatted onto the windshield, there was a flash of light off our port and behind us. Was that lightning or a boat's strobe? I'd noticed a pair of field glasses stowed in a pouch under the captain's seat. I pulled them out, hung on to the wheel with one hand, and began scanning. Nothing. Waves now big enough that we slid down their troughs and up their heights like an amusement park ride, except we weren't amused.

"Let me drive," he said. "You must be tired."

"I need to go check on Belle and find lifejackets." Rocking and rolling with the boat, I clung to anything I could hang on to—time to batten the hatches.

Belle sat on a bunk, clutching its metal frame. Under the soot from our firefight, her face was pinched with pain.

"It's getting bad out there, Lor," she said, "But I'm praying."

She hated rough water even more than I. We'd both experienced enough stormy seas to last a lifetime.

Apprehension gnawed me. "This isn't the book of John or something," I yelled.

I knew I was taking my fear out on her. "We won't see Jesus out there walking toward us on the water. We're in the middle of this mess, alone."

"Nope." Belle staggered upright and yelled right back at me, "I'm not alone. One of the bennies of becoming his child is his promise never to leave us. He's here, and I know if this little boat goes down, and the Coast Guard doesn't get to us in time, he'll be there with me, too, doing his own underwater rescue, taking me to heaven to be with him."

She sank back onto the narrow bed. My fright and irritation turned to worry as I looked at her drawn face and glassy eyes.

I felt her forehead, too warm.

"You sick or something?"

"It's the leg I injured in the explosion. It's hurting like the dickens."

Without asking, I wrapped an arm around the metal bed rail to steady myself, removed her boot, and pulled up the cuff of her pants. Her calf was swollen, and the torn, injured flesh looked shiny pink. A faint red streak traced upward an inch or two above the gash.

"Don't have my survival bag, anymore, no first aid supplies," she said sadly. "I had some antibiotics left over from when my dogs got the worst end of a porcupine encounter on our hike last summer."

"That's right, but sweetie," I said, "You're not a pooch."

"My vet friend, Carl, said it was penicillin, same thing doctors give to humans. Besides, it was just for serious survival emergencies. I need my survival bag."

"You know Jay got the radio running long enough for me to call the Coast Guard? They should be here, soon. Meanwhile, let's get these lifejackets on, and I'll look around and see if I can find a first aid kit."

I searched through the messy cabin but didn't even find a Band-Aid.

Jay yelled.

As I stumbled onto deck, bringing his life vest with me, I saw him pointing at something off our stern.

A big, blocky, seiner plowed through the waves, heading in our direction. I scrambled up onto the bridge and grabbed the binoculars again. Behind us, the boat's powerful searchlight sliced through the fog.

"It's the *ViKing Revenge*," Jay said.

"We're in trouble," I quavered.

Despair drenched me. I sagged to the deck.

Crap, crap, crap. We can't get away. We're going to die for nothing, I won't see my boys getting married, no more making art, Belle won't get to watch her son graduate, I won't ever have a real date with Jay.

Something white-hot sizzled inside me, sparking one intimidated nerve after another, channeling a firestorm of determination.

A boat full of bullies coming to capture or kill us, for what? Because they thought they could. In fact, they controlled our entire lives for the past several days. We'd spent hours trying to deal with thugs who subjected us to their tyrannical demands.

We didn't ask for this, and I will not lie down and take it.

"I'm so done with these guys," I said, grabbing the railing and springing to my feet. Anger crackled inside me; I felt strangely energized. "If we have to set this boat afire and burn it down to the water to keep them off us, let's do it. I've had enough. I want to fight back."

Jay gave me a long, appraising look, smiled grimly, and said, "Yes, ma'am."

"First order of business," he continued, strapping on the life preserver. "Take stock of anything and everything we can turn into a weapon. Next, fortify our defenses. After that, make battle plans."

Back in the cabin, I saw Belle curled on the bunk. She appeared to be asleep, until I called her name. She sat up.

"It's the *ViKing Revenge*. It's coming after us, and I am not going quietly, my friend."

"Right," she said, "It's the principle of the thing. I'm with you. I don't want to go, quietly, either. How can I help?"

We were so busy in the next several minutes searching through the cabin, under the bunks, and in the hold, I hadn't noticed the wind lessening. Not even close to calm, but we weren't doing the roller coaster thing, anymore.

We drug out two, very sharp, fish filleting knives, three rolls of duct tape, one full fire extinguisher, six long coils of rope of various thicknesses, an empty wine bottle, an expensive, self-inflating, rubber raft, and four flare guns with six cartridges each.

We piled our finds on the cabin floor.

As the wind calmed, Jay increased our speed. The larger, less stream-lined *ViKing Revenge* labored through the swells, so it was still a substantial distance behind us. Coast Guard might reach us in time. I told Jay we piled the items we found on the cabin floor.

He turned the wheel over to me, went below, and pulled all the hold covers off, placing them port and starboard as barriers to bullets; using yards of duct tape to help keep them in place.

Belle duct-taped one filet knife to the handle of a broom and set the other where we could reach it.

No Coast Guard in sight. The *ViKing Revenge* steadily grew nearer, still out of accurate gun range, but it wouldn't be long before they'd close that distance.

Belle stepped onto the bridge, claiming she was feeling better. Her slow movements and pale, sweaty face made me doubt, but I said nothing.

Jay suggested we have a quick tailboard and discuss strategy in case the Coast Guard didn't get to us by the time the *ViKing Revenge* drove within shooting range. We made our battle plans. Jay and Belle climbed back off the bridge and, loosening coils of the rope we'd found, tied them to the net in several places. To help make the net less visible, Jay cut the buoys off the end. He pulled several yards of web from the loaded reel at my instruction and piled it on deck at the stern.

I loaded the flare guns and placed the extra cartridges within easy reach.

By now, the rain had stopped, and mushy haze settled so thickly over the water I could no longer see the big boat stalking us.

Unsure which direction to go, I relied on the compass. With the fog came more placid seas, so I ran the engine as hard as I dared.

The mist lifted as rain sputtered again. It was now full dark. Cresting a wave, we saw the lights of the *ViKing Revenge* behind us. Much closer and gaining every minute. There were two men on deck, and I wondered how many more, below. Fear bit at me, threatening to strangle my resolve.

We had two rifles, a pistol, revolver, and a minimal amount of ammunition. Yes, we had flare guns and a bayonet-like weapon made from a broom handle, but seriously? We were three people, one injured, in a fish boat. Outnumbered and outgunned.

I've got to stay focused. We've got a plan, and we've got our wits. This is about surviving until the Coast Guard arrives.

Jay said, "We need to operate the boat from inside, now. They're almost close enough to start firing."

Belle climbed down and began steering from inside the cabin. Before Jay and I followed her, we unlocked the large net reel, thankful darkness covered our movements.

The boat, closing in, repeatedly blasted an air horn as if to trumpet its superior size and power. Inside, Jay pushed up a hatch near the cabin door and, keeping hidden, reported the seiner's movements. We would first work at outmaneuvering it, to buy time, knowing the bigger boat could not turn as sharp as ours.

Gunfire. Bullets smacked into our craft.

"Go left," Jay instructed.

Belle yanked the wheel.

"Now right," he said.

Back and forth we careened, bouncing and bobbing. Outside, wood and fiberglass cracked and clattered onto the deck.

CHAPTER 33

"Blew the top off our mast," Jay reported. "Keep our speed up. We'll keep dancing with 'em."

"Why haven't they unloaded on us, yet?" I asked to no one in particular, as we see-sawed through the waves.

"Maybe they've been ordered to bring us back to Vlodir," Jay said.

So, he can kill us.

"Now," I said to Belle, after we watched the bigger boat for a few more minutes, "Slow her down, but turn left and then right in a wide zigzag. It's time for the net trick."

Jay and I continued to guide Belle as we allowed the bigger boat to gain on us, bringing it into position.

We crawled back on deck again. I crouched, remaining hidden, ready at the port side of the reel. Jay threw the pile of net over the roller on the stern where it slid into the ocean behind us, then he moved forward, grabbed the starboard side of the reel, and we spun it together, watching it release streaming yards of webbing over the stern and into the water. As the reel turned faster and faster, the net unwound into the sea where it trailed, nearly invisible in the darkness. We crept back into the relative safety of the cabin and watched the fathoms of nylon web, cork line, lead line, and yards of tangled rope snaking out into the waves, becoming a shape that curved back and forth in sweeping undulations behind us. The weight of the net in the water slowed our boat. The *ViKing Revenge* grew closer by the second.

"If there are commercial fishermen on that boat, they'll catch on to what we're trying to do," Belle said anxiously.

With everything in me, I hope not. This net trick will be our only chance to get away.

My legs shook. Jay held the filet knife in one hand and a flare gun in another.

Staring through the crack in the hatch, we could see the boat increase speed. They seemed intent on crushing our little craft.

We could do nothing but wait, watch, listen, and hope. The fifty-eight-foot seiner barreled toward us, not slowing down, engine roaring, cutting a swath of foam and spray.

Watching for the exact moment, there! Back up and out of the cabin, Jay raced. With the filet knife, he feverishly sawed through the backer rope that kept the end of the net tied to the boat. Bullets whistled over us, a few striking the bridge. Jay cut through just as the reel emptied. The rest of the net disappeared into the waves behind us, about the same time the *ViKing Revenge* ran over the other end. The men running the seiner were obviously not fishermen.

"Go," I yelled to Belle, as Jay crashed back into the cabin.

She shoved the throttle all the way forward, and our little boat bounded ahead. We grabbed for a handhold, unable to take our eyes off the craft looming in our wake.

At first, we saw nothing, heard nothing. We bounced, our boat rising and pounding onto the waves as we ran before the seiner.

Then, cacophony. Over the sounds from our boat, over the wind and rain, over the crashing waves, came the high, howling, protest of a big, powerful diesel, strangling. Yards of gill net and wads of rope wrapped, twisted, and tangled around a massive prop and keel as the heavy craft drove forward. Bearing down upon us, the seiner roared like a monster. The noise changed from bellowing to grumbles, and the diesel stalled.

The ignoramus driving the *ViKing Revenge* restarted the engine, throwing the transmission back into gear, which is about the worst thing you can do when your prop and keel are net wrapped.

Again, it thundered to life. Shifting light over their deck showed a cloud of oily smoke. It appeared the driver was attempting to force the crippled boat into reverse. A strange whistling, followed by mechanical growls and groans echoed across the waves, and their engine stopped again.

About that time, I realized we weren't moving forward, either. And just like that, our engine made a small, almost apologetic cough and died.

Their motor came to life, one last agonized time, and the racket was unearthly. A howling, squealing mechanical ogre dying, spewing smoke, ripping and tearing itself to pieces. Silence.

The three of us worked feverishly, trying to start our engine.

After long, panic-driven seconds of checking connections, pushing on this and pulling on that, I rapped on the glass cover of the fuel gauge. Still aimed at full. Why hadn't I noticed? The pointer didn't budge.

"The gauge isn't working," I shouted. "I think we're out of diesel."

"We're going to need to figure this out, pretty quick," Belle said, peering through the hatch. "I see two guys in an Achilles inflatable heading for us."

Jay lugged a plastic fuel container from the fo's'cle.

"I'm betting you have an idea how to get us running, again," he said. "Let me know if there's something I can do; otherwise, I'll hold them off while you work your magic." He smiled.

How can he be so relaxed?

I said, "Can't get back to the fuel tanks with bullets flying around, so we're going to have to rig something else. Lucky the engine on this old thing is the same as the engine on the first boat Brad and I fished, a 3208 Cat. I might be able to fix our problem. Drag the can to the rear of the cabin, and I'll get started."

Still watching through the hatch, Belle said, "That inflatable is getting closer all the time."

"Be right with you, Belle," Jay called, as he tugged the container over to where I pointed.

My legs stopped trembling as I concentrated on the task at hand. Here was a problem I knew something about.

I used the filet knife to cut the fuel line where it came from the big tank in the hold, making as much hose available as I could. I braced the full jug so it couldn't tip over and shoved the end of the hose down into the fuel. This unwieldy container was now our tank. I needed a crescent wrench and remembered seeing a toolbox under the sink. I yanked it out just as the shooting started in earnest. Bullets strafed our bridge and thwacked into our boat. I ducked.

"The guys on the seiner are trying to cover the raft so they can board us," Jay said.

"Shoot?" Belle yelled.

"Need to conserve our ammo, wait'll I say," Jay replied.

I removed two wrenches from the box. The boat rose and fell as I stumbled toward the engine.

I've got to fix this. Please help me, God.

I cracked three injector lines open with the larger wrench. Moved around to the front of the engine and grabbed the hand pump located on the fuel filter assembly. I maniacally worked the pump, noticing, a positive sign; it became more difficult to manipulate as it filled with fluid. I moved back to the injection lines, seeing bubbles form where I had opened them. So far, so good. Soon fuel leaked out.

"You hit the inflatable," Belle shouted.

"Looks like that third flare set it on fire," Jay said.

More bullets hit the cabin. A Plexiglass window burst inward. I turned around as pieces sprayed into the galley, one narrowly missing Jay.

"Stay as low as you can," he called.

"They've put another inflatable in the water," Belle said.

Jay fired off another flare. I tightened the injector lines, worked the pump a few more turns, and made sure the pump knob was screwed down tight. I knew I didn't have to bleed the injector lines on all the cylinders to restart it. It was time to get going.

Men fired from the second inflatable, but with constantly shifting waves, most bullets were going wide.

I cranked the engine. It started, sounding timid. It wasn't going to produce much power until the other five cylinders pumped air from the rest of the injector lines, and I worried, knowing that would take precious moments.

More bullets smacked us. I felt a sharp sting as a chip of wood grazed my neck.

The engine picked up more rpm, sounding gradually stronger, letting me know the air was almost out of the lines.

"Now," Jay called, and rifle shots boomed through the cabin.

"Got him," Belle yelled.

Another volley of bullets came at us. One zipped between the boards shattering a window, and another thwacked into the pilot's chair where I worked. Shards scattered.

I waited, tense, as our diesel picked up a few more cylinders. Our engine was running and coming up to speed, ready to move us forward, but now we had another problem.

I saw green boots on the gangway ledge to the right of me in front of the broken cabin window. Someone was on our boat. The second they passed, I peeked out. Another inflatable had somehow circled us and was right up against our starboard side. Two men climbed onto our deck. We had three bad guys on board, plus two more in an inflatable that Jay and Belle were holding off. The one in green boots was out there close to my window, but I couldn't see him anymore.

"Good shot," Belle hollered, "Second inflatable on fire."

Green Boots was coming back. I grabbed the makeshift bayonet and shoved with all my strength out the broken window, at the same time, yelling, "Hang on," to Belle and Jay. I juiced the throttle, jamming it forward, and spun the steering wheel.

Green Boots yelled, wrenched his foot away, lost his balance, and fell off our bow into the ocean.

Two burning inflatables, four men floundering or dead in the ocean, and two bad guys on our boat by the time we got moving.

Grabbing a flare gun, I hunkered behind the wooden protection Jay had put up, my heart thrumming like a rock-n-roll drum. Knew I was steering erratically, but I couldn't do any better one-handed while loading flares. I could barely see through the boards that blocked the windows, and wondered how Jay and Belle could hit anything, hampered as they were.

I glimpsed the stern end of the *ViKing Revenge* as we tore by. It sat much lower in the water. Flames bloomed at its stern. Was it sinking?

"The rats on deck will be through our door in no time," Belle said. Her voice sounded far away.

"Stop driving, Loren. You and Belle need to move into the bow in front of the engine, now," Jay yelled as he crouched, reloading.

I turned with my flare gun, hollering, "You first," just as they blew the door open.

Jay was near the floor; Belle was in the bunk area, but I looked straight at the space where the cabin door had stood one second earlier. A hulking man shape filled the opening. I fired.

I don't think the instructions on the flare gun package recommend this.

I'm still not sure how it worked, whether the flare blew through the man, or what happened, exactly, but it exploded around him, or in him, and bright white sparks and fluorescent orange and green glittery lights spun and twirled into the night as he disappeared, shrieking, over the side of the boat.

In a movie, this is where there would be an ever so slight pause, as the audience was given a second to appreciate the special effects. That flare exploding was almost beautiful, in a horrifying way. Maybe it's because I'm a painter and fascinated by light and color; but I was momentarily transfixed.

The bad guy that took his place was not. Aimed right at me, his pistol boomed twice as I flung myself against the cabin wall, and Belle jumped in front of me. Then Jay rammed the shooter.

I was on the floor of the cabin. Belle lay across me. I could make out shapes, two men, fighting.

The shooter, no gun now, kicks out at Jay. Jay, twisting away, lands a roundhouse to the guy's face. Shooter kicks Jay backward onto the deck. Jay tumbles into the hold, jumps up, grabs the shooter, rotates his leg, and sends him sprawling into the cabin. A wave rocks the boat, and Jay loses his balance on the cabin stairs. The shooter, up again, now on top, head butts Jay's face. His hands now squeezing Jay's throat. Jay's legs somehow coming up, knocking him aside. Jay, again bouncing to his feet like a cat, delivers a kick to the man's head that sends him cracking onto the stairs with his neck at an odd angle. The bad guy goes still as a mannequin.

Jay, face bloody, leaning over Belle and me, calling our names, did he say, "Loren, honey?" His voice fading away.

I try to speak her name, but nothing will come out. My voice will not work. "Belle? Belle?"

Pain, a sledgehammer, pounding, pounding. Murmurs, voices, quiet, darkness. Faint electronic sounds, a repetitive beeping.

As my brain focused, I looked around, realizing I was in a hospital room, tubes and wires running everywhere.

Bandages here, bandages there, with the smell of disinfectant layered over everything. I couldn't make any sense of it. As I tried to figure out where I was, a man dressed in scrubs entered my room.

"I'm Lanny, your nurse," he said. "Let's see how you're doing."

He looked mid-twenties, with short blond hair and a faint blue rose tattoo on his forearm.

"Full name and date of birth," he asked, lifting my left arm and examining the cast and gauze swathing my hand and wrist. He touched something painful, high on my shoulder. "Where do you live, and what day is it?"

I got all the answers right, except for the day. My turn to ask questions, "Where am I? Where's Belle and Jay?"

"Doc will be in soon, and you can talk with her."

He turned out the light and left.

I slept.

Minutes or hours later, a slight noise. I came awake, heart thumping. Where was I?

CHAPTER 34

Awoman walked in, brisk, businesslike, short gray hair, surgical mask over her tanned features, wearing a white coat over a blue coverall type uniform.

Mask off, she said, "I'm Doctor Pelkie. Let's talk about your injuries."

I pulled myself to a sitting position, feeling slow, old, and exhausted.

She lifted a chart off a clip on my bed, sat on a metal chair as she flipped through it, saying, "You were shot through the left hand and shoulder." Her voice was severe, almost accusatory.

Somewhere inside my brain, I protested, *hey, this isn't my fault.*

I was too groggy to speak, so I remained mute, listening to her list my medical issues.

"Let's see—surgery on your left hand. The bullet entered through your palm, ripping it apart. Apparently, you held your hand up, somehow, because the bullet that went through it buried in your left shoulder. We removed it, of course. You have damaged muscle and ligaments in your shoulder, which should heal well with therapy. It looks like there was prior injury to that shoulder, a dislocation there. The hand is the real problem. Getting it well will take a lot more time; you'll probably need more surgery and lots of physical therapy."

That sounded dismal. I lifted my arm, staring at the cast.

"We removed some Plexiglass bits from your back and sewed up a cut on your left arm. We noticed half-healed burns on your hands and a few areas on your head with missing hair. X-rays show a broken bone, er, cuboid on your right foot."

"Questions?" she asked briskly, writing on a chart.

"Where are Belle and Jay?"

"Lieutenant Colonel Carrel needed his thigh wound dressed. He had a short surgery with stitches put in the muscles surrounding his puncture. We gave him antibiotics, and he is sleeping off a sedative."

"How's Belle? When can I see her?"

"Melody Belle Engiak is in a coma. Gunshot wound to her head. She's in critical condition."

I couldn't get my breath.

Belle deliberately jumped in front of me. She took my bullet.

Tears blinded me. Reaching for the edge of the blanket, I wiped my eyes.

"Your friend sustained a life-threatening gunshot injury. She has one broken and two cracked ribs, torn muscle from an older bullet injury to her lower right leg, and an infected gash on her left calf. She's a fighter, however, and we'll hope for the best."

"I've got to go to her."

I was halfway out of bed, looking for something I could throw on. My face must have shown my distress, because the doctor's voice softened, not quite so clipped and formal as she said, "You need to stay in bed for now." She looked at me, "Do you know where you are?

I looked around. Palest grey green paint on all surfaces.

Do the walls curve near their top, or is that residual effects from whatever meds they gave me? I'm guessing military.

"You're in a US Navy submarine," Dr. Pelkie said, not waiting for my response. "We're transporting you to a hospital in Anchorage. You'll be able to contact family from there. Ms. Engiak will be flown to Virginia Mason Medical Center in Seattle."

"What about Jay?"

"He will leave for Washington. Coast Guard has a helicopter on its way now to pick him up."

"Can I see him before he leaves?"

"I'll see if he's awake."

"Are we under water, right now?"

"No."

Dr. Pelkie's professional briskness had returned. She said, "Try to rest," and walked toward the door.

"I want to see my friend, Belle," I called after her. My voice sounded scratchy.

She turned, smiling, "That's not possible right now, but I'm sure you'll see her soon."

The doctor was wrong.

I slept.

Man's voice speaking. The aroma of food, something with tomato and garlic.

I opened my eyes. Jay was passing a covered dish in front of my face and calling my name.

"Do I need to yodel to get you to wake up?" His smile brightened the room.

He set a tray on my lap and opened the container. Steam from lasagna warmed my face.

"Have you eaten?"

"A few minutes ago," he replied, sitting on the metal chair. He was in clean clothes, tan button-down shirt, and baggy khaki pants.

I slid the lasagna to the other side of the tray. No way I could swallow around the knot of dread in my throat.

"Please tell me what you know about Belle." My voice quavered, but I didn't care.

He leaned toward me, eyes kind. "Doc told you she's in a coma, right?"

I nodded.

"They will fly her to Virginia Mason to deal with her head injury. We won't know how severe the problem is for a while. She'll need more tests. They've got her stabilized, but she needs brain surgery, and they did not equip this sub to deal with high tech, micro procedures, or long-term recovery issues."

"I'm so worried she may never get…" I stopped, leaned back on the pillow, and covered my face with my hands. I sobbed.

Jay stood and wrapped his arms around me.

"She'll be under expert medical care. I know the doctors will do everything they can to help her get well."

"Dr. Pelkie said a helicopter will be here soon, for you."

"I'll fly to Elmendorf Airforce Base, then on to DC. I need to report. There's a lot of work to do, down there. This missile situation has been a fiasco. It'll take months to get everything sorted."

Should I ask if I'll ever see him, again?

I decided on a safer topic. "Last I saw, you were all over the boat fighting the big Russian that shot Belle and me."

"Let's just say he didn't make it."

"What about the *ViKing Revenge?*"

"They got the injured young man off it, just before it sank."

After a moment, I asked, "What happened to the fish boat we were on?"

"Coast Guard was towing it to Kodiak, last I heard. I'm sure they'll try to find the owner."

Someone stuck their head in the door and said, "Lieutenant Colonel Carrel, your chopper's landed."

Jay kissed my forehead and ran his fingers down my face.

"Don't forget me, Loren. Get all healed up. I'll be back."

He rushed through the door, then returned just as suddenly.

"When Belle wakes up, let her know the Coast Guard found her brother trying to escape with what they called a 'big floating packet.' They hauled him aboard and searched him and the bag. They found a wallet and cell phone inside with Belle's name. There were two kilos of cocaine as well, with Cody's fingerprints all over them. Coast Guard said he had hyperthermia, and the only thing that saved him was someone noticed the bright red sack bobbing on the waves. He's got partially amputated fingers, said some guy started chopping on them. He confessed to stealing the cocaine and asked to be taken to rehab. Anyway, he's going to jail. I spilled the beans on his recent activities."

Cody's still alive because he had his sister's "Santa sack." Belle saved him, once again, and he'll live, while she's in a coma, fighting for her life. Inexplicable.

"Jay, I know you'll be crazy busy; but please don't forget Wind Dancer. Now's not the time, but at some point, we'll need to discuss her situation. I can't stand to think of that old woman out there, alone."

"I won't forget," Jay said. "I'll keep you posted. Meanwhile, you get well."

He kissed me, again, his lips on mine this time, warm with promise.

"I really need to see, Belle, Jay."

"You will soon, I'm sure."

But Jay was wrong, too.

Six months after that August event, my life was more or less back to normal. I stood in front of my living room window watching snow fall in late February. After my adventure and accident, my boys left their jobs, studies, and girlfriends, and flew home, one at a time, where they drove me to physical therapy, cooked, managed my chores, hung my art show, and did everything they could think of to make my life easier. We had real, live, enjoyable conversations; and managed it without emojis. Reading, drinking tea, and watching the many birds crowding my feeders was my main activity for a while, but I gradually got up and around and back into life.

My elderly friend from the library, Jess, brought me a Bible. Surprising myself, I read a few chapters every morning. After three surgeries, two stainless steel pins, and hours of painful exercises, my left hand was somewhat curled and stiff, but doing well enough. My foot healed almost good as new, my burns didn't leave deep scars, and my hair grew in again. I began painting, working on an ocean wave series, entitled "Storms."

One Monday morning, I got a phone call from the Homer police station asking me to stop by their office to talk with someone from D.C. about my "experience" the previous August.

An unsmiling Chief Harvin introduced me to three official-looking men sitting around a table in a private room. He led me to an empty chair and left.

Two of the men were from the Department of Homeland Security, and the other was FBI. After asking my name, where I lived, and what kind of art I made, they spent the next three hours impressing on me the advisability of my complete silence, warning me of my patriotic duty, and hinting of embarrassment and more that could fall upon me, if I were to talk about my experiences from the previous summer. The more they talked, the more I realized the level of chagrin, confusion, and panic, government heads must be suffering over Charlene Chametz's treachery and the missile debacle. The more they lectured, the less I believed them. They had already circulated the "official" story about a gas leak explosion, head injury, and drunk hunters and wanted me to agree to stick to their script. What they weren't saying, what few of any rank or responsibility was ever going to admit: how vulnerable we, in these great United States really are. Nor would they talk about the fact that there are citizens of our country energetically working for the downfall of the U.S., some of these in leadership positions, some elected officials. No, this "mix-up," as they called it, this hacking into our military's computers was "an anomaly" and "entirely unprecedented." My patriotic duty, they repeated, was silence.

"I'd like to ask something," I said, as the session ended, and the men stood, gathering their briefcases and coats.

"Were all the bad guys rounded up?"

The three men glanced at each other and away. Mr. FBI got very busy shuffling papers, and one of the Homeland Security employees walked toward the door as if I hadn't spoken. The other, Mr. Barnes, paused, giving me a toothy smile. With his closely spaced eyes and prominent canines, he had a decidedly predatory look.

"Yes," he said, "The ones that weren't already neutralized we took into custody. Glad to report that's all over. You can go back and make your nice little paintings with no worries."

I left the police station, shut my car door too hard, and tore out of the parking lot.

Go back and make my nice little paintings? How patronizing can they get? A lot of official lying going on.

I wondered if they'd visited Belle with their veiled threats, bland expressions, and plastic smiles.

Not wanting to take my anger home, I drove down to the spit. This narrow gravel finger sticks about four and a half miles out into Kachemak Bay and has a harbor where work and pleasure boats hide out from bad weather or tie up until taken out next time. The spit is also where tourists flock in spring and summer for souvenirs, fishing charters, food, and entertainment.

I carried a camera in my car and decided to take a walk on the floating docks between the boats. I thought I might get a few picturesque photos of snow piled on commercial fish tenders or landing craft.

The end of the spit was busy, nothing unusual, boats being repaired, fresh catch unloading at the dock, business transacted. I ambled along, enjoying the sights, my winter coat keeping the damp breeze away. As the late February sun disappeared, I shot a variety: buoy laden scows, working people, a toddler holding a small dog, and a crabby sea lion.

Later, in my studio, I transferred the photos from my camera to my laptop and, going through each, searched for images I could turn into a painting.

A picture of six men backlit by the setting sun caught my attention. The dazzling light against their dark silhouetted shapes attracted me. All the men were in natural poses, backs to me, struggling to unload crab pots. All of them, but one. It was so bright I hadn't noticed him when I hurriedly snapped the picture. I hadn't wanted to hang around and get in their way as they worked.

I zoomed in on the guy. Stocky, not young, heavily bearded, he was bundled in a heavy coat with a thick, toboggan-type hat pulled low on his forehead.

His face. What was the deal with his eyes? I couldn't look away.

When I zoomed in further, the picture became too blurry to see more detail. I zoomed back out to where the photo seemed clear. That man's expression: he was staring death rays straight at me. Just the light, I decided, feeling suddenly chilled. I clicked on the next photograph.

Each month I received an email from Jay. He wrote he'd been able to help Wind Dancer move to senior housing near Kenai. They staffed the facility with dedicated professionals who provided excellent mental health help. He was still searching for her husband and family. In every email, Jay asked how I was doing but never volunteered much about himself. I had no idea where he was. He seemed busy, distracted, and very far away. Our short-lived relationship, if I could call it that, had helped us get through those tortuous days, but not much more. I followed his lead and kept my replies short and newsy, nothing personal.

I miss him, but I don't really know him, and I'm not going to offer my heart to some distant man any more than I'm going to set a newborn husky pup out in a snowbank.

CHAPTER 35

Eight months after the August event, mid-April, my anxiety attacks were worse. My elderly friend Jess moved to Florida to be with her daughter, I quit my volunteer job at the library. I was still painting my way through my "Storm" series. My paintings were neither "little" nor "nice," but making them seemed to be what I needed to do.

I began attending a series of art events at Homer's high school theatre. The songs, drama, and funny stories distracted me, helped me forget. After the show one evening, the director tried to enlist me as their next speaker. By the time I, with mumbled excuses, extricated myself and left, everyone else was gone, the parking lot empty. In the blurry evening light, a man hunched in the shadows against the side of the building. He didn't move as I hurried past. I couldn't see his face, but I shivered, sure his eyes were following me.

I didn't attend any more art happenings.

In May, nine months after the August misadventure, with dreams of explosions and flying body parts playing like horror movies in my head night after night, I sought help from Dolly, a professional counselor.

Dolly was a superb listener. She didn't speak a lot, but what she said carried the strength of experience, wisdom, and kindness. I was eaten with guilt over Belle taking that bullet meant for me. Most of my social connections were shut down, and I had begun to believe someone was watching or following me. I stayed at home more and more.

Belle was still in Seattle, working her way through rehabilitation. I hadn't seen her in almost a year. She was getting better, she assured me, but it was a slow process. She was excited about each improvement and was currently thrilled she didn't need to use a walker, anymore. Her son, Jake, was there, finishing the school year, helping her, and enjoying city life. Refusing to let me visit, she said she wanted a painting or two that I had done while she recuperated. Belle was cheerful on the phone, but when tired, her sentences sometimes came out garbled. After hearing her stutter and forget her words through a conversation describing Cody's legal battles, I dropped out of counseling, sick with remorse.

But the dreams plagued me. I asked if I could come back.

"Of course," Dolly said. "Come on, already."

My first session back, it came pouring out—months of bottled regret. I hadn't been able to admit my guilty feelings, even to myself.

"Can you write me a prescription for some kind of sleep aid?"

Dolly's eyes softened. "I can write you one for about three weeks, but it won't take the place of working through your anxieties."

I took one pill that night and slept like a rock. However, I still had bad dreams, so I put the pills in my medicine cabinet and decided to keep plugging away at the counseling. Next time, I was the one asking Dolly to pray for me. After subsequent visits with her, I began to feel less apprehensive.

I stayed home most of June, painted and did yard work, driving to town for my counselling sessions or when I needed groceries or picked up my mail.

By late July, my fear induced attacks were almost gone. One Friday afternoon, I hopped aboard a vintage, recommissioned sailboat with artist friends. We were pushed by a jaunty breeze across Kachemak Bay to Halibut Cove, where we spent the evening enjoying live music and a lovely dinner. We rode back, sunset colors in our eyes, feeling the bliss. Relaxed and happy after my outing, I walked through my front door, locked it, and headed into the kitchen for some ginger kombucha.

Relaxed and happy, that is, until I saw the blocky male installed brazenly at my dining room table. The guy whose eyes contained all the kindness of frost-covered nail heads. The man with the devil horn.

His thick lips pulled taut in a smile that looked as inviting as the edge of a bloody skinning knife.

Crap and double crap.

Paralyzed, my mouth dry, I wondered fleetingly how I could be sweating and feeling icy cold at the same time.

Why isn't he dead or in jail?

The man glaring at me in the harbor photo. The man skulking in the shadows outside the school. Vlodir Rafenski, Russian military official with whom our Secretary of State committed high treason. Vlodir, the Russian general who called me "rabbit," shook me like a rag doll, then dropped me on the floor. That big-league bad guy who tried to fire off one of our missiles but failed.

He's probably not in the best of moods. I'll bet he can't go back to Russia, and he won't want to be discovered in the US, so what's his plan?

"What do you want?" My voice sounded steady. That was kind of amazing because every muscle in my entire body under my second hand, embroidered, purple, earth mother, hippie dress was sucked up tight, and vibrating like a new strung violin.

"I want you to drive me into Canada."

"If I won't?"

"I will kill you."

"Why don't you drive yourself?"

"I can't drive a car and hike across the border, same time. I need a driver and a car. You're my driver. Sit here." He pointed imperiously to a chair, my chair, like it was his. "Listen."

I was sure he had several ways he could kill me, right there. I sat. It didn't take long for me to ascertain what he wanted. It was illegal, of course, and dangerous, but had been done before. He said I was to drive within a couple miles of the US/Canada border and let him out. He would hike in a roundabout way through the forest and sneak across an unguarded part of the border. I would cross in my car with my passport, my paperwork, everything legitimate and legal, then wait for him about three miles into Canada along the highway. Drive to somewhere near Whitehorse and drop him off. He said he had people waiting for him.

He'll kill me when he's done with me. Once in Canada, I'm pretty much dead.

"Look," I said, stalling, "People will miss me, people will know I'm gone."

"No, Loren, they won't. You do nothing. You stay home for days on end, you never see friends, there's no one around, no family, no husband, no lover. No one to miss you when you're gone."

How does he know my name?

"You don't know my life," I sputtered.

"I've been waiting here since last October, fitting in, making friends, watching you, asking about you. This is such a small town. You go nowhere; you do nothing. Who care if you drive to Canada?"

"I have family," I insisted, indignantly. "They care about me. And, yes, I do all kinds of things. I'm an artist. I make art. I finished six paintings last winter."

Why am I defending myself to this demon?

He leaped from the chair, knocking it over, blaring, "You are nothing, Rabbit. You smear paint on canvas. I make war, I make governments rise or fall."

At that point, I should have shut up, but, well, I didn't. I gulped a big swig of my fermented tea. "If you're so important, Vlodir," I shouted, standing up and pointing my finger like a weapon at his rage-splotched face, "Why are you the one running and hiding like a rabbit? Why aren't you in Russia, making governments rise and fall?"

Crap. Shouldn't have said that.

He lunged. My drink went flying. I darted around the end of the table.

He stopped and glared at me; I glared right back. I actually think I bared my teeth. His laughter, which was much scarier than his yelling, sounded like a garbage disposal grinding through a glass jar.

"I guess you're a rabbit that fights, eh?"

"Look," I said, remembering Belle's 'sooth the savage' tone, and borrowing it, "I will drive you to Canada, but I've got to get cash from the bank and let a friend know I'm taking a short trip, so she won't get worried."

"No phone calls," Vlodir said. "Also, you will leave your cell phone here."

"I will email her. You can read the email. She expects me to email her every day, and if I don't, she might send police."

"Who is this person?"

"My friend, Belle, who was with me at the lodge. They shot her in the head, and she is in Seattle, recuperating."

"Another stupid woman, she is nothing, who care? Write email. Then we go."

"I need to wait until the bank opens tomorrow, so I can get cash."

"No, we go tonight. You write email, I watch."

I wrote:

Dear Melody Belle,
(I hoped the formal greeting and use of her first name would get her attention.)
I boated to Halibut Cove to help at an art fundraising clam dinner tonight. The chef is a devil, he steamed the clams in dirty seaweed. Please ask John Paul to help us by firing that chef. You must remember digging clams on our 4th-grade class field trip, where we filled the bully's pants with seaweed. Won't write for a few days. Taking a car trip. Remember to tell John Paul.
Love, Loren.

Vlodir hung over my shoulder, breathing down my neck. He stunk. He read my email aloud in a singsong, mocking manner.

"'Pants filled with seaweed,' very stupid letter, but no surprise, you can send."

I sent the email.

"Time to go," he said.

"I need to get my passport and pack."

"I need to follow you and watch. You try nothing," he said.

Up the stairs we trooped. I grabbed an overnight bag, took my passport from a drawer, pulled on jeans under my flowing dress, and, turning my back, flipped it over my head and wriggled into a long baggy top, not caring if he was watching or not. I shoved my feet into socks and hiking shoes and hurried into the bathroom. Vlodir pushed in behind me.

"Pretty nice house you live in, Rabbit," he said.

I said nothing, opening the cabinet over the sink. I was just about to grab my toothbrush when I saw the sleeping pills Dolly had prescribed for me.

Turning, I said, "I need to use the lavatory before we go; you can see I have no weapon; please let me have a moment of privacy."

His expression was ugly as he backed out of the bathroom. "At lodge, I gave you time, and you cheated me and ran off. Now you have one minute."

I did what I needed to do, flushed the commode, and under cover of the noise, grabbed the pills, dumping them out of their container into a pocket on my tunic.

We headed north. I used a credit card and filled my car at a gas station in Ninilchik, hoping to see someone I could signal for help. The little town was quiet. Soldotna was asleep as well, and there was almost no traffic, coming or going. The Russian scanned the road. He watched every car going by and every move I made. I suspected he had a gun. There were no words between us. I tried to come up with conversation, anything that might make him see me as human, until he told me rabbits don't talk, and to shut my mouth.

The early morning summer sun was lighting the sky, when bleary and dry-mouthed, I said I needed to stop for coffee and a restroom break.

Vlodir said, "Pay attention, Rabbit. You try something; I shoot you and many others."

He has a gun.

I pulled into Wild Harry's in Cooper Landing. Four a.m., but the place bustled with sport anglers buying lattes and doughnuts before they headed to the Russian River to fish for salmon. I visited the restroom. Vlodir followed and would have entered behind me, except some hefty woman pushed past him, chiding, "This is 'Ladies,' can't you read?"

I had no chance to say anything, because she turned and left almost as soon as she entered, smacking him with the door. He cursed. I reached into my pocket, crushing sleeping pills between my fingers, rushed out, and got in line for our coffee.

With his hat jammed down to his eyebrows, his scruffy beard and wild expression, Vlodir didn't look much different from some of the combat fishermen grabbing morning snacks around us. He pressed right up against me, and his fingers dug into my arm. I paid for our coffee using my card. I hoped to be given a paper receipt I had to sign, so I could put an S.O.S. on it, but Harry's credit card machine, was the no signature needed, type.

Had Belle gotten my email? It was a long shot, but I hoped she was well enough to remember the childish codeword, "seaweed," we'd created way back in fourth grade, which was our signal to one another we needed help.

On the highway once more, we drank our coffee—more silence. Several miles up the road, Vlodir told me to pull over. I hoped he would walk into the trees so I could put some of the powdered sleeping pills into his drink or drive off without him, but he aimed his pistol at my belly and did his business standing in the open door right beside my car. An apple green pickup roared by, honking and waving.

Crap. How am I supposed to get away from him without getting myself or innocent bystanders hurt, or worse?

I drove, both hands on the wheel, hunched forward in concentration.

Why does Vlodir think I'll drive over into Canada, wait for him and drive him, anywhere? Surely, he knows I could drop him off and race to the border and tell the authorities what he's up to. There's someone else in on his escape plan. I've got to get away before he joins up with his accomplice.

CHAPTER 36

I remembered a self-defense class I'd taken in college. The instructor said that almost anything could be used as a weapon and that everyone, no matter how tough they seem, is vulnerable in some way. She also said women usually procrastinated longer and took more from their attackers before defending themselves, which often led to their death.

So, what were Vlodir's vulnerable areas? Physically, his nose, eyes, neck, groin and knees. Because he was sitting, his bottom half was pretty well protected, so attacking his crotch or anything lower was out for now. What could I do to his head before he could shoot me?

And what can I use as a weapon?

Nothing in my car, except a camera and snow scraper in the trunk. Too far away for me to get to, however. Should I drive recklessly and get pulled over?

Vlodir interrupted my thoughts by saying, "You stop in Girdwood."

"You mean stop at the big gas station where the road takes off to Girdwood?"

"No gas station. You will drive into Girdwood to 112 Alpine Avenue."

There's no reason to get off the main highway and drive clear up there, so that's got to be where the other person enters the picture.

I knew I had to come up with something, soon. We were traveling north on the Seward highway, about twenty miles from where it would intersect with the only road that led to Girdwood, a cozy skiing village nestled near

Alyeska mountain. My hands were talons on the steering wheel. I was breathing too fast.

Can't let him know I'm terrified.

A pebble thrown by a passing bus hit my side window. I jerked away and looked down. I noticed a small, cylinder-shaped container in the plastic pocket of my door.

What is that?

I shifted in my seat, pretended to be repositioning myself, smoothed my tunic with my left hand, and then let it slide lower, turning the object over. A label read 'Warning!' in bright orange letters. I remembered. Bear spray. Forgotten in my car for about three years.

I glanced away and rubbed the side of my face, combing my right hand through my hair, hoping Vlodir hadn't noticed my activity.

He continued to watch traffic, his head turning again and again as he scanned every vehicle near us.

I had my weapon, now what? A mile or two later, I decided. I would say I needed an immediate stop, pull over, spray Vlodir with bear repellent, abandon my car and run out on the pavement. It was Friday morning, and traffic was heavy coming from Anchorage due to dipnet season opening on the Kenai River. Surely, someone would stop for me.

Part of that plan worked, anyway. I whipped the car over to the side of the road, yelling, "Going to be sick!"

Throwing my door wide, I grabbed the spray, shoved it into Vlodir's face, depressed the trigger, and dropped it. I was half out the door when the Russian grabbed my leg, punched and gouged it until I screamed. He yanked me back inside and slapped me so hard my nose spurted blood. The bear spray hadn't gone off.

"Give up, stupid rabbit," he growled, twisting my ankle. He pinched my right wrist and squeezed until I expected to hear something break.

"No more, or I kill you right here."

I drove back onto the highway, crying silently, wiping my bloody nose on my sleeve.

Vlodir picked up the container of bear spray and read, "Warning!" He repeated this in a high, quavering voice.

"I'm so frightened," he jeered, and threw the spray at me. As his arm started up, I instinctively ducked, jerking the wheel, veering wildly, almost losing control of my car. Instead of striking me, the container hit the inside mirror. The plastic lid flew off, the nozzle broke, and the acrid stuff, under pressure, shot out of the can, while the container ricocheted right back at Vlodir. He tried to pick it up and cover the hole, only hosing himself more. My eyes burning, I careened off the road next to an abandoned motel.

The Russian fought to get his door open, his face dripping with the noxious fluid. Eyes streaming, he made choking noises, wheezing and coughing. He opened his mouth, gagging, sucking air, having trouble breathing. So was I. He jerked on the door handle, finally pawing it open, scrambling to get out. Through tear-blurred eyes, I kicked out with my right leg, pummeling him viciously on the backside, shoving as hard as I could, managing to knock him onto the pavement. Desperate to escape, I stomped the gas pedal with my left foot. The front passenger door hung open. Vlodir's coat caught on something, and the vehicle lurched forward and ran partially over him. He screamed. In full flight mode and panic, I jammed the accelerator. The car drug him along the gravel before his coat ripped away. I heard his angry howl as I reached over, slammed the passenger door, righted myself under the steering wheel, zipped back onto the highway, and tore off. His pistol shot shattered my rear window.

I did not look behind me. Wind whipped through my rig. Barreling up the road, I squinted through gallons of tears and slung snot everywhere. Fortunately, the bear spray that hit me was light, residual. The container fell out of the car with Vlodir, so after about ten minutes, I could breathe easier. Reaching the Girdwood turnoff and gas station, I rolled by the pumps and drove around to the back of the mall where Alaska State Troopers had an office.

I rubbed my face on my sleeve and hurried into the building. Blood and tears smeared me into a disheveled mess, and I hoped my appearance wouldn't go against me.

The troopers told me I needed to stay there while they verified my story. I told them Vlodir had a gun and an accomplice in Girdwood. Too keyed up to sit, I paced the room, waiting. Near the location I described, they found a man with torn clothing, scratches down the side of his face, and what appeared to be a broken ankle, crawling around in the bushes, cursing. Calling himself Vic Dempsey, he claimed we were married, lived in Homer, and had a domestic dispute driving to Anchorage. He said I'd thrown away his passport and driver's license, he was trying to find them, and he loved his feisty wife and didn't want to press charges. Could we go our way? The officers seized his gun and hauled him in. That evening, his accomplice, a woman they said resembled me, was arrested.

At my request, the troopers called Chief of Police Harvin in Homer. They locked Vlodir and me in separate rooms for over three hours while they untangled our stories.

I asked to speak to the Chief and, during a brief conversation, requested that he notify Lieutenant Colonel Jay Carrel. I said both the FBI and Department of Homeland Security could help.

"As wild as all this sounds," I said, "It's a matter of extreme importance. I'm talking national security importance. Vlodir Rafenski is a Russian military fugitive and terrorist."

Chief Harvin's wife and Belle were good friends; maybe that's why he believed me.

I don't know exactly what did the trick, but I stayed in a beautiful mountain lodge near Girdwood at the government's expense that night. The next morning Lieutenant Colonel Jay Carrel walked into the lobby and greeted me with enthusiasm.

He said he brought good news and better news. Vlodir Rafenski and his partner in crime, Carla H., an underground rabble rouser with anarchist and drug running ties, would be prosecuted. Carla immediately turned state's evidence to lighten her sentence. Because she was about my size, age and coloring, the plan had been to kill me somewhere north of Anchorage and use my car and passport to get Vlodir into Canada. The Russian government had disavowed any knowledge of Rafenski or his actions, no surprise. Speaker of the House Chametz would stand trial for treason, and a worldwide hunt was on for the rest of the terrorists involved in causing the missile crisis and the drug running operation.

"What's your, 'better news?'" I asked, finishing my blueberry muffin as we walked out to his rental vehicle.

"Well, for one thing, I get to drive you home, and I'm going to stop the car, and kiss you about every five miles… like this."

He demonstrated.

When we could breathe again, he said, "We'll get your car fixed and have it brought to you. I have to go back to Washington for around six weeks to get this missile event buttoned up, but after that, I'm retiring, moving to Alaska, and going partners with my cousin, Daley. I want to be closer to my mother…and you."

"Your… your… mother?"

"Wind Dancer is my mother, Loren. I found my mom."

"No. Seriously? I don't even know what to say."

He continued, "One more thing. Belle, is who got in touch with me. She sent me dozens of messages and made quite a lot of noise with local law enforcement. She said you were in trouble, something about an email and a secret code word 'seaweed' and a bully in fourth grade. You'll have to fill me in on that one; sounds very interesting."

The next day Jay flew off.

Three weeks slipped by. Our summer was going, going, almost gone.

And then came the news about Belle.

After seventeen days in a coma, harrowing weeks in intensive care, two brain-related surgeries, and hours of extensive rehabilitation, she was coming home. We hadn't seen each other since the gun battle on the little fishing boat -crossing Shelikof.

Belle took my bullet. She knew I wasn't ready to die. Will she resent me because of all she's suffered? Can we still be friends?

Tonight, is a quiet, unremarkable August evening. Tonight, marks the anniversary that began the most frightening days of my life. Tonight, I'm uncertain, even though my physical injuries seem to have healed, and tonight when the faint clatter drifts into my studio, I hold my breath. A staccato flutter, and for a micro instant, I freeze. My heart jumps.

But I gather my courage and make myself move forward even though dread whispers at me. I've learned that brave people know fear, too; but they make themselves go ahead and do what needs to be done, anyway. I trace the noise from my studio up the oak stairs into a bedroom where an enormous, emerald-winged moth rattles against a window. Relieved, I open the louvered glass to free the frantic insect, but the next instant, stumble back at the sudden appearance of a helicopter overhead in the evening dusk. As it disappears into the mist, I remember moments from last summer that left me with scars on my body and a few in my emotions, as well. Instead of reliving those times, however, I look at my watch, shake off my apprehension, and decide I'd better get to the airport. Belle will arrive soon, and I'm her ride.

EPILOGUE

Here she comes, strolling across the tarmac, fancy designer clothes, a short fancy hairstyle, swinging a fancy cane. Jake is walking behind her, lugging, of all things, her bright red survival bag. His face is almost as red as the bag. I can tell she's loaded it, as usual. I stand there, taking her in.

"Get over here," she screams at me, "I've missed you even more than I missed these mountains."

We hug for a long time. Then we pull back and look each other over. Yes, we're both a little more scarred and a little more scuffed, but we've made it this far through life, we figured things out, we survived. It didn't kill us, and we might even be stronger. We laugh and cry and hug some more.

And when she says, right out loud in the terminal in front of everyone, "I've just got to tell Jesus, thank you, right now;" I don't object, I don't pull away. I stand silent and listen, not caring who hears us, because I've decided I want him to be my friend, too, and I'm sure she can introduce me.

THE END

www.ingramcontent.com/pod-product-compliance
Lightning Source LLC
Chambersburg PA
CBHW051633260626
47170CB00004B/1159